MW00896462

CIRCLES IN HELL SERIES
Hell's Super
A Cold Day In Hell
Deal With The Devil
The Reluctant Demon
I'm No Angel

I'm No Angel

(Circles in Hell, Book Five)

by

Mark Cain

ISBN-13: 978-1981970247

All rights reserved. No part of this book may be reproduced or transmitted in any form or by any means, electronic or mechanical, including photocopying, recording, or by any information storage and retrieval system, without permission in writing from the copyright owner.

'I'm No Angel' is published by Perdition Press, which can be contacted at:

hellssuper@hotmail.com

'I'm No Angel' is the copyright of the author, Mark Cain, 2018. All rights are reserved.

This is a work of fiction. All of the characters, organizations or events portrayed in this novel are either products of the imagination or are used fictitiously.

Cover art by Dan Wolfe (www.doodledojo.co.uk)

To all of you who asked what Steve would do next.

Chapter 1

The white clouds glowed with a brilliant radiance, an effect caused by the proximity of the Holy Realm. They billowed beside the Pearly Gates. And then, as if a hand parted them, a gap opened in their midst, revealing a solitary figure, clad in a shimmering suit of gray. Resolute he was, and heroic in his own way, though the receding hairline undercut the effect somewhat.

That was me. 'Twas I.

Feeling more than a bit spiffy, I wandered to the tall podium before the Gates, where a robed figure with a flowing white beard awaited. He looked at me approvingly. "Looking good, Steve."

"You really think so?" I stared down at my silver Oxfords. "Are the pants too long?"

Saint Peter shook his head. "No. You want the trousers to break slightly on your shoes. Here," he said, reaching in his desk, pulling out a full-length mirror and setting it upright on the cloudy surface. "See for yourself."

How he could fit a six-foot mirror in a desk drawer was a bit of a miracle, but then, he was a saint, and miracles were his stock-in-trade. Yet, that he had such a thing at all seemed a bit incongruous, considering the whole Sin of Pride thing. You wouldn't think a saint cared much about his appearance.

Still, he was right. The length of the slacks looked spot-on, pressing ever-so-slightly against the Oxfords. I buttoned the coat and, turning, looked over my shoulder. The fabric hung just right on my frame. "Perfect!" I exhaled.

Peter frowned. "Not quite. Turn around." I did, and he quickly loosened the skinny bit of charcoal-colored fabric that ornamented my silver shirt. "Who taught you how to tie a tie? A three year old?"

I blushed. "I was never very good at that. In life, I generally avoided ties like the plague. When I had to wear one, I used a clip-on."

"Classy," he murmured. "Now watch carefully." I followed his hands as they rapidly retied the thing into a perfect full Windsor. "The trick is to start with the skinny end a few inches shorter than the fat end. Got it?"

"Got it. Urp!" I choked when he cinched up the knot to the notch formed by the front of my buttoned collar.

"Sorry," he said, loosening things a bit. "Better?"

"Yes," I said. "Actually this is a lot more comfortable that what I wore in life."

"That's another mistake humans make." Peter tsked. "So many mistakes you humans make."

"We humans?" I said with amusement. "As I recall, you used to be human yourself."

Peter thought about it a sec then nodded. "Yes, that's true, I suppose, but it was before the invention of the tie."

I looked in the mirror and adjusted the knot slightly. "But which, of our numerous failings, are you referring to now?"

"You tend to buy shirts with the collars half an inch too small. There's no reason to wander around choking, right?"

I grinned. "Right. Oh, and thanks. You do good work."

Saint Peter arched an eyebrow. "As good as Beelzebub?"

"I'd hate to have to live off the difference."

"You're dead, Steve."

"You know what I mean. You'd both have made great tailors, if you hadn't, ah, chosen different lines of work. It was really nice of you, though, to make me the suit. I could have gotten gray cloth downstairs, but Hell's gray is more the result of grime than quality fabric. This stuff practically gleams," I said admiringly. "Thanks again."

The old saint smoothed down my lapels. "You're welcome. Consider it a little payback for all the decades I treated you, well ..."

"Like shit?" I offered.

Peter frowned. "Such language! Not up here."

It was my turn to blush. "Sorry. Old habits, you know."

"Well, now that you're one of the Saved and not one of the Damned, you really need to clean up that foul mouth of yours. Set an example, if you know what I mean."

"I do," I said slowly. "But I'm not sure it will make much difference downstairs when I'm trying to ease the suffering of the Damned. He ... heck. There's so much swearing down there that I doubt anyone would be improved by my example. Or even notice, for that matter."

Pete pursed his lips. "Well, at least try to tone it down some. And remember: no swearing up here."

I nodded quickly. "Right. Well, I'd better get going. Flo's expecting me for dinner."

"Wait!" said the saint, reaching back into his desk, which seemed to be as well stocked as Fibber McGee's closet. "I have a few more accessories." He pulled out a handkerchief, folded it expertly and inserted it in the pocket on my coat. "I'll let you study how I folded it later. Perhaps with Florence's help, you'll figure it out."

"Okay." Flo was very good at such niceties.

"Also," he said, fishing around in a pocket – yes, even a saint likes pockets, though this one wore no slacks under that robe of his – until he found what he was searching for. He smiled as he pulled out a small Swiss Army knife, the kind you might put on a keychain. "Here. You don't have duct tape any longer, but everyone can use a Swiss Army knife."

I grinned and pocketed it. "Thanks. I …"

"Oh, and one more thing." Peter opened another of the seemingly endless drawers in his desk, extracting a shiny gray hat.

"A matching fedora?" I said, absurdly pleased. I placed it on my head and, with a glance in the mirror, adjusted the hat to sit at a slightly saucy angle. "Not quite a halo."

"No, though it does glow a little. And it suits you."

"The whole outfit is swell!" I enthused then began to make my way toward Hell's Escalator.

"One question," Peter said behind me. "Why gray instead of white?"

I shrugged. "I'm no angel. There's still a bit of bad in me, since I didn't go through the prewash cycle for Heaven."

"Prewash cycle?" Peter said, puzzled. Then he brightened. "Oh, you mean the purge of evil that happens before you enter Heaven."

"Yeah. I'm glad, though, that I was finally judged by you, and all those witnesses, both fernal and infernal …"

"I don't think fernal is a word."

"Divine, then," I amended. "Anyway, I'm glad to know definitively that I'm more good than bad, but, well, like I said, I'm no angel. I think the gray suits me."

"You know," Saint Peter said with a chuckle, "I do too."

"Later, Pete."

Heaven's Concierge flinched. He hated being called Pete, but he knew of my penchant for shortening people's names, so he let it pass. "Later. Give my love to Florence."

"Will do," I said, as I stepped onto the Escalator that would take me down to Hell.

Chapter 2

The Escalator descended at a steep pitch, steeper than what you would find on a terrestrial version of a moving staircase, but this was the main method of descending into the bowels of Hell, and, well, those bowels were pretty damn deep, eight miles down before stopping on the Sahara-like surface of Level Eight. To get there expeditiously, steep was pretty much *de rigueur*. Since the Ninth Circle was reserved for Satan, his assistant and the four Traitors (Cain, Judas, Hitler and Screech Boy), the Escalator didn't go there. Still, the moving stairs would take a typical soul about as low as it could go.

For the first few yards riding on the Escalator, one could look back and see a bit of Gates Level, an ever-shrinking patch of blue and wispy white. While this sight had long since lost its novelty for me, most of the newly-damned couldn't help but glance back with regret, like Lot's wife taking a final look at her old home before getting Sodom-ized, that is, being turned into a pillar of salt, or perhaps more aptly, Orpheus checking out his darling Eurydice, only to lose her to the land of Hades, which fittingly was the pre-Christian version of Hell. Yes, humans seem compelled to look back with longing or regret, so the newly-damned invariably watched that eye of light close, their option for salvation disappear forever. And when the last view of GL winked out, those poor souls were left with nothing but a dull gray gloom that deepened with each passing yard, a growing dark and a growing dread.

The substratum for Gates Level seemed almost paper thin, gauze-like, remarkable considering the size of Peter's operation. Well, most of that subsurface was thin, though there was a large bulbous portion, like a mud daubers' nest, attached to the underside. That was the location of Level 0.5, where the black Styx flowed through a cavern of glistening obsidian, where Charon, immortal Ferryman of the Dead, transported the occasional damned VIP soul to Hell.

The Escalator was traveling in its deliberate, juggernaut fashion toward the far edge of Level One. I knew this from my years as a damned soul, though at present I couldn't see One at all. Generally the Damned had spectacular views of the horrific landscape of each circle in Hell, but this particular stretch of moving stairs was enclosed on the sides by tall panes of one-way glass. These panes were completely opaque from the outside and, this high up, very nearly so from the inside as well. Only as the Damned approached the surface of the First Circle could they see through the glass and appreciate what they were missing.

The glass serves three purposes. One, it protects the Virtuous Pagans and Unbaptized Infants on Level One, aka Limbo, from the dreary sight of the newly-damned, who are, admittedly, some pretty depressed individuals. Two, as the Escalator approaches the surface, the glass allows riders a last-minute, fleeting yet enticing view of the First Circle, which is the only really pleasant bit of real estate in all of Hell. In Limbo, the VPs and UIs are spending a fairly enjoyable Eternity playing golf, getting massages, rock climbing, swimming, those sort of things. Level One is a well-earned, permanent vacation for its inhabitants, who were after all pretty good eggs in their lives. That's why we call them *virtuous* pagans in the first place, as opposed to snarky pagans or bastard pagans or, well, you get the idea.

Which brings me to the third and most important function of the tall, thick glass. It keeps the newly-damned from leaping off the Escalator and escaping to Limbo, which by anyone's estimation beats the snot out of the other circles in Hell. Not allowed of course. After all, the Damned are not really pagans, except in the most figurative sense of the word. Still, on occasion I have witnessed desperate souls try to scrabble up and over the glass. The windows are quite slick, though. All these individuals succeed at is ruining their nails, which make some pretty unpleasant screeching noises against the featureless, unyielding barrier of glass.

Ponk!

Oh, yeah. The glass serves a fourth purpose. Every once in a great while, an errant golf ball strikes a pane. When this happens, a virtuous pagan has made a rare, bad drive off the tee. (The pagans are very good golfers, which makes sense if you think about it, since they have lots of time to practice.) If not for the glass, a bad shot would end up in the rough. This way, the ball ricochets off and lands back on the fairway, making it a snap to salvage par.

The gray faded to black. We had dropped beneath the surface of One. Black, blinding and hellaciously hot were the cores of the Circles of Hell. There was no light again until I reached the first switchback, the point where the Escalator turned in the opposite direction and dipped into the upper atmosphere, if atmosphere it could be called, of the Second Circle, where the Lustful were perpetually punished. From there the Escalator continued its inexorable journey deeper and deeper into the penal colony of the Damned, the original Devil's Island.

Pretty fucking depressing, no?

Oops. There I go again, ruining the mood, along with a perfectly good descriptive section, with my swearing. Ah, well. I was never good at keeping a straight face for very long. I swear,

I ... Well, I guess I do, and I can't blame it on being one of the Damned any longer.

In Hell, everyone swears. Even mutes, who sign out their profanities, usually with ASL (American Sign Language), but sometimes with semaphore or signal flags. Even Morse Code. Sounds like a lot of trouble, I know, but profanity has been decreed down here, by order of Big Red himself. That would be Satan. Everyone has to participate.

Being a saved soul makes me exempt from the requirement, but in life I'd had a bit of the old salty tongue anyway, and while I hardly swore like a sailor, off-colored words had punctuated my speech since about fifth grade. That's when most boys discover curse words, as we all know, though at that age, the kids are more interested in body parts (mostly pee-pees and butts) and the stuff that comes out of them, like wee-wee and poop. Especially poop. I don't know why poop is so fascinating to ten-year-old boys. It just is.

So I'd been swearing for a long time, about a hundred years I estimate, if you combined my life on Earth with that of being one of the Damned in Hell. Past tense, of course. With that much practice in the fine art of obscenity, this was going to be a difficult habit to break.

I was still in a bit of shock about the rapid reversal of my fortunes. Dead in my early forties, sixty years spent as one of the Damned, a few months as a demon. And then it all changed again, and I was saved, thanks to Saint Peter and winning a two out of three coin toss challenge. That had happened only a few days ago.

So much change, so quickly. I felt like I had whiplash or something.

Yet now I was saved. A sheep, not a goat. I no longer had my demon powers, except for a bit of invulnerability, thanks to the protections offered me by the Accords. Oh, and my vision was a little better than before, too. I saw things more clearly, though maybe that was just the wisdom of a saved soul. I saw things as they really were. Generally, anyway. I'm sure if Satan put his mind to it, he could still trick me, just like in the old days, but I doubted anyone else could pull it off.

Why I'm not in Heaven is out of choice. Like my girlfriend, Florence Nightingale, I've decided to stay in Hell and ease the suffering of others. Besides, I've never learned to play the harp. All those strings: way too confusing. And frankly, Heaven, the whole idea of it, well, it's a bit intimidating to me. What if I didn't fit in? What if I walked through the Pearly Gates, bought one of those cloud bungalows that I'm sure they must have in some Heavenly subdivision, then did something impossibly gauche, like put pink flamingos in my front yard or prop up a thundercloud on cinder blocks in the driveway, all because I'd picked up some bad habits in my sixty years of damnation? And there goes the neighborhood. No, I'm just not ready for all that pressure. In Hell, at least I know the rules.

The panes of gray glass were gone, and I had an unimpeded view of the Second Circle of Hell. In the distance was Mount Erebus, a cruel white spike that hung from the underbelly of Level One. Farther away still was a stormy sea, the ocean of Prometheus, where the ancient titan from Greek myth was serving as an object lesson in eternal torment. Somewhere, a mile or so away, Sisyphus was rolling his rock, Bessie, up his hill. I couldn't see him, but I knew he was there. He was always there.

The Fire Pits of Two glowed beneath me, and black smoke embraced the Escalator with arms of soot. I coughed. The fumes from the fire pit were particularly noxious today; they reeked of overcooked human flesh. Polyphemus must have thrown a few extra on the barbie.

From the Throat of Hell (the collective holes in the center of Each Circle of Hell) came a flash of black lightning. Hell was the only place in the universe where you could see black lightning, except of course in the pages of a DC comic. It was pretty impressive, a sable bolt of electricity against a forlorn gray sky. There was the crash of thunder, and a dark figure jetted from the Throat, flying like a bat out of Hell.

BOOH was headed toward Lustland, probably carrying some important document from Satan for Asmodeus, the prince of Hell who oversaw this circle. At the sight of my batty friend, I sighed. With gain often comes loss, and I worried that my new status as one of the Saved wouldn't allow for a relationship with Satan's courier-in-chief. In the blink of an eye, BOOH disappeared into the heart of Lustland, City of Lust, where my former paramour, Lilith, who is the nicest succubus you could ever hope to meet, by the way, lived and worked.

Reno, the demon who animated the Escalator, had recently changed his trajectory – a common occurrence around here. Last time I rode down, the Escalator had touched ground on Two near Sisyphus and Polyphemus. Today though we were headed for our usual landing spot, downtown Lustland, not far from the corporate offices of Lust Unlimited.

Speaking of said demon: the hard black handrails of the Escalator began to undulate. He was attempting to destabilize some newly-damned individuals who were riding about fifty yards ahead of and beneath me. These souls shouldn't have been there at all, considering how long Peter and I had visited without interruption, but they had probably tried to escape their fates by running up the Escalator. It never worked, though it could slow your descent a skosh.

I'd long ago learned how to maintain my balance when the Escalator started rocking. The newbies, though, were struggling to stay upright, trying not to get pitched to the metal treads, or worse, over the sides to fall a thousand feet, splat, onto the surface of Level Two.

I frowned. These unfortunates shouldn't have to put up with Reno's shenanigans. After all, they had just been damned to Hell and were probably still in shock, and the last thing they needed was an owie because the Escalator was being cranky. This was my first opportunity – as a newly-saved soul on a mission of mercy in the Underworld – to relieve a little suffering. I slapped my hands hard on the two plastic railings. "Stop it!" I said sternly.

"What? Oh, right, right. Those stupid Accords," grumbled a voice beneath my feet. The Escalator handrails immediately settled down. "Fuck you, Minion!" snapped the voice.

"You too, Reno," I said cheerily.

You might wonder about Reno. In life, he had been one of the inventors of the Escalator, so when he became a demon, he got the gig. This is not unlike what happened to Otis, who ran the Elevator down here.

"You know you can't pull those sorts of shenanigans when I'm around. You could risk hurting me, ya know."

"Like I give a shit."

"Such language!" I said, in mock outrage. "And in front of a saved soul. My, my. You know that's completely against the Accords also, right?"

The Accords I keep referring to govern the relations between Heaven and Hell and their respective inhabitants. As a saved soul, I was untouchable. That included protection from unwanted demon sass.

Reno let out another grumble — this one rattled the Escalator — but he held his tongue.

I grinned. *This is going to be fun.*

I trotted down the steps to the nearest soul ahead of me. Most of the newly damned had managed to keep their footing, but this one had fallen, so I helped her to her feet.

She looked at me in surprise but didn't speak. I think she really *was* in shock.

The woman was young, maybe her mid-twenties, and in good shape metaphysically, all things considered. People usually look pretty terrible when they get here, either from old age or some damage they incurred as part of their final moments on earth — like being in a car crash. But she was okay, except for her limp, dirty blonde hair and some bleary tattoos that had been applied by someone who was less than a master of the craft. Her eyes were bloodshot, probably from crying, though there was a rheumy quality to them. She could have O.D.ed her way to the Afterlife.

The water works began. I patted her back, in an awkward attempt at consolation. "There, there."

"H … Hell!" she gasped between her sobs. "Oh, god, it really exists!"

I shrugged. "'fraid so. Sucks, doesn't it?"

She nodded and started crying again. "I, I was raised Episcopalian," she said between sobs, "but I never really believed in all of this. It just seemed so, so unlikely." She looked up at me. "You know, a soul that outlives death, an omniscient Creator, angels, saints, devils, demons, and oh crap … Hell and damnation!"

I couldn't think of what else to do, so I held her and let her cry. "This must be hard to take in," I said finally, "but yes, there really is a Heaven." I said this last word, still marveling that my saved-soul status allowed me to voice it aloud. "And there really is a Hell. Unfortunately, you got consigned to the basement."

She sniffled. "But, but why? I ... I wasn't such a bad person."

Damned if I know. Probably lost a coin toss with Saint Peter.

I frowned. That damn coin. It had been the cause of sixty years of personal torment. I hated what it had done to me, what it had probably done to this young woman and countless others as well. I shook my head.

"It could be that lack-of-faith thing you just referenced, but really, I don't know. What I *do* know is that everything is part of the Divine Plan. If it's any consolation, there are a number of good people in Hell."

"Then why are they here?"

"Again," I said, shrugging, "all I've got for you is Divine Plan."

She looked at me speculatively. "You look awfully well-dressed for a damned soul."

"I'm not damned." I exhaled softly. "It's a long story, which we don't have time for, it appears." We had reached the surface of Level Two, and I felt her body pull away from me, not of her own volition but through the intervention of some invisible, overpowering force. Apparently she was to be consigned to this level. I hopped off the Escalator with her.

A rank of pitchfork-wielding demons – the welcoming committee on this level – was heading toward her, but I waved them back. They shot me some dirty looks but stepped away. I gave them a mock salute, then turned back to the devastated young woman.

"Look," I said quietly, trying to calm her down. "It won't be easy for you. It's not easy for anyone. This is Hell, and you will suffer. Everyone suffers here. But there is a bright side."

"Bright side?" she gasped, a frown carving way-too-deep ridges into her young brow. "In Hell?"

I nodded. "Amazingly, here, in the most unexpected of places, you will find an occasional kindness. Not from them," I said, glowering at the demons, "but from the ranks of the Damned. There you will find friendship, camaraderie."

"What ... What should I do?" She said, still sniveling.

"Persevere. Expect the worst, which is usually what will happen, and savor the occasional unexpected moments of reprieve."

"That's it?" She said, an edge of frustration in her voice. "Persevere?"

She's getting peeved. Good. Anger is better than despair.

"Yes," I said gently, kissing her forehead in a form of benediction. "And hope. Oh, and one more thing."

"Wha ... what's that?"

With one hand, I raised her chin so that we were looking into each other's eyes. "Never let the bastards beat you down."

The young woman's face hardened. She swallowed hard and nodded. "Right. Thanks."

"And don't say th ..." But it was too late. She was on the ground with a pie in her face.

She'd learn in time. I helped her to her feet, handing her my handkerchief to wipe away the cream. "Keep it," I said, when she tried to give my hankie back. "I can get more. Take care of yourself."

She started to thank me again, but I put a finger to my lips, shushing her. Her eyes widened, then she nodded. The woman put her own finger to trembling lips. Yes, she'd learn. With a sad smile, I turned back to the Escalator.

As I began my descent, I heard her scream. The demons had surrounded her. I sighed as the Escalator carried me out of earshot.

Chapter 3

My heart was heavy as I stepped off the Escalator onto Level Five.

I had just performed my first act of kindness. Well, it wasn't exactly my first. I mean, *surely* sometime in my forty odd years on planet Earth I'd been nice to somebody. And since coming to Hell, I know I'd been kind to Orson, Flo, Louis – even Tommy Edison, at least a time or two. But when I put on the new suit, I'd begun a career as an angel of mercy, or if not that exalted an agent for good, at least a saved soul providing comfort to the Damned of Hell. So, the young woman on the Escalator was the first person I'd helped in my new capacity.

Didn't seem like I did much for her, though. The thought was discouraging.

I walked past my old office, a forlorn single-wide trailer that was the headquarters for Hell's Plant Maintenance Department.

Maybe I should talk this through with Orson. He's always a good sounding board.

The door to the office popped open, and Orson and Tom, with a large pane of plate glass between them, practically ran down the stairs. "Hey guys," I began.

"Hi, Steve!" Orson said, without breaking stride. "Can't talk now. Gotta get this up to Asmodeus on Two ASAP!"

"Yeah!" Tom gasped, struggling to keep up with his boss. "We've already screwed up the job once. He'll gut us if we aren't there pronto!"

They probably weren't exaggerating. Disembowelment was a favorite torment among devils and demons, especially devil princes, like Asmodeus. Why, I remember my first disembowelment like it was yesterday. Astoreth had me and

Orson in his house, setting up a wet bar. We'd encountered a bit of trouble running the pipes to the sink. When we didn't get it right after three times – It's always three, by the way. Christian theology is built around that number – he disemboweled the both of us, then for fun, swapped our intestines. For a month, I couldn't get enough escargot. Orson, for his part, had a craving for Twizzlers, a personal favorite of mine. Then Astoreth showed up and switched things back. Needless to say, this was not a kindness on his part. It just gave him the opportunity to rip open our bellies again. Besides, we still hadn't gotten that stupid wet bar working right, so he had some justification, I suppose.

At least I got my taste for Twizzlers back. And I got to stop eating those yucky snails.

Mem'ries light the corners of my mind.

But enough reminiscing.

I watched Orson and Edison dash up a side street, heading for the Elevator. In seconds they were gone. I hoped Otis would cut them a break and pick them up right away, though he was seldom so accommodating.

Too bad, I thought, a little disappointed. I'd hoped to be able to visit a while, but no such luck.

With a sigh, I headed toward the Victorian Quarter. In a few blocks, the drab but modern industrial portion of the Fifth Circle – tastelessly decorated by Hell's management with sprawling factories patterned after those in the Rust Belt – gave way to, by comparison, a quaint neighborhood of cobbled streets, brownstones fronting said streets, and horse-drawn carriages. There was an unusual number of the latter out today, and traffic was snarled, always a bad thing, but predictable in a situation where blind drivers were directing the efforts of equally blind horses.

A phaeton (Cool word, huh?), which is a snappy equine-powered two-seater, sort of like the Victorian version of a convertible, raced around the corner. Its horse was most definitely not blind, judging from the way it was weaving its way through traffic. Driving the phaeton was a demon in a morning coat and top hat, holes cut through the beaver fur of his stove pipe to accommodate a particularly cruel set of horns. In his hand was a whip, which he was applying liberally, not to the horse, but to something, or rather someone, he was dragging behind the carriage.

"Ow, ow, ow!" cried the poor unfortunate, both from the sting of the whip and all that bumping up and down on the cobblestones. I recognized both dragger and draggee. Benjamin Disraeli had become a demon shortly after I got here. The man being dragged — Man in drag? No, that means something else, I think — was William Gladstone, Disraeli's one-time political nemesis. In seconds they rounded another corner and were gone.

It must have been nice for Disraeli. In life, he'd hated Gladstone. Someone told me that an opportunity to torture Gladstone was in fact the chief reason Disraeli had agreed to join the Devil and Demon Corps in the first place. Of course, the antipathy between the two was mutual — Benji and Billy had loathed each other for two centuries — and if Gladstone instead had been asked to join the D&D Corps, I'm sure Disraeli would be the one dangling by one leg from the back of a phaeton.

I shook my head. That would have been a good tormentation to stop, but the carriage had been moving too fast, and I no longer possessed my demonic super speed. With another sigh, I crossed the street.

Here, Victorian versions of bag ladies were practically mobbing the sidewalk. These smelly and seedy old hags, with hair like damp dishrags, blotchy complexions, and blackened teeth, could be very aggressive. They had to be. If they didn't reach their quotas, they'd spend the night dangling upside down inside the dome of a facsimile of St. Paul's Cathedral, accompanying a large bat colony that also spent its night hanging upside down in the dome. All that blood running to their heads: that's probably why their complexions had all those blotches.

Oh, I'm talking about the bag ladies here, not their winged roomies.

To help them meet their sales targets, I tried to buy an item from everyone. A box of matches here (three hundred dollars), a wormy apple there (a thousand), a rose for Flo. The final item cost ten thousand, even though it was pale and withered; still, it's the thought that counts. I knew I wouldn't be able to keep up what amounted to a philanthropic enterprise. I no longer was on expense account, now that I wasn't working for Satan. Soon my pockets would be empty, and I'd have to get around the Underworld without any money. Didn't know what I'd do then.

I'll have to ask Flo how she manages.

Finally I was able to break away from the lady merchants. With my meager assortment of purchases in hand, I hurried to the entrance of Flo's brownstone. I stepped inside just in time to see the old man from 2G career down the stairs, landing with a splat face down before me. His cane followed in short order, deliberately tearing a hole in his slacks and lodging itself in the one body orifice large enough to accommodate it. Poor fellow. Bad enough that his gouty left leg was swollen to the size of a golf bag, requiring the cane in the first place, but then the damn stick had turned on him. Every day he had to negotiate these stairs, and I wondered how often falling down them was part of

25

the routine. With great care, I extracted the cane then helped the man to his feet. He nodded his thanks to me, looked accusingly at the walking stick then used it to hobble to the door. I shook my head.

Halfway up the stairs, I stopped to use my new pocket knife to tighten a screw on a loose brass rod that was helping to hold the runner on the stairs in place. With luck, the old man wouldn't trip on the morrow. Maybe not even on the stairs. In seconds, the task was done.

What a marvel! Back in the day, when I was damned, and fixing things was my job, that would have taken me an hour. Take away the ill fortune suffered by all the Damned, and I seem to do okay as a handyman. Guess I actually developed some skills over the past sixty years.

The door to Flo's apartment is never locked. Devils and demons show no respect for privacy, so it does little good to secure a door in Hell. Generally, though, Flo's unusual status down here keeps the bad guys out.

There *had* been a few incidents in the past, but one of the Damned – specifically me – had always been involved, so Satan must have felt he had some wiggle room to infiltrate her private sanctum. Now that not just one but two saved souls lived in the place, I was fairly confident we would have our privacy. Flo's FloZone, the special quality she possessed that was like a force field or something, repelling evildoers, was now being reinforced by my own Steve-o-Zone. It probably wasn't as powerful as hers – hell, she was a much better person than I ever could be – but I was a saved soul too, and that had to count for something.

I opened the door, stepped inside and found myself in our cozy flat. *Our flat: how odd to think of it that way.* I wondered idly who'd gotten stuck with my old sixth-floor walkup studio.

Ugh. What a vermin-infested dump that *was.* Still, the roaches had been nice to me sometimes, well, not nice, but at least they usually stayed out of my way, except for their perpetual chittering. And they'd been a constant if mildly repulsive source of nighttime companionship. But that was then, and this was now, and my new roommate was a whole lot more pleasant to hang out with than all those crunchy six-legged critters had been.

Florence wasn't home yet. It was a little early for her to be back from the hospital, but she'd arrive soon, so I put on the kettle for tea time. Then I plopped heavily in the living room chair I'd recently claimed as my own in order to do some hard thinking about my new status in the Underworld.

Which is where Florence Nightingale, my personal angel of mercy, found me when she opened the door some ten minutes later. "Steve? Is something wrong?"

I looked up, distracted. "Uh, no. I guess not. Why do you ask?"

She smiled at me uncertainly. "The kettle?"

"What? The kettle? Oh!" The kettle was screaming in the background. I hadn't even heard it, I was so deep in thought. "The kettle!" I said again, this time with more urgency, and I hurried to take it off the stove's burner. Removing the lid, I stared down at a dry metal bottom. "Sorry. I'll have to boil some more water."

"Never mind," Flo said, putting a small paper bag on the kitchen table. She reached in the sack and pulled out a bottle of Tanqueray. "I thought we'd do something different tonight."

"Cocktail hour? Where'd you get the gin?" I asked in astonishment. Finding decent gin in Hell was harder than getting a compliment down here.

"A devil was trying to get on my good side," she answered primly. "I tried to say no, but, well, you and I both like gin."

"What devil?" I asked, suddenly jealous. "Not Asmodeus?"

She chuckled. "No, TNK-el."

"Oh, no surprise there." TNK-el was a dinky little devil who had the hots for Flo. "Hope he doesn't expect much in return for his gift."

"I promised to have coffee with him tomorrow. Well," she added, "I'll have coffee, and he'll probably have ..."

"Yeah, I know," I said, absently, going for a couple of glasses. "A grape Slurpee."

"Exactly." Florence kissed me on the cheek. "Since I made the supreme sacrifice, could I also make the drink selection?"

"Sure," I said, pausing before the two martini glasses I was reaching for. "What'll ya have, beautiful?" I deadpanned, in my best bartender voice.

"A tonic and gin?"

"You got it," I said, grabbing two low ball glasses instead. From the freezer, I scored some ice cubes for each one, then, rummaging around in the fridge, found an unopened bottle of tonic and a lime. "Say, where do you get all this good stuff? I can never find anything fresh in Hell."

"Saint Peter puts together a weekly package for me and sends it down by light beam."

I started to grab my new pocket knife to cut the lime but thought better of it, remembering how I'd just used it to tighten a screw holding down a runner with some pretty disgusting stains on it. I'd have to remember to wash my new possession. From the wooden block on the counter, I removed a paring knife and sliced two wedges out of the lime. Flo liked lots of citrus juice in her drink, so I gave one slice a generous squeeze before dropping it in her glass. For me, the lime was just for

28

color – no point undercutting the flavor of a good gin – so my wedge sat on top of the rocks, a little green boat stuck in an ice floe. "Maybe we can ask him to add Tanqueray to your weekly care package."

"Do you really think we need to have that much gin in the house?" she asked, unpinning her nurse's cap and placing it on the table. "I still like my tea time, you know. I thought this could be an exception."

"Okay," I said, somewhat deflated. I mean, tea is fine, I guess, but I'd take a good martini at the end of the day anytime over some lousy hot water infused with leaves from a shrub. Still, just having the luxury of tea time with the woman I loved was good enough for me.

Besides, maybe I could spike my tea with gin. I frowned. *No, that doesn't sound good even to* me.

In moments, the drinks were made, and we settled in the living room. Flo took her first sip, and her eyes widened, which was usually her reaction whenever she drank spirits – as opposed to just being one, which she was pretty used to by now. "Not exactly a tonic and gin, dear."

"Well," I shrugged. "What would you rather taste: quinine or the complex botanicals of Tanqueray?"

"Well, when you put it that way ..."

Whew!

"Now," Flo said, putting down her glass, "what were you thinking about when I came in? Lovely suit, by the way."

"Yeah." I looked down at my new duds. "There's a matching fedora too," which I'd put on a shelf in the coat closet. I frowned. "As to your question, I was just thinking about an encounter I'd had on the Escalator." I described to Flo the young woman's understandable fear at beginning an afterlife of eternal damnation. "Poor thing. She didn't even know why she had been consigned to Hell."

"Unfortunately, that's not an uncommon occurrence down here." She looked at me quizzically. "Why the thundercloud face, Steve?"

"What? Oh, just a little bit of empathy for her plight. She probably came out on the losing end of a coin toss, just like me." I said all this calmly enough, but I didn't feel calm, and I knew my face was turning red.

Flo rolled her eyes. "Not the coin again. Can't you let that go?"

"Sorry," I said, embarrassed yet defiant, "but no, I can't. I spent sixty years as one of the Damned because of that dumb quarter, and it turns out I wasn't even supposed to."

"I understand, really," she said softly, touching my hand. "I just hate to see you upset over it. Now, you were telling me about the woman on the Escalator. You got off with her on Two and ...?"

I took a deep breath, willing away my anger. "And, after a few words of advice, I left her there, surrounded by demons. I felt so ... so helpless."

Flo sighed. "I know the feeling. I do everything possible to ease the suffering of those poor, benighted souls in the hospital, but at some point, I simply cannot shield them from their damnation. Finding out what you can and cannot do to help in Hell, discovering your limits and making peace with them, is perhaps the biggest challenge of those in our situation."

I took a slug of my drink, hoping the gin would smooth away the edges of my frustration. It helped, if only marginally. "As far as I know, you and I are the only two people in our situation."

"Yes, of course. For my own part, I have become somewhat reconciled to my limits." She looked at me thoughtfully. "I only hope that you can too, in time."

"Why do you say it that way?"

She gave me a rueful grin. "Oh, come now, Steve. After all you've done, challenging and besting even Satan himself, do you think you are going to have an easy time 'settling?'"

I stroked my chin in thought. "Suppose not."

Flo kicked off her shoes. I scooped up her feet, placed them on my lap and began massaging them. In moments she was sighing again, this time in pleasure.

I looked at her speculatively. "Have anything else that needs rubbing?"

"Why Steve Minion, you scamp!" she said in mock outrage. Flo stood and took my hand. "Still, if it will bring comfort to you ..."

"Oh, it will, it will." We shared a long kiss then headed for the bedroom.

Flo and I have a lot of sex. Not as much as Lilith and I used to have, but back then I was a demon and my stamina was better. Still, five or six times a day is more than most couples, I believe. Certainly it exceeds the American national average. It goes without saying that sex with Flo beats the crap, ah, crud, out of sex among the Damned, since coitus for most everyone else down here is, by Devil diktat, unpleasant at best and horrific at worst. If you could get it up at all, I mean.

I know what you're thinking. Typical guy. Can't get his head out of his shorts. But it's not just me. If anything, Florence Nightingale has a bigger libido than I do. I've always thought that it's because she went through life a virgin, and only recently discovered the pleasures of the ectoflesh. Still, our sex life was just icing on the cake of a wonderful relationship.

31

Just icing. My favorite flavor, though. Hers too, I think.

Feeling the need to replenish our vital juices, we decided on steak for dinner. When I first moved in with Flo, I had wanted to get a grill so I could help with the cooking. (I'd never been a very good "inside" cook.) Finding a grill in Hell is no problem. The place is littered with them. But we didn't have a porch or any other outside space to put it, and even though we were in Hell, where safety regulations tended to be on the lax side, our building code didn't allow a grill to be placed inside. Still, I decided I'd always cook the steaks, even if it meant I'd just have to use the oven's broiler instead.

After dinner, we had a quiet evening reading in the living room. Well, Flo read. Me, I was too distracted. I needed to figure out this whole "give comfort to the Damned" thing. I wasn't sure if offering a few kind words here and there was going to cut it for me.

I determined on the morrow … "On the morrow?" That's the second, no, now third time I've used the expression. I'm starting to sound like Flo. Anyway, I determined the next day to explore the possibilities.

Then we hit the sack. Many times.

Afterwards, Flo, face pink with the flush of our lovemaking, fell right to sleep. Not me, though. Wide awake, I lay on my back, hands behind my head, elbows pointing up toward the coved ceiling. My eyes were not able to see very much in the faint light, so my imagination created imaginary designs, whirls and curlicues and mazes … and circles that looked like hundreds of malicious quarters.

But mostly mazes. I was trying to solve a puzzle, and not the one I'd been thinking about for most of the day. To be sure, I still hadn't figured out how I would help the Damned in Hell. What was puzzling me at that moment, though, was *why* it was so important to me to find the right way to help, something that was meaningful to me.

Why aren't I content just to help others?

I frowned, realizing that I never *had* been content. In life, nothing was ever good enough. And then I was damned, during which time everything pretty much sucked. When I got promoted to demon, my lot in the afterlife definitely improved, though it came at the cost of harming others. That cost was simply too high for me, so I was actually less satisfied as a demon than as one of the Damned.

And now I'm saved. Shit, I could be in Heaven if I wanted. Well, maybe not until I did something about this potty mouth of mine, but still.

Heaven was available to me anytime I wanted to go. That was the ultimate human desire, that and eating a really good BLT. You'd think my saved-soul status, an open invitation to enter the Gates of Heaven, would have me satisfied at last. But I feared even that wouldn't content me, which might have been another reason why I was holding off going to Paradise. Not to mention my quiet conviction that I wasn't a good enough person to be allowed in Heaven, that I wouldn't fit in and ...

See? Never satisfied.

Perhaps it's the nature of the human condition, I concluded, never to be content. It was like breathing. You wanted that rush of air into your lungs, desperately wanted it, yet as soon as you'd breathed your fill, you wanted to empty those lungs as fast as possible. And when you were done, you couldn't wait to fill them again. Never content with the current state.

Damn it!

A soft sigh brought me out of these gloomy thoughts. Flo lay beside me, a lock of chestnut hair draped over her elegant neck. She must have been dreaming, but if so, I reflected, it was the dream of an innocent. She looked so peaceful, lying beside me. It made me smile.

Turning on my side, I spooned Flo, kissed her neck. Holding her lightly in my grasp, I closed my eyes and tried to match her gentle breathing. In no time I felt sleepy. Just before I drifted off, I smiled again, thinking that in moments like this, maybe it *was* possible for me to find a measure of contentment.

Chapter 4

"**H**ow is it that you can look like a Hollywood movie star in a nurse's uniform?"

I was lying in bed, watching Flo slip into her dress. She always got up before me. My insomnia of the previous evening was an aberration. After sixty years of not being able to sleep worth a damn, my "saved" status had cured this particular Hell-induced malady. Now, I reveled in being able to catch my Zees, and, after she left for the hospital, I would often lounge in bed for an hour or two, drinking coffee and working a crossword puzzle.

Flo leaned over and kissed me. "My uniform is a simple dress, though," she paused, a little puzzled, "I confess it seems to fit me more snugly than what I wore in life, especially through the bodice and around my hips. Still, I've worn this for so many years that I no longer pay much attention to my attire. Do I look acceptable?" she asked, presenting herself for my inspection.

"Absolutely! You look fine. I wouldn't change a thing." Her dress *was* snug, tight in all the right places, showing off her killer figure. This was Satan's doing, I knew. While the Earl of Hell could neither hurt nor impede Florence Nightingale in her activities down here, he seemed to have a modicum of control over items about which she seemed to have little interest. Item one: she appeared as she did in her early twenties, when she was a great beauty, heavily courted but never wed. Item two: her clothes were intended to show off her substantial physical assets to best effect.

In this way, she became an untouchable beauty. Most every man in Hell, and a fair number of women too, had the hots for her, a fact about which she was completely unaware. That Satan was using Flo in this way to mildly torture many of the Damned had been obvious to me for years, but she was oblivious. (Funny how just sticking "l i" in the middle of "obvious" completely changes the word's meaning, isn't it?) Since *I* liked seeing her in her nurse's uniform too, especially now that she was not an off-limits lady, this was one of the few times when Satan and I were in agreement.

Flo smiled. "Well, then, I won't worry about it," she said, kissing me again, this time a big wet one that ended with me trying to pull her back in bed. "None of that, now. I'm late as it is. You'll just have to wait until I get home."

"Oh, okay," I said, disappointed.

"That's the lad. Have a good day, darling."

"Thanks," I said, finally crawling from the bed. "I think I'll get myself out soon as well, see what good I can do today."

"Best of luck." She left the bedroom. In moments, I heard the front door close behind her.

I headed into the bathroom and turned on the shower. The water was clean and warm, a far cry from the filthy frigidity I had encountered during my sixty years of damnation.

It's funny how often the word "good" popped into my mind now that I was saved. I still lived in the most miserable domain imaginable, but aside from the gruesome landscape, the smell and the frequent screams from the Damned, my life, or afterlife, was indeed pretty damn good.

Oops. I really have to watch the profanities. I'm one of the white hats now.

Normally I took a long shower – it was just such a luxury – but today I was in a hurry to get started. After toweling off, I slipped on my skivvies, shaved my puss, combed back what little hair I had and brushed the old pearly whites. I dressed quickly, not having to spend time selecting a wardrobe for the day. In that regard, my afterlife wasn't much different from when I was Hell's Super and had to wear the same coveralls all the time. From now on, though, it was gray suit all the way. The tie didn't give me much trouble, because yesterday I'd simply loosened the knot and slipped the loop over my head without untying things. As I reversed the action this morning, I felt a bit of guilt. It didn't seem proper for me to be cheating, but I quickly shrugged it off. I may have been a saved soul, but I would never be the paragon of virtue Flo was.

I'm me. Mostly good, a little bad, and a whole lot of trouble. I grinned. Today I'd start the trouble in earnest, only this time, it would be against all the bad guys down here, of which there was a considerable number.

The bag ladies were just beginning to show up on the street corners, and I hurried down the cobblestone so that none of them could snag me with a sales pitch. There was a whizzing in the air, and instinctively I ducked. A trash bag had been thrown out a window.

It's not as if we have curbside pickup in Hell. Still, people have to get rid of their garbage somehow, and this was as good a way as any, though it became one more projectile the Damned had to dodge.

The sack went splat on the pavement beside me, the fetid aroma of rotting fish heads and spoiled tripe rising from the split paper. Trotting down the street, I wondered what would have happened if I'd just stood there. Would the bag have hit me? Would it have been deflected by some invisible hand? Somehow I doubted that second possibility. A damned human likely threw the bag to the street, not a devil or a demon, and while I was ostensibly immune to the bad guys, one of my own kind might have been able to inflict harm on me.

I didn't know for sure. I didn't intend to find out.

The day, or the Underworld's version of one, was still early. In my time as Hell's Super, I'd been an early riser. Truth be told, I was like that even during my lifetime, so though I said I'd slept in, it was still fairly early in Hell's day when I crossed over into the industrial section of the Fifth Circle.

My target was Orson's trailer. He would still be involved in the morning's review and prioritization of work orders. As I neared the office of the Plant Maintenance Department, I saw Edison exit the building. He was heading toward Parts. We waved at each other.

Up the steps I went. Reaching for the knob, I hesitated. I wasn't worried about it coming off in my hand, as it had done almost every morning for sixty years. A wave of nostalgia had hit me. This used to be my office, my domain, but now I felt like an interloper. I didn't really belong here anymore. My fist knuckled up; I'd knock on the door. No. That didn't feel right either. Instead I opened the door a crack and stuck my head in. "Anyone home?"

Orson was sitting at his desk, performing triage on the work orders. He'd usually handled this when I was Hell's Super. Orson had been doing it a long time and was better at it than me. And it was actually the assistant's job, anyway, though I guess my rotund friend didn't yet trust Tom's instincts. Edison was certainly more adept at diagnosing and fixing things that broke in Hell, even though as an assistant he wouldn't be allowed to actually do said fixing, yet he lacked Orson's political instincts, essential when trying to choose the handful of tasks to attempt from the mountain of work orders that came in daily. I wondered if my friend would ever be able to bring himself to delegate a task he had performed so well for so long.

I nodded to myself. *He probably will eventually. If nothing else, Beezy will make him, since it's supposed to be Edison's job now. Besides, no one is supposed to perform a task well down here, and I guess that would include work order triage.*

At the sound of my voice, Orson looked up. "Steve!" he said, shoving back in his chair and hurrying toward me. He gave me a big bear hug. "Great to see you, pal!"

I should have seen that coming. Orson was on the ground, his hair smoking from a blast of Hellfire, the shattered remains of a deftly-thrown lemon cream pie blinding him momentarily. Whichever demon had tossed that one was a real pro. He hadn't even gotten a drop of filling on my new suit.

Instinctively, I reached to my coat pocket for my handkerchief, then remembered I'd left it the previous day with the young woman on Two. I'd have to request a pile of hankies from Peter. I had a feeling I'd be needing them.

I looked around the room for a substitute, but Orson had already used his sleeve to wipe away the goo. He was squinting – the lemon juice stung his eyes – but he was smiling too. He started to say something, but I shushed him.

"It's good to see you Orson," I said, helping him off the floor.

He nodded. "Would you like some coffee?" he asked, going over to the Mr. Coffee and pulling out the "I'M NOT WITH STUPID. I AM STUPID" mug.

For some reason, the sight of my old mug brought tears to my eyes. Now it was my turn to need a handkerchief. "Yeah," I said. "I would."

Now, the coffee in Plant Maintenance is known throughout the nine Circles of Hell as just about the worst brew imaginable. It is so bad that demons occasionally bring in their charges, like that Juan Valdez character from the Folger's Coffee commercials, and force them to drink it. Plant Maintenance coffee is malice-in-a-mug. I think it is so bad because in our lifetimes both Orson and I had loved the old bean.

For this reason, I eyed the black brew suspiciously. Still, coffee is coffee, and I'm an addict. I took an experimental sip then chuckled.

"What?" Orson asked, as he took a slug from his own mug.

"How's the coffee today?" I asked mildly.

He rolled his eyes. "About the same as usual, I guess. Tastes like hell."

I grinned. "Would it surprise you to know that to me it tastes wonderful, like the coffee in New Orleans, with a strong flavor of chicory?"

"Really?" he said, marveling. "I guess that's one of the benefits of being saved."

I looked at my friend with respect. "You didn't say that with any bitterness at all."

Orson shrugged. "That's because I don't feel bitter, or not about this anyway. Shit, Steve, you deserved to gain your salvation. You certainly put up with enough crap to earn it, being forced to become a demon, defying Satan, evading the hordes of Hell."

"Don't forget winning a two out of three coin toss."

"That too."

I sat down on Orson's stool, well, actually Edison's stool now, since it was reserved for the Plant Maintenance assistant, and took another sip. "Still, which is it? An interesting philosophical conundrum."

"Yes," said my friend. "Fair or only fair-seeming for you, foul or only foul-seeming for me?"

"You sound like some character in Shakespeare."

"That would be 'fair is foul, and foul is fair.'" He grinned. "Or perhaps, the quality of coffee is not strained. It droppeth as the gentle rain from hea… hea…"

"Don't try. You'll burst something. Or allow me. Ahem." *Let's see. How does that go? Oh, yeah.* "The quality of coffee is not strained. It droppeth as the gentle rain from heaven upon the place beneath."

There was a rumble from, I would have guessed, three or four circles down. Beezy or Satan, one of the two. "Oh, keep your shirt on," I grumbled back. "Besides," I continued to my friend, "it's more like dirty water falling from a Mr. Coffee filter upon the carafe beneath."

"But which is it?"

"You mean, 'are you a good witch or a bad witch?'"

Orson shook his head. "You can't go three minutes without referencing 'The Wizard of Oz.'"

I arched an eyebrow. "Or you the Bard. But to return to the topic at hand, Is the coffee good but your taste buds have been twisted to make it taste bad to you? Or is it bad, but since I can't have bad, it only seems good to me?"

"Not sure it matters. In this case, the perception is the reality. For both of us." Orson sat back down at his desk and continued his triage of work orders.

Now, under normal circumstances, that would been considered rude, but I understood. If he didn't keep working, he'd get in trouble with Beelzebub. "Go ahead and talk, Steve. I can do this and listen at the same time. What's up?"

Smiling, I ran my hand over my old mug. (The coffee cup, I mean, not my face, though I do that sometimes too.) "Mostly I just wanted to see you. We haven't talked in a while, not really since I underwent my demonectomy."

Orson didn't look up from his work orders, but he chuckled. "I suppose that's the medical term for the surgical removal of the demon within you."

"Yep," I said with a grin. "Saint Peter performed the operation himself."

"Well, he owed you," Orson grumbled. "As poorly as he's treated you over the years."

"These days, he's going overboard to try to make it up to me. Like making me this cool suit."

"Very nice. Oh," my friend said, staring closely at a work order. "The gutters on Hecate's house are clogged again. Guess we'll need to get to that soon." He put the work order in a small stack on the right side of his desktop. A much larger stack was building to the left. The big pile included the jobs he and Edison would ignore.

"Peter and I are getting along pretty well these days," I continued. "He's really not a bad guy once you get past his gargantuan ego."

"Humph. Sin of Pride, just like you and me. So why isn't *he* down here in Hell?"

"Extenuating circumstances, like being the first pope, the first patriarch, an apostle and of course a good buddy of Jesus ..."

Orson looked up, scandalized, and the ground rumbled at our feet again. In under two minutes, I'd twice casually violated a fundamental rule of the Netherworld. "Cool it, Steve," he said, looking down nervously. "You know you can't use that kind of language here!"

"Well, I can, even if you can't, but I'll lay off. Wouldn't want to shake the fabric of Hell's reality ... very much," I added with an impish grin.

"So that's what it's going to be, then, huh? Just like Flo?"

"Well," I said, rubbing my chin. "Maybe not exactly like Flo. She gives comfort to the Damned. I want to do that too but, well, I'm no goody two-shoes. I wouldn't mind giving Hell's Powers that Be a little bit of payback. Still," I added, looking down at the palms of my hands, "to tell the truth, I haven't quite figured out how I'm going to do that."

The door to the office opened, and Edison came in, loaded up with one giant bulb for Hell's Gate, flashing to repair some devil or demon's roof, a big pretzel and a bag of roasted chestnuts. He put down the big items, and walked over to Orson. "You were right. Harpo was where you said he'd be."

Harpo Marx was spending his eternity as a street vendor. Orson had a fondness for old chestnuts. Edison handed him the bag, then looked down at his own pretzel. "I didn't bring anything for you. I'm sorr ..."

"No!" I shouted. "Don't say that!" On reflex, I stood in front of him, and was rewarded by watching the bolt of flame and banana cream pie heading toward Edison's head each deflect wildly to the side then make rapid U-turns. In a second they disappeared from my view. There was an explosion followed by a loud splat.

"Ow! Crap!" said a voice in the distance.

Well, that was interesting.

The guys thought so too. "Spiffy!" Tom said. "Who was on the receiving end, do you think?"

"Some demon, I imagine," I answered. "With few exceptions, all pies in Hell are thrown by demons. I learned that when I was in Beast Barracks."

"What's Beast Barracks?" Orson asked.

"Boot camp for new demons," I said, feeling a bit wistful for that time in my afterlife. In many ways, Beast Barracks had been the best part of being a demon. The easy camaraderie with the other recruits was a memory I would treasure forever.

"Well," Orson said. "I didn't know it was possible to do a reverse whammy like that."

"Apparently it is for me. Hell's torments may not touch one of the Saved," I said, raising my chin in an attempt to look at least marginally dignified. "The Accords that govern the relationships among all heavenly and infernal creatures won't allow it. Since the demon couldn't hit you, Tommy, without going through me, he reversed himself." And got smacked by his own punishment. I chuckled.

"Pretty good," Edison agreed. "Uh, would you like a piece of my pretzel?"

And down he went. After Edison quit cursing, he looked up at me questioningly.

"Sorry. It only works if I'm fast enough." I helped him up. "And keep your pretzel. Thanks, though."

No pie for me.

"Well, I guess I'd better let you guys get back to work. I need to get out there and figure out how I'm going to make a difference down here. It's ... say, can I ask you two a question before I go?"

Orson and Tommy looked at each other and shrugged. "Sure," said the big guy.

"Do you guys remember the moment when Saint Peter damned you?"

"Why do you ask?" Edison asked.

Good question. Why am *I asking?* "Just curious, I guess. What do you remember?"

Orson leaned back in his chair and thought for a moment. "You know, it's all a bit hazy. I remember standing in front of Peter. He opened the Book of Life and ran his finger down the page." My friend shook his head, as if the action would rustle up elusive memories. "That's all I can recall. Next thing I knew, I was standing on the Escalator heading down."

"What about you, Tom?"

"I can do a little better than that," Edison said slowly, "but not much. I actually remember Saint Peter telling me I was damned, but I don't remember him looking me up in the Book at all." Edison sat heavily upon his stool, closed his eyes and concentrated. At last he opened them and looked at me. "Sorry. That's it. It's as if the piece of my brain storing that particular memory has been walled off."

I nodded. *I bet anything Peter used that stupid quarter to decide both of their fates.*

"Steve?" Orson said, interrupting my thoughts. "You okay?"

"Huh? Oh yeah." I looked at my watch, kind of an irrelevant thing to do in an eternal afterlife, but it was a habit of mine that had pursued me beyond the grave. "Later guys."

"Later!" they said in unison.

They were back at their work order review as I pulled the door behind me.

Chapter 5

My talk with Orson and Edison left me unsettled. What they had told me was not a revelation. The memory of my own damnation had also been fuzzy until Peter had helped me recall it some months ago. That's when I'd first learned that he frequently used a coin toss to settle borderline cases. Yet it was troubling that something as important as the disposition of a soul – of so many souls – would be left to chance.

With an effort, I shoved the conversation from my mind. There was a task at hand. I needed to figure out how to be a good deed doer in Hell.

What to do? What to do?

I was walking the sidewalk, across the street from the oil refinery. To my right, in the distance, the Toaster, Hell's Hospital, loomed over the Parts Department, where Dora, my old comrade in damnation, was leaning on her counter smoking a cigarette. With no opportunity for a good deed in sight, I decided to stop by and say hi to the old battle-ax.

Dora and I hadn't spent any time together since that fateful day Flo went missing, the day Satan tricked me into becoming a demon. When she spotted me, she was so surprised she almost dropped her cigarette. "Steve? Is that you?"

"Yeah, Dora. Cough, cough. How are you?" She was smoking Newports, not her regular brand, which was Kools, but probably all she could get today. Newports always struck me as more cloying than its competition in the menthol-laced cigarette market space. Poor Dora hated mint and menthol, but Kools was the lesser of two evils, so if she was smoking Newports, she was having an extra bad day.

The old hag shrugged. "I'm in Hell, but what else is new?" She eyed me carefully. "Besides you, I mean. Pretty spiffy suit."

"Thanks. Saint Peter made it for me."

"So, it's true then? You're really a saved soul, like Orson said?"

"Yeah," I said modestly. "Got lucky, I guess."

Dora fished out another Newport, lit it with the glowing stub of her old one then flicked it to the pavement. The old one, of course, since flipping the new one to the ground would have been stupid as well as wasteful. Not that Hell gives a crap about the judicious use of anything, though Satan does appreciate littering. By way of example: there was a pile of Dora's butts on the asphalt.

Cigarette butts, I mean. It's not like she has spares of the other kind. I don't know anyone who does, though that could be handy in certain situations, I suppose, like to provide blessed relief in the aftermath of a doubleheader spent on some concrete bleachers, or if you needed to replace the butt you'd worn out during a long ride on one of those minuscule bicycle seats. You get the idea.

But back to Dora. She wasn't normally one to be impressed by anything. She's seen it all, or so she said. Even Dora, though, jaded old reptile that she was, seemed interested in what had happened to me. "Let me get this straight. First, you're damned, like me. Then you become a demon, which I'd always heard was irreversible. And now you're *saved*?"

I stuck my hands in my trouser pockets, glanced down at the pavement, shuffled my feet a little. "When you say it like that, it *does* sound pretty bizarre."

"Bizarre? Fucking amazing, if you ask me." She took a long drag on her cigarette, eyeing me appraisingly. "What now?"

I leaned on Dora's counter, and for a wonder, she let me. Normally, Dora only allowed Dora to do that. "I'm trying to figure that out. You know how Flo came to Hell on her own, even though she's saved and could go to Heaven anytime?"

"Yeah."

"Well, I'm no Florence Nightingale …"

She snorted. "Ain't that the truth?"

"Hey! But you're right. She's the goodest, I mean, the best person I've ever known. I'm not in her league, but I'm going to try to take a page from her book."

Dora looked at me uncomprehendingly. "Meaning…?"

"You know. Flo is spending Eternity easing suffering in the hospital. I want to do something similar."

"Like what? Clean bedpans?"

"Hey!"

"Hey? I throw out a perfectly good insult, and your best comeback is hey? It's also the second time in thirty seconds you used it. Funny, I would have thought a big-deal saved soul like yourself would talk a little more eloquently. Weren't you some hotshot academic in life?"

"I was." My chest swelled with pride. "I was an economist."

Dora snorted again. "Oh, that explains it."

"Hey!" *Guess I do overuse that word.* "I mean, why do you say that?"

"Well," she said, slowly. "It's not like you were literate or anything, like an English or History major."

"Wait a minute," I protested. "I'll have you know I was the author of over fifty scholarly articles in the best peer-reviewed journals of my field. I also wrote three very well-received books."

"All in economics?"

"Well, sure."

"All filled with words like money supply and income per capita and business cycles? GDP, CPI, WXYZ? That kind of shit?"

"Not that last one of course, but the rest, sure. That's the vocabulary of an economist."

"Yeah, but it ain't English. You don't seem so good with English."

For some reason, my feelings were hurt. I kicked at the ground. "Now you're just being mean."

"Oh, quit pouting, Steve. I'm just messing with you." She started laughing, then erupted into a nasty nicotine hack. "Seriously, though, COUGH, why do you talk like a longshoreman? You once told me you felt dumbed down by damnation."

"That's right," I said, nodding.

"But you're saved now and should be smart again. So shouldn't you talk, I don't know, a little more refined?"

"I ..." Hmm. She had a point. I shrugged. "I, I guess I just got used to talking this way. You know, I was a handyman down here a lot longer than I was an economist. Old habits die hard. Besides, it just seems more genuine, you know?"

Dora pulled out another Newport and lit it with the one that had now turned to ash. "Yeah, it does. It *is*. All in all, I'd rather hear everyday talk than a bunch of four syllable words. And then there's empty words and phrases like 'wherefore,' 'in point of fact' and 'it goes without saying.'" She waved vaguely in the air. "You know, shit like that."

I grimaced. Academics did indeed talk that way. Hell, *I* used to talk like that, tossing out phrases at work and in party conversation that sounded impressive but were completely devoid of meaning. "I know exactly what you mean. I guess I agree with you, and ... wait a minute, what were we talking about?"

"Damned if I know. Something about 'Hey.'"

"Hey? Oh yeah," I said, remembering. "I was telling you about wanting to help make things easier on the Damned, like Flo does."

Dora blew a smoke ring. "Any ideas what you'd do?"

"So far, only one." I frowned.

"What is it?"

"Easier for me to show you."

"So show," she said, yawning. I guess she was getting bored with the conversation.

"Okay. Say something nice to me."

Dora looked at me with disgust. "Now, why would I do that? Even if I wanted to, you know what would happen."

I winked at her. "Do you trust me?"

"Not particularly. Oh, don't give me that hurt puppy dog look. I trust you as much as I trust anyone, which is not very much." She paused, thinking about our past history. In all the decades we'd worked together, I'd always been straight with her. "Okay, maybe I trust you a little more than most of the jokers down here."

I smiled. "Thanks. I take that as high praise, coming from you." In life, Dora had been a shark, metaphorically anyway. A predator. Predators tend not to have lots of buddies. "So say something nice. Something you mean. It has to be sincere, you know."

Dora looked as if she'd just swallowed something disagreeable. Having to be nice went against character for her. The hellacious consequences she was expecting if she complimented me wasn't much of an incentive either. Still, to her credit, she nodded. "Why the hell not? What's one more humiliation down here anyway? Doesn't really matter in the scheme of things, I guess. Okay, here goes." She cleared her throat. "I, well, I like you. You and Orson, and Flo of course, are my favorite people in all of Hell." Then Dora closed her eyes, waiting for the inevitable punishment.

In a flash I was standing before her. For some reason, I closed my eyes too, probably from sixty years of conditioning. That's why I felt rather than saw the Hellfire, hot on my schnozzle. The heat quickly receded, though. Then came the whizzing sound of a newly-launched pie; the swooshing grew louder then abruptly softer.

"Shit!" came a voice in the distance. "Twice in one morning!"

Well, what do you know? It must have been the same demon who tried to take pot shots at Edison.

Apparently, Dora had opened her eyes just in time to watch the pie reverse course. She flicked a bit of ash from her cigarette. "A back-flying pie. Interesting. How'd you do that?"

I shrugged. "Oh, I just took advantage of the situation. Just like Flo, I'm a saved soul now. No demon or devil is allowed to harm me. Not sure Flo ever used her saved status as an offensive weapon, but it seems to work."

Dora seemed unimpressed. "Humph. So this is your grand plan? You're going to wander around the Circles deflecting Hellfire?"

"Don't forget the pies!" I protested, but she was right. It was an unimpressive use of my new status.

"Still," she added, with a wicked grin, "it was fun to watch you do it."

Just not particularly noteworthy. I frowned again.

"Well, I guess I should let you get back to work," I said. Not that she seemed to have anything to do. "Oh, as long as I have you, let me ask you a question."

"All right. I guess."

"Do you remember the moment of your damnation?"

Now, Dora has never been very good at swearing, but my question unleashed a flow of obscene invective that would have done a demon proud. "Yeah," she said, chewing through her still-burning cigarette then spitting it on the sidewalk. "What about it?"

"Well," I said slowly, regretting resurrecting what, for Dora, was obviously an unpleasant memory, "could you tell me exactly how it went down?"

"You mean how *I* went down. Like everyone else, I guess. That snotty saint opened his great big book, found my name, and said, 'I regret to inform you that you have been damned for all Eternity. Please take the Escalator to my left. You'll know when to get off.'" Dora finished her brief account with another round of cursing.

Well. That wasn't really much of a surprise. Not everyone could be damned by coin toss. In my years observing the goings-on at Gates Level, I'd personally seen Peter give the bad news, and occasional good news, to many people, straight from the Book of Life. Despite my feelings about that quarter of his, I knew he only employed it in a minority of cases.

And if anyone deserved Hell, it was Dora. After all, in life she'd run a paycheck loan business. What could be worse, at least this side of a serial killer?

"Sorry to bring up a bad memory," I said lamely. I knew it was bad, because Dora had gone a whole thirty seconds without a cigarette.

"Buzz off, Steve," she said with a grumble, lighting another Newport. "I've got to get back to my inventory." Dora turned from the doorway and waddled to the far recesses of the Parts warehouse.

As requested, I buzzed off, spending the rest of the day wandering the streets of Five, occasionally blocking a pie, chasing off the odd demon, that sort of thing. Pretty paltry fare, though it wasn't all flames and baked goods. I had a few opportunities to perform other acts of kindness. For example, a demon tried to push one of the Damned into a wheelbarrow of excrement, but I blocked the way with my body. Finally the demon got bored and wandered off muttering.

I even got a mime out of a thorn bush; he had been performing "man pulling a rope" in there. Looked pretty painful. But as soon as I got him out of the thick of things, the wind pick up and dumped him back in. When I tried to pull out the mime a second time, he gestured an emphatic no. He was so agitated he actually spoke out loud. "Please. It's better for me to just stay in here. Being thrown back in hurts much more." I nodded, leaving him there to continue his performance.

This was all very discouraging.

I was just getting ready to hang things up for the day and head home when I spotted a young girl in a frayed and tattered shift, sitting on a curb, crying disconsolately. I went up to her. Kneeling down to be at her eye level, I asked, "What's wrong?"

She sniffed. "I ... I have to go inside that building there," she said, indicating a sausage factory behind her. "And I just know something awful will happen when I do."

I'd toured a sausage factory once and knew how the stuff was made. "I'm sure you're right. You'll probably lose your lunch. But ..." I added quickly, "would it help if I went inside with you?"

The naïf looked at me wide-eyed. "Would you do that? For me?"

I smiled. "Sure. Come on."

The crying lessened, and she extended her hand. "Help me up?"

"My pleasure," I said, helping her to her feet. Then, arm in arm we headed toward the factory door. We opened it and stepped into blackness. The door slammed behind us.

A light came on, illuminating a large and very familiar rosewood desk. The arm holding mine tightened.

"Gaaah!"

The girl was gone. In her place was a boa constrictor. It gave my arm a final wrenching squeeze before dropping to the floor. Then it transformed into …

"Satan! You!"

"Yes. Me." The Earl of Hell walked around the desk, where his favorite red La-Z-Boy popped out of the floor. He sat down as a king might take to his throne. Unusually, though, he did not kick back, raising the footrest. He just gripped the sides of the chair, staring at me with undisguised hatred.

The feeling was mutual. For sixty years, Satan had been the architect of my damnation. He had battered and broken me in this very room, again and again, made me suffer the indignities of the cowed and servile. Against my will, mostly, he had turned me into a demon, separating me from almost all of the few friends I'd managed to make down here. And then when I had a second chance for redemption, he tried to cheat by rigging Saint Peter's coin toss. Only divine intervention had prevented him from getting his way.

But a Higher Power *had* intervened. I was saved and, I reflected, no longer under the thumb of Hell's ruler. I got all squinty-eyed myself as I looked at Satan with a loathing that matched his own. "What do *you* want?" I hissed.

I was particularly proud of the hiss. That was one of Satan's signature moves, you know, and I enjoyed throwing it back in his face.

Satan's hands clenched, and his claws dug deep into the red leather of his La-Z-Boy. "You know exactly. I want you the hell out of my domain!"

Putting my hands behind me, I began to pace the floor, trying to project a casual attitude. I even put my back to Satan. It was a risk – you turn your back on one of the most powerful beings in the universe at your own peril – but I was counting on my Steve-o-Zone to protect me. Besides, I was tired of being intimidated by this guy. Nothing shows you don't fear someone more than turning your back to him; it's about as dismissive a gesture as there is.

Of course, I really did fear him. Satan scared me shitless, always had, but it was a phobia I resolved to work on, starting at that very moment. Because he could no longer read my mind – and because I was working really hard not to tremble or collapse in fear or something equally craven – Big Red might not know how I felt.

"You're not fooling me, Minion. It's a nice act, but you'll never lose your fear of *me*! Bwahahahahahaha!" As I looked back at him, he raised his hands above his head and shot Hellfire into the air. Then he began to morph rapidly among a variety of his aspects, a cobra, a dragon, television static, a floating head not dissimilar to the one used by the wizard in 'The Wizard of Oz.' He ended with one of my least favorite of his incarnations: Azazel. "How about this one, eh? I think this one scares you most of all. Ah. AH AH AH!"

Azazel, even down to the fake-o creepy laugh. The devil form he had assumed when he tricked me into becoming a demon. Back then, yes, it had terrified me. Now, knowing it was all part of an elaborate con, it only pissed me off. I growled at him, sounding a little like I did back in my demon days. It startled him. "Nice try, you fucker."

"How *dare* you?" he said in outrage. "Have you forgotten your place? I am the Lord of Hell, you know."

I placed my palms on his desktop and leaned toward him. "So what?" I said, a savage intensity in my voice that surprised even me. "I'm a saved soul. I figure that makes me at least one step higher in the celestial pecking order than you."

Satan looked as if he'd been slapped. I smiled. "And I'm not going anywhere. Me and Flo..."

"Flo and I..."he corrected reflexively. Satan was almost as much a stickler for grammar as Orson. "Me and Flo," I repeated, knowing it would bug him. I grinned evilly. "We're going to stay down here and do everything in our power to thwart you."

Satan stood up abruptly, his recliner shooting backward until it disappeared into the gloom at the rear of his office. "Listen, you poor excuse for a saved soul! I have put up with Nightingale for a hundred and fifty years. In all that time, yes, she has been a constant irritation, but nothing more than that. And she at least really is a good soul. I respect her integrity."

I narrowed my eyes. "You used to say you respected mine."

Satan made a stack of papers appear on his desk. With a swipe of his hand, he knocked them to the floor.

He was always one for dramatic effect.

"Maybe I did at one time. Now I feel nothing but disdain for you. Who do you think you're kidding, you fake? I may be evil, but I've never pretended to be anything but what I am."

"Not so!" I responded heatedly. "Prince of Lies, remember?"

"Well," he hesitated. "Yes, but deceit is part of who I am. You, you're supposedly a good soul. Give me a break! I know devils who are better people than you are."

I nodded. "Like Beelzebub." Beezy was the only devil in Hell I respected.

"Yes, like Beelzebub. You, though, sir, are nothing but a fraud. You never should have been given a second chance at the coin toss!"

"And you shouldn't have tried to cheat!" I bellowed, feeling my face turn red.

Surprisingly, the Prince of Hell flinched. "What ... what are you talking about?"

"Oh, come on," I said with a grumble. "I saw you try to blow the quarter over so that it would land 'heads' up, making me lose the toss. Shit, everybody there saw it!"

Satan exhaled softly. "Oh, that. Right, right. I forgot."

Huh? Satan never forgets. I eyed him with suspicion.

But Satan was eyeing me as well, or rather glaring at me. "I stand by my earlier statement. You're a fraud."

I frowned. In a way, he was right. I was not a bad person, but I wasn't a particularly good one either. "Maybe," I said slowly. "Maybe you're right. Maybe I'm not that much of a good guy right now, but I'm going to spend the rest of Eternity trying to become one."

"Humph." Satan motioned behind him, and his La-Z-Boy raced forward to scoop him up. "Good luck with your plans for self-improvement. You have a long way to go before you'll be worth more than the carpet beneath my desk. And speaking of going, why don't you take said plans and work them in some place other than my domain? Deflecting a bunch of pies. Brother." For a moment, he looked uncertain, as if considering something new, but then he shook his head. "It's funny, I suppose, but I doubt it helps to burnish your soul to a fine luster. Yes, Heaven would be a better place for you. I sure as hell don't want you down here!"

"Nice try, horn head," I said, earning me one of Satan's patented snarls. He almost never wore his devil horns, finding them on the gauche side. I cleared my throat and continued. "I'm going to stay right here."

Satan transformed from his Azazel persona back to the man-in-black look, complete with Agent Smith sunglasses. These he now slipped down his nose, presenting me a view of the black version of his eyes. (Sometimes they were red.) They were like bottomless wells; one could get lost in those eyes, trying to find the depths of their evil. "Minion," he said softly, but with a voice that promised violence. "Leave Hell now or suffer great harm."

"You can't harm me, and you know it."

The Lord of Hell cursed under his breath. "Maybe not, but I can harm those you care about. Not Nightingale, but everyone else: Orson, Braille, Pinkerton and the others."

I swallowed hard. This was something I'd been afraid of from the very beginning, that Satan, unable to hurt me, would turn up the heat on my friends. I searched my mind for an answer to this. Then it came to me, and I smiled. "You can't, and you know that too."

Satan rocketed from his chair, sending his recliner back into the darkness. He picked up his desk and threw it out of sight. "You go too far! The damned souls are *mine*, by divine decree. The manner and extent of their torment is up to me alone to decide."

Now for my big bluff. "If you hurt them because you're mad at me, then you hurt me, and that is against the Accords." I really didn't know this for a fact, but it was logical. It had to be why Flo was able to have friendships down here.

"Argh!" Satan screamed in frustration.

I'm right. Whew. It had been a huge risk, calling his bluff, but I was glad I'd done it.

"Enough of this! Begone!" Satan waved his hand at me.

There was a familiar tingle, just like I used to feel whenever I teleported, but nothing happened. Seems Satan couldn't even do anything as benign as send me away.

And he knew it, if the frown on his face was any indication. "You can see yourself out," he said stiffly. Then his desk and chair flew back into place and he sat down, picking up a pile of paperwork. The room faded to black.

And the doors leading to his waiting area opened. I stepped through, then they slammed behind me.

Hard.

Chapter 6

Bruce the Bedeviled, Satan's personal assistant, was at his desk. He was staring at me with contempt. "Hello, traitor."

Bruce was a newly-made demon. When I renounced my demonism, or my demonosity, or whatever the hell it's called, all of the D&D Corps accounted me a turncoat. Well, I didn't exactly know if they *all* thought I was a traitor. Maximus, a friend of mine from demon boot camp, might not have. And Lord Beelzebub, who had been my boss and mentor for sixty years, really didn't take the evil "Bwahaha etc." devil thing too seriously. To him, being number two in Hell was nothing more than a job, one he was very good at, but at the end of the day just what he was supposed to be doing in the grand scheme of things. So he probably didn't take my resignation from the Corps personally either.

Most other devils and demons, though, must have felt like Bruce, that I had turned up my nose at the greatest gift Satan could offer, to be made a demon, and a powerful one at that. To them, my transgression was unforgivable.

"Hello, Bruce," I said mildly. "Like my suit?"

Bruce was always the fashion plate. "Why, yes, very much, I..." He caught himself and frowned. "Don't bandy words with me, you, you traitor."

"You already said that. Need to work on your snappy repartee, my friend."

His eyes narrowed, and he frowned. "I am not your friend, Minion. I wasn't when you were damned, I wasn't even when you were a demon, so I'm sure as hell not going to be one now. Just get out of here."

"Okay," I said, whistling, and headed to the Elevator. I pressed the button.

"Fat chance," said a disembodied voice. It was Otis, the demon of the Elevator. "You can stand there throughout Eternity, for all I care."

"Oh, come on, Otis. You've got to pick me up sometime. It's the rules."

The demon growled. "Maybe so. But I might make you wait two or three days."

I pointed back to the office I'd just exited. "You'd better not do that. Satan wants me out of here, pronto."

"No I don't!" boomed a voice from behind the double doors. "I just wanted you out of my office. You can rot where you stand, for all I care. Leave him there, Otis. Go run some errands."

The demon elevator chortled. "Yes sir. See you around, chump!"

"YOU DARE!"

"Not you sir!" Otis said hurriedly. "I was talking to *this* chump."

Oops.

"Not that you're a chump too, your Greatness, I only meant ..."

Satan's office doors blew open, and a blast of Hellfire erupted from within. It turned the Elevator doors to slag. I heard a yelp and then a whoosh as Otis took off at top speed. If he was smart, he'd head to Gates Level and park it there for a while.

"What about me, sir?" Bruce asked, staring into the cavernous black space behind the open doors. "I don't want to even look at this, this traitor!"

I grinned. "Makes three times, Bruce."

"Shut up, Minion!" boomed the Earl of Hell's voice. "And quit messing with my employee. As for you, Bruce, just focus on your filing. You'll be fine." The Devil's doors slammed shut again.

Bruce looked at a two-foot pile of paperwork – probably contracts for people's souls – and gritted his teeth. Can't say I blamed him. Filing always sucked for me too.

I shrugged and started a circumnavigation of the front office. There wasn't much to see. The office was decorated, incongruously I'd always thought, in white. White shag carpet, a white desk for Bruce, white file drawers built into an equally white wall. Even the outside of Satan's office doors were like snow.

There was one exception to the décor: a single stainless steel door. I tried the knob, even though I knew it would be locked. This was, after all, the entrance to the traitors' cell block. I wrapped a couple of times.

"Knock, knock."

"Uh, who's there?" said a gravelly voice.

Aha. Adam's eldest likes knock knock jokes. "Raisin," I replied, not missing a beat.

"Raisin who?"

"Raisin Cain."

"Arggh!" howled the voice.

"Get away from that door!" Bruce snapped.

"Whatever." I wandered to the center of the room and stared up through the Throat of Hell. There wasn't much to see. The ceiling to the room was maybe twelve feet up, where the beginning of the Throat, a hole thirty feet in diameter, opened. It was jet black, a stark contrast to the rest of the room, but if I stood dead center (couldn't rightly stand "live" center, not being alive anymore) beneath the hole, I could make out a patch of white in the center. That would be where the hole broke through into the Eighth Circle of Hell. That was pretty high up.

Hmm. Nope. No exit that way.

So, Otis was gone, and Bruce was trying very hard to pretend I didn't exist.

Shit. How the hell am I going to get out of here? No Stairs, no access to the Elevator, no way to climb up to and then out through the Throat of Hell. The Escalator doesn't even come down here. If it did, I could at least have run up it, though that would have been a bitch, a mile-long jog on electric stairs moving in the opposite direction.

I caught myself, realizing I needed to get out of here quickly. My language was turning to gutter talk. Satan may not have been able to harm me, but he was a bad influence.

This was a bit of a dilemma. Other than my magical lucky charm, that is to say, my protection from harm, as opposed to a boxful of cereal or anything like that, I had no superpowers. I'd lost them all when I'd stopped being a demon. Then I brightened. *I do have another superpower left. My mouth.*

I walked back over to Satan's assistant, who was putting a fat dossier into the "R" drawer, paying me no mind. The knock knock joke had given me an idea.

I poked him with my finger. "Hey Bruce, did you know that Satan runs the IRS back on Earth?"

The demon looked up at me, confused. "No, I ..."

"He must, because everyone knows the devil takes many forms."

Somewhere in the Universe there was a rimshot. I'm sure it was for me. Meanwhile, from Satan's office came a sound like thunder. I smiled. "Hey Bruce."

He groaned. "What now?"

63

"What did Bill Murray say when he met Satan?"

Bruce slipped another file into a drawer. He was doing his best to ignore me. "I'm sure I have no idea."

"I ain't afraid of no goats. Yuk yuk!"

Satan hates to be called a goat, though I thought I heard the stomping of his cloven hooves after my punch line. "QUIT PLAYING STRAIGHT MAN TO THIS JERK!"

"No, Bill Murray didn't play 'The Jerk,'" I yelled back. "That was Steve Martin! Have you forgotten all that movie trivia I taught you back in the day?"

"INSOLENT HUMAN!"

"And Bill Murray could not have said that!" Bruce protested, coming to the defense of his boss. "I remember now! Murray and the entire cast of 'Ghostbusters' went to Heaven."

I shrugged. "Who cares? A joke's a joke. Speaking of jokes, Have you heard about the dyslexic devil worshipper? He sold his soul to Santa."

Ugh. Even I cringed at that one. Bruce buried his head in his hands, while the sound of an incipient storm grew in Satan's office.

"Oh, Bruce," I said, checking out his wardrobe. Satan's assistant was dressed in a white turtleneck and equally white Nehru jacket. It was a bit of a throwback to Sixties fashions, but those were the styles he favored. He even had on a pair of slacks, never a guarantee with demons, who don't always want to have their tails scrunched by a bunch of fabric over their butts. Bruce, however, would never be caught dead without his slacks on, at least not while at work. Who knew what he did on his off time? Whenever I saw him, though, he was always perfectly dressed. His slacks matched his jacket: ice cream colored, which is to say vanilla, of course, because Neapolitan would have just looked goofy. "You know your men's fashion houses pretty well, don't you?"

He looked up. This new angle confused him. "Uh, yes. I suppose so."

I nodded. "Tell me then. Have you ever seen Satan in Armani?"

This was just the kind of puzzler to throw at Bruce. He frowned. "No, I don't believe so."

"Of course not. The Devil Wears Prada."

The office doors opened again, and a second blast of Hellfire shot through the opening, this time directly at me. About a foot from my face, though, the flames made an abrupt U-turn. Satan's doors slammed shut in a hurry, and the fire bounced harmlessly off them.

Hmm. I must really be getting to him. Time to up the ante. But with what? I'm fresh out of devil jokes. Ah, I know.

I sat on the edge of Bruce's desk. This always infuriated him, which of course is why I did it.

"Get your saved butt off my furniture!" he hissed in a way only a demon or devil could.

Instead, I leaned in closer. "Did you know that Satan is really stupid?"

"What? No I ..."

"If he had another brain, that would make one."

The floor began to rock. Satan is the Sin of Pride personified. He hates to be called stupid, or at least, so I assumed. I doubt if anyone had ever dared to do it before. I continued.

"Satan is an idiot. He's dumber than a pet rock. ... You know, don't you, that Satan tempted Adam and Eve to eat from the tree bearing the fruit containing the knowledge of good and evil."

"Of course," Bruce grumbled in irritation. "Everybody knows that. Now would you shut up and leave me alone? I have work to do." He threw a file at me, but it boomeranged, flew into his face and smacked him one.

"Ow!"

"What you may not know," I continued, as if none of that had happened, "is that many call that 'the stupid tree,' because eating from it resulted in humans doing a bunch of really stupid things. Anyway, after Satan tempted them, he fell out of the stupid tree and hit every branch on the way down."

Horns blew in the distance. Maybe they were supposed to be battle horns, but they sounded more like an "AWOOGAH!" to me.

Oh, boy. That last joke was pretty tortured, but I really wanted to get the Adam and Eve thing in there. Now to switch gears.

"I'm kidding, of course. Satan must actually be very smart."

Bruce sighed in relief.

I grinned cruelly. "He has to be. He has an intellect that is rivaled only by green vegetables."

I'm on a roll. "Satan has an IQ of one. Unfortunately it takes at least a two to be able to belch. Yep, if stupid were sand, Satan would be the Sahara."

The Ninth Circle of Hell rocked so hard, it was pitched to a forty-five degree angle, and Bruce went crashing to the carpet. I noticed with satisfaction that I had no problem keeping my feet under me.

I glanced at Satan's office doors. *Now to put him away.*

"Let's face it, Bruce. Everyone in Hell knows how stupid Satan is. Why, he's so dumb he makes Adramelech looks like a rocket scientist."

66

Bruce was horrified. Adramelech, an arch demon, was widely acknowledged to be the dumbest creature in all the nine Circles of Hell.

The Ninth Circle seemed to be upside down now, and Bruce was clutching desperately to his desk top, which curiously had remained in place, as had I. "Please, Steve," he whispered plaintively. "Please sto …"

I almost felt sorry for the twerpy little demon. One more should do it. "Satan is so stupid he makes Digger (the second dumbest critter down here) look like a Nobel laureate."

"BOOH!" Satan screamed from inside his office. In about a second, BOOH flew down, which is to say up, alighting on the carpet. He looked a little confused by the changed perspective, but it was hard to befuddle the Bat out of Hell, especially since he spent half his existence hanging upside down anyway. He adjusted quickly.

"Get that asshole out of here!"

BOOH looked at Bruce.

"NOT THAT ASSHOLE! The other one. Minion! Drop him on Eight. That big-mouthed SOB can take the Stairs home!"

I laughed uncontrollably during the entire ride to Level Eight.

Chapter 7

BOOH set me down behind a sand dune next to Camelot. That's an establishment that sells used dromedaries at the bazaar operating perpetually on Eight. It also offers hourly parking, but the rates are exorbitant, even by Hell's standards.

I was still chuckling as BOOH settled down on the ground next to me. He looked worried.

I wiped the tears from my eyes, then patted him companionably. "Oh, relax, pal. I just told a few jokes."

"Skree? Urm?"

"Because it was the only way I could think of to get out of the Ninth Circle. Satan wouldn't let me use the Elevator, so I improvised. Funny. I've always had a knack for making myself irritating to others, even the Lord of Hell, apparently." It was a strange point of pride, but I shrugged. In this situation I'd take it.

BOOH exhaled. "Skree."

"Yeah," I agreed. "So, how are you? Don't worry," I said, seeing BOOH look around nervously. "No one can see us talking here, and Satan can't read your mind or mine, so we should be good."

"Uh, urm," he hesitated.

I looked at my batty friend. "Are you feeling guilty for associating with me?"

BOOH's ears flattened, which they always did when he was angry or conflicted or had ear mites. In this case it was probably option two. He looked at me and nodded.

Pursing my lips, I thought for a second. "BOOH, everyone in Hell, even Satan, knows that you are a morally neutral creature, like Switzerland with fangs, right?"

"Urm."

"Okay, if that's the case, then you can't be caught in a moral dilemma. You're not doing anything wrong, because right and wrong don't actually apply to you."

BOOH sat down with a thump. I don't think he'd considered the situation from that perspective. My friend was deep in thought for a minute, and I kept quiet, letting him process my words. Finally he made his decision. He looked at me and nodded. "Ur...urm!"

"That's the spirit! I don't want you to get in trouble, though, so let's have our occasional tête-à-têtes on the qt, okay?"

"Skree."

That settled, I lay down and began to make sand angels. They're like snow angels except, well, made in sand, of which we had plenty on Level Eight. As I swirled my arms back and forth, making angel wings in the white powder, I marveled at my new suit; the fabric was just amazing. It never got dirty, never got wrinkled. Yep, Peter did very good work. I wondered if he had also made Flo's nurse's uniform. She never looked disheveled either. *Or perhaps it's just one more benefit of being a saved soul. No need to do laundry or dry cleaning. That alone is a little bit of Heaven.*

BOOH watched me for a few secs, shrugged and started making sand angels also – big ones. My friend has a touch of what I assume to be mange on his back, and the desert floor probably made a pretty good back scratcher.

That done, we stood up. The sand fell from my clothes as if they were made of Teflon. BOOH stretched out his wings and did a shake and a jig. Sand flew from his fur; the resulting

69

breeze made me feel like I was in Haiti in the middle of a hurricane. BOOH's sand also fell harmlessly from my suit.

We spent ten minutes, crouched back on the ground, playing a few rounds of Tic-Tac-Toe. After that, we played some Twenty Questions then argued about which Circle would win the most medals in the upcoming Hellish Olympics.

The giant bat looked at his wrist, just like I'd done with Orson and Edison earlier in the day. There was no watch there, but the meaning was clear. He had to get back to work. I nodded. "Of course. Listen, since I can't track your comings and goings, maybe you can keep an eye on mine. If you see me in a place where we might have a little privacy, drop in for a visit, okay?"

"Urm. Skree." BOOH tousled my hair with one of the two small hands attached to his wings. (Oh, that's one hand per side; two on the same wing would have been creepy.) Then my friend took to the skies.

And there I was, alone on Level Eight. I had a three mile hike up the Stairway to Heaven to get back to Flo's flat on Five, and I wasn't looking forward to getting my exercise on the mother of all StairMasters.

Please note two letters are capitalized in the name of that product: S&M. That seems really appropriate to me.

But I digress. Frequently.

Not being quite ready to hoof it up the Stairs, I decided to pay a call on my former mentor, Beelzebub. The thought filled me with trepidation. We were on opposite sides now, and I had no idea what kind of a reception I'd get. He couldn't hurt me, except emotionally, I reflected, but because I actually cared for the ancient devil, he could do that pretty effectively.

That I could have feelings for one of the great icons of evil would strike almost anyone as odd. I should have hated him, but I didn't, for I knew Beelzebub's great secret. He was evil because his job required him to be, sort of like a collection agent, but off-the-clock he was a pretty decent person. And he was wise, philosophical even. Deep. Despite these virtues, I had no idea how he would react to me showing up on his doorstep. Still, I had to come face to face with him sooner or later, if only to find out where we stood in our relationship. Now was as good a time as any.

I walked around the dune and crossed the camel lot, making a direct beeline for his office. Devils, demons and Damned alike parted before me, and I felt like Moses crossing the Red Sea, or in this case, I suppose, the Dead Sea. Everyone gave me plenty of clearance, except one individual, who was so focused on her trash pickup duties that she hadn't noticed me.

The soul in question was an unusual sight for Hell: a nun in full habit. I figured she must have died before Vatican Two. After that, many religious sisters began to wear modern clothing, always dignified, but the more colorful, the better.

Can't say I blame them. Black and white may always be fashionable, but wearing the same thing every day, year in, year out, gets old. I speak from experience.

This woman, however, was dressed in the traditional habit of a nun, Ursuline I think, at least judging from the wimple she wore. She must have been roasting in the full-length, mostly black outfit, especially on Eight, which is one of the hotter circles in Hell, yet she didn't show her discomfort. She simply went about her business, sweeping up dirt and manure, dumping them in a barrel that she would periodically push across the sand to the next cleanup location.

I watched her work for a minute. Diligent, focused, uncomplaining. Just like most of the nuns I had known in my lifetime.

Her presence in Hell troubled me. There of course must be members of the Catholic orders who don't make it to Heaven, but I had run across very few of them in my sixty year sojourn in the Circles of Hell, and those I had met usually had been male. The women religious of the Roman Catholic Church had been some of the finest, most spiritual human beings I had known in my lifetime, taking vows of poverty, chastity and obedience. What's more, they really lived by those vows.

I couldn't help myself. "Excuse me. Hello? Hello?"

The woman, who seemed to be about seventy, though you can never tell down here, looked up from her broom and dustpan, seeing me for the first time. "Oh, I'm sorry," she said politely, a slight southern drawl adding a molasses sweetness to her voice. "I didn't realize I was in your way."

"Not at all, sister," I said with a smile. "I was just surprised to see you here."

She smiled softly in return. "I'm always here. It's my job to keep the bazaar clean. I've been doing it for over a hundred years."

"I didn't mean here, here," I said, pointing to the activity of the bazaar then made a broad sweep of my hand. "I meant in Hell. How did that happen to you?"

The woman shrugged. "It's not my place to question the judgment of the L …"

She struggled to say the word, even though she would have been punished for mentioning the divine, but she was intent upon doing it anyway. With a gesture, I shushed her. "I understand, but, well, were you a good person in life?"

"I tried to be. I spent fifty years giving comfort to terminally ill patients in a hospital in rural Louisiana."

"Did you keep your vows?"

"Yes, of course."

I looked at her with confusion. "And yet you ended up here. There must have been *some* reason for it."

There was a brief flash of lightning in her eyes, which she quickly repressed. "Perhaps, perhaps it was my temper. In life, it would flare occasionally." She bit her lip. "Watching people die from cancer. It was … difficult." The sister looked more sad than angry.

Maybe. Maybe her temper qualified as the cardinal sin of Wrath. I didn't believe it, though.

"Since coming to Hell, I've learned to master that particular character flaw, or at least, I hope I have." She made a somewhat regretful smile. "Excuse me, but I must return to my labors now."

"Of course, but, before I leave you alone, may I ask your name?"

She looked at me questioningly. Names weren't particularly important in the afterlife, especially if you were unlikely to encounter someone a second time. She shrugged. "I was born Jeanette Lansford, but my name as an Ursuline was Mary Theresa."

"Do you remember the date of your death?"

Mary Theresa was silent for a moment, thinking. "February 2, 1935. Now, I really must get back to work."

"Of course. Thank you for talking with me."

"Take care, young man," she said with another smile, a smile so gentle it nearly broke my heart. Then she dropped dustpan and broom into her barrel, dragged all to a spot thirty feet away and began to clean the surrounding area.

I looked at her once more, frowning.

There is no way that woman belongs in Hell. Something is very wrong here, and I bet a quarter I know what it is. I repeated the woman's names and death date a couple of times, committing them to memory, then continued my walk to the office of Beelzebub.

In a couple of minutes, I reached the large, squat, screened-in pavilion that was Beezy's command central. From fifty feet away, the walls looked solid, but as I approached, I could begin to see through the screening. The Patron Devil of Gluttony, all seven feet and seven hundred pounds of him, sat at his desk, readers on the tip of his nose, studying some report from one of the many departments in Hell that reported to him. If nothing else, Beezy was a hard-working administrator. I reached up to knock on one of the posts supporting the roof and providing a frame onto which the screening was attached. Before I'd made a sound, he said, "Come in, Minion."

Well. How did he know I was even there? He can't read my mind anymore. Or at least I don't think he can, since Satan can't.

I pivoted left and headed to the revolving door, spinning inside, letting in a couple of dozen insects, but leaving hundreds more on the outside. Beezy was in no mood to be bothered by them. He simply stared at the new buggables. There was a sizzle, and their carcasses fell to the floor.

"I may not be able to read your mind any longer," Beelzebub said evenly, "but I saw your flashy new suit as soon as you hit the tarmac of Camelot. Have a seat."

I lowered myself onto the single folding chair that was in front of his desk. Then I looked up at him. Beezy's expression was impassive. He took off his glasses and laid them on his desktop. He studied me; I studied him. I was able to look my former boss in the eye without flinching. This was a bit of a feat, considering how much pain and grief he'd given me in the sixty years I'd worked for him. That I was able to do so was one of the few good things that had come out of my months as a demon. That's when I'd really gotten to know the true Beezy.

Finally, Beelzebub broke the silence. "Well?"

I shrugged. "I … I don't know. I was down here and…"

He cleared his throat. "Yes, I know. Satan was just telling me about it. Devil and stupid jokes: really?"

Another shrug. "It was the best I could think of at the time. Satan had tricked me into coming down to his office, but he wasn't letting me use the Elevator. I had to get out of there somehow."

A wisp of a smile floated across his face. "You always did have a smart mouth. Bet you enjoyed that."

"I did," I confessed. "I had to toady up to him for a long time when I was one of the Damned. Needling him felt good. It also got me out of a tight spot."

Beelzebub no longer looked amused. "You realize how proud he is, don't you?"

"Satan?" Shoulder pump. "Sure. Sin of Pride is his hallmark. Well, that and Wrath."

"Then I suppose congratulations are in order. You managed to hurt his feelings."

I looked at Beezy skeptically. "Oh, come on. I didn't think he had any feelings. Other than anger, of course."

Another throat clear. This one made the entire room rumble. "Well, he does. You made him lose face. You've been doing that for some time now, ever since you started failing as a demon."

"Hey! I was a good demon."

Beezy shook his head. "No you weren't. You were a powerful one, but you never had the stuff of a demon."

"Well, that's Satan's own fault for making me one in the first place!" I retorted.

"Yes, and it showed a lot of people that he's fallible. Devils, demons and the folks upstairs. He's mortified. Then you go around calling him stupid. Cruel. Also dangerous, in case you haven't figured that out yet. We're talking about Satan here, you know. If he hated you before, he loathes you now. You just showed him up for the second time in a row. He won't forget."

That I had gotten the better of Satan was only something I'd considered in passing. But I could see what Beezy meant. And I'd just called him stupid – multiple times – and bested him. Again. In the process, I'd made him even more confirmed in his animosity toward me. Even if he couldn't harm me directly, I had a feeling that was a bad move on my part. He was, after all, Satan, and if anyone could find a way to get revenge on me, it would be Big Red. Involuntarily, I shuddered.

The wisp returned. "You're getting the idea, I see. It's never a good idea to piss off Satan. Just like it's not nice to fool Mother Nature."

"Yeah, I guess I understand that now. But, I'm here, and I'm determined to do what I can to make things better in Hell. I was just wondering, though ..."

"Wondering what?"

Suddenly I felt shy, like a boy asking a girl out on a date, or a guy showing another guy how he felt about him, which most of us aren't comfortable doing. Well, some are: emotionally-centered sorts, maybe, like that Dr. Phil character I've heard so much about but have never actually met. Perhaps he could pull it off. But me, well, no one has ever accused me of being centered – a bit askew is more like it – and this situation was a little awkward for me. It didn't help that Beezy was a foot taller than me, so that I had to crane my neck upward like a tourist staring at a skyscraper. His horns, claws and fangs were barriers to heartfelt conversation also. I took a deep breath and took the plunge. "Well, I was wondering how things stand between you and me."

Beezy chuckled softly. "Between me, Satan's right-hand man and best friend for billions of years, and you, my former employee and whipping boy? Steve, come on. You know I can't support what you're doing. In this, we are on opposite sides."

I sat quietly, mourning the loss, of all things, of a devil who had persecuted me for decades. "You hate me," I said bitterly, looking down at my hands.

He snorted softly. "Not at all. I've told you before, my role in Hell is just business for me. I like you. I always have, though I could never show it, but if you think we can pal around now, after all you've done, well, come on."

"No ..." I said slowly. "That would be impossible, I guess."

"I'm afraid so." He paused, thinking. "Still, I will be interested to see what you come up with. You have always been a source of great entertainment for me."

I smiled ruefully. "Well, I'll just have to see if I can continue the trend."

"See you around, Steve," Beelzebub said, slipping his readers back onto his nose. That was a clear dismissal.

"Take care, Beezy," I murmured, getting off my chair and heading for the exit.

"Funny thing about pocket universes," he said quietly, not looking up from the paperwork in his hands. "Once they've been created, they cannot be destroyed."

"Huh?"

"Think about it."

Frowning, I rotated through the revolving door, letting in a fresh batch of flies, mosquitoes and noseeums to pester their Lord. I heard a curse through the screen wall, and a few swift slams. No doubt Beezy had just flattened a dozen bugs with his fly swatter.

I pondered my former boss's words as I walked away. *What did he mean?*

Towering above me was a black monolith that spanned the distance between the Eighth and Seventh circles of Hell. It was the first leg of the Stairway to Heaven. Opening the door to the stairwell, I stepped inside.

Pocket universe. Pocket universe.

I remembered that Erebus resided in a pocket universe. That's why it was an upside-down mountain with upside down gravity. And there was another pocket universe with which I was familiar, a very personal one, from the time when I was a demon.

Could it be?

I concentrated and felt it. It had been there all this time, the private hidey-hole I'd created in my early days as a demon. As easily as I could back in my time at Beast Barracks, I opened it and reached inside. There was only one object in there, but I pulled it out, smiling nostalgically.

It was the red foam rubber hand, forefinger extended, Beezy had given me that day on Earth when we had taken in a ballgame together.

Chapter 8

"**W**ell, I'm still not sure it's a good idea. Why don't you go up and ask Peter?"

It was the next morning. I had gotten up a little earlier than usual, in order to have breakfast with Florence. We were sitting in the living room, drinking coffee. Flo was already dressed for work. I was still in my robe, considering an idea I'd had as to what my next move would be. "I guess I will, though I'll have to deal with Otis again." The thought of parking in front of Hell's Elevator for a couple of hours had little appeal.

"Just be patient. He has to pick you up eventually. It's the law."

I stroked my chin. *That's true.* Even in Hell, there were certain rules.

"Your worst-case scenario is you'll have to take the stairs."

"No, that's no good. Beezy had the treads between One and Gates Level removed months ago so that Peter can't slip down for a quick round of golf."

She took a sip of her coffee. "Didn't you hear? While you were in Beast Barracks, learning whatever a demon needs to know, Saint Peter successfully petitioned to have them replaced. Orson and Thomas finished the work a couple of weeks ago."

"Really? Why would Satan give a crap about what Peter wants?"

"Language, dear."

"Sorry," I said, blushing.

She patted my hand. "Good boy. Peter pointed out to Hell's Management that he had a key for every secure space in

Heaven or Hell, including the Elevator, and could go down to play anytime he wanted. Besides, he threatened to lodge a formal complaint to 'On High' if the stairs weren't fixed. Satan didn't want the hassle, so he put them back in."

Good to know. As long as I stay out of the Ninth Circle, I can keep my mobility. And staying out of Nine shouldn't be a problem. I doubt Satan wants me anywhere near him, after my jokeathon yesterday.

Flo took our two cups into the kitchen and started to fill the sink with water. I followed her. "Leave them. I'll wash the breakfast dishes before leaving."

She dimpled and gave me a quick smooch. "Thank you. I need to get to the hospital and find out if there are any repercussions from my actions yesterday."

While I had been playing with Satan the previous day, Flo had singlehandedly thwarted the entire hospital staff, or the demonic ones anyway, who had planned on giving epidurals to all the patients. This was to be just prior to their participation in the Fifth Circle Marathon, which was one of the Hellish Olympic events that BOOH and I had been discussing. The Olympics, just like their Earthly counterparts, were held every four years, and the hospital always fielded a team, demonic and human, though all damned participants were hobbled in some fashion, be it epidurals or casts or something similar. Predictably, the human team members almost never won anything, but because of Flo's interference, the patients got to run the marathon with their legs working for a change. This resulted in one of them getting the bronze, which must have wreaked havoc with Hell's robust gambling concern.

Ever since Flo told me about it the previous evening, I'd been astonished by her audacity, as well as her effectiveness. "I still can't believe you pulled that off. It was amazing, but ..."

"But what?"

"Well." I hesitated. "Won't they reschedule the epidurals for a later, equally inconvenient time?"

Flo assumed a stern look. "It will have to be much later. The hospital books its major tormentations weeks in advance, and since this one was to have involved almost the entire demonic staff, it may be months before they can try again."

I reached under the sink and pulled out the Dawn, squirting some of the liquid in the water before dumping in the dishes to pre-soak. "But," I said softly, "they *will* do it at some point, won't they?"

She sighed. "Yes, eventually."

"Flo, I keep thinking, 'what's the point?' All we can do is delay the inevitable or make people feel a little better in the aftermath of torment."

"It *is* a dilemma. I've already admitted that. Something I have struggled with for almost one hundred and fifty years, and yet we have to help in some way. Don't we?" She sounded almost as if she were pleading with me to agree.

"Yes, of course," I said hurriedly. "I just wish there were something we could do that would be lasting."

Flo pursed her lips. "Nothing lasts as long as Eternity."

"But every bit helps. And meanwhile, I'm going to see if I can piss off …"

"Language!"

"Sorry. I'm going to see if I can antagonize the Antagonist and his cronies."

"And you think that will help?" she asked, standing before the mirror and securing her nurse's cap to her chestnut tresses with a few hair pins.

"Sure!" I said with enthusiasm. "It will throw the bad guys off their game, and also, if I do it right, there will be a multiplier effect."

"So you say. I hope you are right. Oh!" she said, looking at the clock on the wall. It showed nearly seven thirty.

As you know, clocks generally don't work very well in Hell, but Flo's wall clock was the most accurate timepiece I'd seen down here.

"I must run!" She kissed me on the check. "I'm never this late. Give my love to Peter."

And then she was out the door.

I thought about ignoring the dishes – I hate washing dishes – but I was a saved soul now. A white hat. A goodie two-shoes.

Yuck. When you say it like that …

Besides, I'd promised. They didn't take long, though, and when finished I had the satisfaction of completing my first good deed of the day.

Okay, it wasn't a good deed. It was just some lousy dishes, but if I hadn't done them, Flo would have come home to a dirty kitchen, or maybe even felt she couldn't trust me with the simplest of chores. Regardless, doing the dishes for Florence Nightingale felt sort of like a good deed. Or maybe I was just stretching a point.

I took my shower and got dressed. Now the clock in the kitchen read eight thirty. I frowned. If I wanted to be as much of a do-gooder as Flo, I needed to get back in the habit of rising early.

Maybe I'll start setting an alarm clock, though that seemed like a form of eternal damnation to me. I'd always hated alarm clocks. Well, I decided. I'd just hit the shower right after Flo was done with it. That settled, I had one more task to perform before heading up to see Pete.

I went to the small desk in the living room. Somehow and from somewhere, Flo had scored an old-timey typewriter. It was an Olivetti. I remembered using one like it in college, before word processors and, eventually, personal computers made them obsolete.

I'll have to ask Pete sometime if I could get a laptop or something.

I hadn't had my own PC since my last years on Earth, and I'd never had a laptop, since they weren't very common in the nineties, when I bit the bullet. It would be really cool to have one. A laptop, I mean. Not a bullet.

Meanwhile, there was the Olivetti. I sat in the desk chair, inserted a sheet of paper into the typewriter roller, twisting the knob until I had about an inch of white space above the typing area. Then I began composing my thoughts. Fortunately, I had learned to draft at the keyboard in the final decade of my mortal existence. I was a fast typist, though I usually made tons of mistakes, but being saved seemed to have cured me of that. I didn't make a single typo. I started to hum.

This must be what Heaven is like.

When I was done, I pulled the sheet out of the roller, slipped the page into a Manila folder then headed for the door.

A few blocks away was Hell's Elevator. On reaching the door, I pressed the up button.

"Get lost."

"Come on, Otis, you have to pick me up eventually. You know it."

"Maybe so," said the disembodied voice. "But I'll do it on my own schedule."

Sigh. "Whatever." I sat down to wait. Forty-five minutes later, there was a ding.

Well, that's a lot better than I was expecting.

I opened the door by hand, since only on Nine does it open automatically. At least the door didn't fight me like it used to when I was damned. Otis probably hated that he had to cooperate with me at all. I stepped through and let the door fall closed with a bang.

"Hey, watch it!" Otis grumbled.

"Oh, dear boy," I said with all the sincerity of a politician. "Did I hurt you?"

"Up yours, Minion."

I smiled and punched the button for Gates Level.

"What do you want up there?" he growled.

Now for sixty years, the Elevator had never said a word to me. It just made my life difficult whenever I wanted to go up. Then I became a demon, and I learned its name: Otis. Otis, the demon Elevator, became my good buddy.

Now that I'm no longer one of the Corps, he hates me, yet he won't shut up. I guess he'd gotten used to talking to me.

"None of your business. Besides, I'm a saved soul now, as you very well know. Is it really all that surprising that I want to go up to that better place occasionally?"

Otis grumbled, but he was the only elevator serving the Circles of Hell, after all. Once someone got inside, the demon had to take his passenger where he wanted to go. It was the rules.

DING! went the Elevator's bell again. We had reached Gates Level.

I stepped out into the demilitarized zone between Heaven and Hell. The clouds that tended to hang around this space, usually as white as cotton balls, were an ominous gray, as if they were threatening a thunderstorm. In apprehension, I looked around for Saint Peter.

The weather on Gates Level, while normally quite placid, sometimes reflected the mood of Heaven's Concierge. I became aware of this arcane meteorological fact one time when Orson and I were up on GL replacing – once again – a bulb at the Gates of Hell. Unusually, it wasn't the "Abandon all hope sign" that we were working on. It wasn't even the "Welcome to Hell" sign, but the least important of the three, the one saying "Over Thirty Billion Served." Though, as I recall, the number was more like twenty billion back then.

This was in 1996, not long after I'd died and assumed the role of Hell's Super. I had just fallen off the ladder for the third time, when Gene Kelly came to Heaven. Turns out Pete is a big Kelly fan – he's seen all his movies – and the old saint was really excited to meet the famous dancer.

The Gates Region was pretty spiffy that day. The Pearlies were glowing so brightly that a few angels who were flying by slipped on sunglasses. Behind the Gates, two powerful spot lights were burning. That reminded me of 20th Century Fox, which wasn't quite appropriate, since Kelly did his best movies at MGM, but I suppose bright lights made more sense than a roaring lion up here. But the most impressive phenomena that day, though also the most bizarre, were the clouds. They were clustered together in spinning geometric patterns, hexagons and octagons and the like, as if they were extras in a carefully choreographed Hollywood number, maybe something by Busby Berkeley, who I believe directed Kelly in a movie.

'Take Me Out to the Ballgame' – 1946. I just googled it.

When Kelly showed up, Peter nodded, a slight rain began to fall and the strains of "Singing in the Rain" cranked up. Mr. Kelly looked a bit dazed, which is fairly normal for the newly-dead, who tend to be shaken up by experiencing their own demise, though the bizarre rendition of his most famous number no doubt exacerbated his condition. Saint Peter then gently escorted Kelly to the podium, where, without checking the Book of Life, Heaven's Concierge pronounced his charge to be saved. Pete scored a quick autograph, which he's shown me on more than one occasion. It says, "To Pete. Thanks for everything. — Gene."

I suppose, if I'd just been granted passage to Heaven, I would have been on the thankful side also. And willing to sign my millionth autograph.

It all seemed kind of tacky to me. I mean, here you are, one of the greatest saints of all time, and you order around a bunch of clouds to do your bidding just to get an autograph. Brother.

But the point of the story is that Peter seemed to have some sort of psychic connection with the clouds up here. If they were troubled, then so was he.

In moments, I spotted him. He was pacing behind his podium, and his brow looked as stormy as the clouds surrounding him. I had been right.

"Hey, Pete."

He looked at me and frowned. "Saint Peter."

I notice, in passing, that Peter doesn't mind Gene Kelly calling him Pete. Just me. But I'm not bitter about it.

And not just Peter. We're back to Saint Peter. He must be really upset about something. "Saint Peter," I amended. "What's wrong?"

Peter started pacing even faster. "My relief hasn't arrived!"

"Your relief? Hey, could you stand still a second? You're giving me vertigo."

"What?" I don't think he even realized he'd been pacing. With an effort, he forced himself to calm down. "Sorry. It's just that I'm supposed to play in the finals of a golf tournament on One today. Andrew said he'd cover for me at the desk, but apparently he's been delayed." He chewed his lip. "If I'm late for my tee time, I'll forfeit. I'm favored to win, you know."

I didn't know that, but it didn't surprise me. Peter was a very good golfer, and I didn't think there was a virtuous pagan who could outplay him.

I thought for a second. *Could I help?* "Well, why don't you let me handle things here until Andrew shows up? I'm sure it will only be a few minutes."

Peter looked at me speculatively. "I don't know if I should do that." Though it was obvious he wanted to.

"Why not? Is there some rule against it?"

"Well, no, but it's a very important job, and there's no room for error."

Now it was my turn to frown. "No disrespect intended, but it looks pretty straightforward to me. Someone shows up, you look up that person's name in the book. Hey!" I had a sudden thought. "How do you know who the person is? Do you ask him? And what if he doesn't give you his real name?"

"Now see? It's not as straightforward as you make it out to be. Fortunately, whoever is handling the Book of Life cannot be lied to. You ask for the name of the person standing before you, and once you get it, you know exactly where in the Book to find the listing for that person's life."

"Hmm. I didn't know that, but once I look, it's pretty binary, right? Saved or damned."

Peter fished in his pocket and pulled out his quarter. "You forgot the coin toss."

"Oh, right, right. But see? I can do this, and it will only be for a few minutes. Then Andrew will be here to take over."

"Hmm." Peter looked down at his feet, where a set of golf clubs was crowded against the base of his podium. "Well … okay." Pete rummaged around in his desk, extracting a white cloak not dissimilar from the one he was wearing. I slipped it on over my suit. "Oh, and these," he said, showing me a fake beard and white wig.

I looked at the false hair with distaste. "Do I have to?"

"Yes," he said, handing me the beard, which had ear pieces similar to what eye glasses have. These I slipped onto my ears. The wig was next; it covered my ears, so no one could see how the beard was attached. "People are expecting Saint Peter, so you have to look at least a little like me."

Peter pounced for his golf clubs then handed me his quarter, which, with some reluctance, I accepted, slipping it into a pocket. "Thanks, Steve. I really appreciate it. If you have any problem, just stall until Andrew gets here, and he can sort things out."

I rolled my eyes. "I'm sure I can manage. Oh! Before you go, I was wondering: could you make copies of this flyer," I said, showing him the Manila folder, "and get them posted on some bulletin boards in Heaven?"

"Huh? What do you have?"

I handed Peter my advertisement, which read:

TOURS OF HELL
EXPERIENCED GUIDE
SEE THE STYX, MEET CHARON
WITNESS THE HORRORS OF THE UNDERWORLD
A GREAT VALUE
WHEN: DAILY AT 10 AM
WHERE: MEET OUTSIDE THE GATES

He looked up at me. "You've got to be kidding. Who in his right mind would leave Heaven and go to Hell?"

I shrugged. "No idea. Maybe someone who is bored or just curious about what they'd escaped. In any event, they will be perfectly safe, as you know, and I'll give them a good tour."

Peter looked in longing at the Stairway entrance. It no longer looked like a pile of debris, which is how I had left it at the end of my tenure as Hell's Super. Instead there was a simple stairway entrance made of brick, like what might be found on the roof of a building. Someone had done this in the past couple of days. The possible culprits were the new Hell's Super and his assistant, but I'd seen numerous displays of Orson's skill with mortar and trowel and didn't think it likely. I suspected Beelzebub himself had done the work, due to the quality of the workmanship.

The pretty new entrance wasn't what Peter was longing for but rather what it represented. The Stairway was the fastest way to get to One, since not even Peter could count on Otis arriving in punctual fashion.

Oh, I suppose Pete could have jumped down the Mouth of Hell, but that's not much fun. I speak from personal experience, having done it numerous times when I was a damned soul. At best, the leap is an acquired taste.

Poor Peter. He was so conflicted, he was going to blow a fuse. All these demands at once, the pressures of a job, the finals of a golf match, turning over the Book of Life to a half-crazed former Hellion who had an agenda. He desperately wanted to make that tee time, though.

I finally articulated the heart of his dilemma. "A favor for a favor?" I looked meekly at the conflicted concierge.

"Fine!" he said at last. "It won't hurt anyone who decides to do it."

Peter took the flyer from me with his left hand and in his right a hundred copies appeared. Shit, he was better than a

Xerox machine. Then he tossed the copies straight up. Like paper airplanes, they sliced through the air, shooting over the Pearly Gates. He handed me back my original. "Done. You get to keep your original, though. It was made in Hell and can't cross over. Now, out of my way!"

With that, Peter raced for the entrance to the Stairway. As fast as he was going, I judged he'd make his tee time, no sweat.

Chapter 9

J ust my luck. Not two minutes after Peter left, a crowd of people appeared in the Hereafter to receive their final assignments. Most were slated for Hell, of course. Only a small fraction of the total ever made it through the Pearlies.

You might wonder how souls arrive at Gates Level. A few special ones are escorted personally by Morty, that's Mortimer, also known as the Angel of Death or merely DEATH. Morty is Charon's big brother, and he and I get along okay, well, except for that one time when I was on the receiving end of his ministrations. But since everyone has to go through that, I know it's nothing personal, and I've long since gotten past any bad feelings. Besides, Morty is great at parties, unlike his younger sibling, who doesn't go in for large social functions.

When I say "I was on the receiving end," I don't mean that Morty personally escorted me to Saint Peter's desk upon my death. However, the Grim Reaper has administrative authority over all deaths, even those for other belief systems, such as Hinduism, where he goes by the name of Yama or Yamaraj. Same guy. All the various pilots, copilots, train engineers, bus drivers, serving staff, porters, pursers, even the afterlife's versions of Aramark and Skychef, who prepare and then stuff those repulsive meals into little aluminum foil covered trays, all of these transportation professionals and ancillary service agencies report to Mortimer. Morty is a *very* big deal in the afterlife.

And occasionally, just occasionally, he personally leads a hot shot by hand up to Gates Level. When this happens, it's really quite impressive, two spirits, floating through the air, approaching the light, clouds parting for them to reveal the celestial sorting room overseen by Saint Peter. Hot shot might mean a very good guy, like Father Damien of leper colony fame, but just as easily a bad guy. I'm pretty sure that's how Mussolini got here. That's what someone told me, though of course it was before my time.

Sometimes, the recently departed simply appear on Gates Level out of thin air. They're dead, and then the next instant they are standing before Heaven's Concierge. But this method of transport is only for people with strong constitutions. Dying on its own is already a bit discombobulating and, coupled with teleportation, would trigger extreme vertigo in most people. The last thing Peter wants is someone barfing on a cloud because the dearly departed got nauseous from extreme post mortem turbulence, so teleportation is usually reserved for fighter pilots, astronauts and divorce lawyers. You know: unflappable sorts.

Most of us, though, to ease the transition from the physical to the metaphysical, travel by analogues of transport that would have been familiar in life. For example, Gates Level has a terminal with trains arriving from all over the Earth. Each one is magical, like the Polar Express, though no presents or morning-after glasses of eggnog. There's also a bus stop, heliport, even an airport. I came by plane, though fortunately it was before the TSA was established. That's the Thereafter Safety Administration. I always hated standing in lines, and that can be bad enough at Gates Level. To have to cool your heels twice, and after you'd just died, which is inconvenient on its own, well, that additional wait must be tedious. But there's progress for you.

Right as I took my place at Saint Peter's desk, before the Book of Life, the 10:15 flight from JFK landed, followed closely by the arrival of the Wiener Walzer, a massively long passenger

92

train that ran from Budapest, Vienna, Zurich and Prague all the way to Gates Level. I should note that the Earthbound version of this train makes exactly the same stops, except for the last one, of course.

Between the arrivals of the plane and the train, I was soon in the thick of it. Fortunately, my many years as Hell's Super helped me through any language issues. I could speak almost any tongue you threw at me, or at least those of countries where the populations were predominately Jewish, Christian or Muslim. That covered a lot of ground.

Another bit of good fortune: the job was as straightforward as I thought. At first, all the people milled around, not knowing what the heck to do, but then they saw me. While I felt ridiculous in my Saint Peter outfit, like a badly-suited Santa Claus in a mall during Christmastime, I must have looked more like the heavenly arbiter than I thought. Or perhaps it was just a matter of expectations. The newly-dead, well, the newly-dead Christians anyway, expected Saint Peter at this point in their journey, so anyone who vaguely looked the part was given the benefit of a doubt. Whatever the reason, they politely queued up before the desk. Then the lemming effect kicked in, and Muslims and Jews followed suit. There wasn't even any cutting in line, since probably everyone thought that might not make a good first impression on the guy who had their Eternal fates beneath his fingertips.

I'm not tall, though I'm not short, and my frame is on the slight side. These traits hardly provide me with the gravitas people might expect from Saint Peter, and in truth, Pete is quite tall and powerfully built; he looms above most of those he judges. Still, I did my best, channeling my inner Darth Vader – not the evil stuff, but the towering presence, including the "Luke, I am your father," voice. You know. This required me to

93

stand on my tiptoes, which fortunately was not noticeable beneath the long robe, and speak half an octave below normal.

With each person, I asked for a name, looked the recently departed up in the Book of Life, and gave the news. Generally it was bad, which was troubling to me, since I'd been on the receiving end of that myself once. Occasionally, I got to tell a do-goodnik he or she was going to Heaven. That was pretty cool. It's nice to make someone's day.

Remarkable, though, was how often the fates of the people before me were in doubt, that is, beside a name I would frequently find a great big question mark, instead of the sheep (saved) or goat (damned) icons with which I quickly became familiar. When I hit a question mark, there was nothing for it. Out came Pete's quarter. More often than not, those people whose fates were determined by the toss seemed to end up on the losing end. This seemed odd to me.

When I processed a soul, I made a note next to the appropriate name in the margin of the Book of Life. A check went beside names that were clearly marked saved or damned, a smiley-face or frowny-face next to question mark entries, saved by a coin toss or damned by one respectively. The vast majority of completed entries in the Book of Life had the initials SP next to them. That was either for Saint Peter or Simon Peter. Same guy, so it didn't matter. Occasionally I spotted an "AP," which must have stood for Saint Andrew, or, rather, Andrew Prōtoklētos, which is Greek for "First-Called," and also what those of the Orthodox faith call him. Following Pete and Andy's examples, I put an SM next to the name of each person I processed, figuring Peter would know that was me, rather than, say, sadomasochism, which I notice is turning out to be a frequently-used word in this narrative, especially the masochism part.

Each time I gave a soul bad news, there was a blinding flash. That was when the good in their souls separated from the bad and fled to the Well of [Damned] Souls, where it waited on the off chance that Heaven might want to begin a recycling program.

That has never happened. The only real use of castoff soul stuff is to fuel Hell's HVAC system, but very few people know about that. Satan tries to keep his poaching quiet so as to avoid a PR debacle.

So, I was judging people left and right, working as fast as I ever had. Things were going okay, I guess; only once did I get asked why I sounded like James Earl Jones with a throat condition, but that guy ended up going to Hell anyway, so it was no big deal. Still, I wished Andrew would come and take over. Something must have delayed him more than he or Peter had expected.

I had been processing souls as fast as I could for about thirty minutes when I hit a quiet patch. For the nonce, Gates Level was completely devoid of people needing judgment.

While waiting for the next onslaught, which would come from the Hong Kong Hyperloop, I opened the Book of Life and checked a few names. As I suspected, both Orson and Edison's fates had been determined by the coin. Then I thought to look up Mary Theresa. Same thing. That she had even required the arbitration of Pete's quarter was surprising in the first place — her temper really didn't seem extreme or sinful enough to consign her to Hell — but, even so, how could she not have won that coin toss?

Frowning, I pulled the quarter out of my pocket and started flipping it. Twenty throws later, I had counted nine heads and eleven tails. Pretty close to fifty-fifty, which would lead me to believe that the quarter was okay. Yet, I considered, troubled, when the coin tosses really counted, that is, when salvation and damnation were the stakes, my brief experience as Decider-in-Chief seemed to indicate that the outcomes were not distributed anywhere close to fifty-fifty. The split seemed more like sixty-forty or even seventy-thirty in the damned to saved ratio. I wasn't really sure though, since I'd been so busy during the sorting that I hadn't had time to keep a record.

Hmm. That doesn't make sense.

On a whim, I rummaged through Pete's desk, extracting a number one pencil and a blank piece of onion skin (the paper kind, not the vegetable variety). With the pencil, I made an impression of each side of the quarter onto the paper.

I folded the sheet and slipped it in my inside coat pocket just as Andrew exited the Pearly Gates and headed my way. With a sigh of relief, I hung Pete's "On Break. Back Soon" sign on the front of the podium then went to meet Andy. The clouds gave us a bit of cover, so those waiting in line couldn't see us make the exchange. "Boy, am I glad to see you," I said, peeling off the wig and beard and slipping out of the robe. I handed all that stuff to him.

I did not know Saint Andrew well, but I had met him once when doing some maintenance work up here. He resembled Peter, which was unsurprising, since they were brothers. Andrew certainly didn't need to wear the getup I did in order to fool the crowd. He turned to a cloud bank and opened what looked like a gym locker, dropping the garments inside.

"Steve Minion, what are you doing impersonating Simon?"

As I've said before, and as you might have learned anyway from Sunday school, Simon was the name Peter grew up with, and anyone who knew the Keeper of the Book of Life back in his mortal years tended to call him Simon, except the Lord, of course, who usually called him Simon Peter.

"Oh, he was worried about missing his tee time, so I volunteered to cover until you got here."

Andrew smiled. He was by nature of a less prickly demeanor than Peter, easier to get along with. "That was nice of you. So your good deeds are going to extend to individuals other than damned souls now?"

That was a new thought. "Hadn't occurred to me, but why not? If I can help someone out, I will, I guess."

He looked at me appraisingly. "The suit. It looks good on you."

"Thanks!" I said with enthusiasm. "This fabric is amazing. It never gets soiled, never gets wrinkled." I told him about making sand angels the previous day. "And the sand just fell off."

"That's what it's supposed to do. I provided Simon with the fabric, you know." He said it modestly, but I could tell he was fishing for a compliment.

"Really? Well it's incredible. What's the secret?"

"Scotch guard."

"You mean that stuff that comes in an aerosol can?"

Andrew casually examined his fingernails. "No, I mean I blessed the fabric before I gave it to Simon to work with."

"Ah." That explained things. Andrew was the patron Saint of Scotland, after all. "Well, anyway, thanks."

"You're welcome."

"And now that you're here, I'll be heading out." I turned to go.

He grabbed my arm. "Wait, Steve. Do you have the coin?"

It was still in my palm. "You know," I said slowly, handing the quarter over to Andy, "there's something weird about this thing."

"What do you mean?" he asked, examining the coin for a moment before placing it in a pocket of his robe. "Doesn't it flip anymore?"

"Oh, sure, that's not the problem. It's just that …" I frowned.

"It's just that what?"

"Well," I said hesitantly, "it seems to me that there are more people who get damned than saved when a coin toss is required."

He looked at me skeptically. "I'm sure it's your imagination. Simon's been using this quarter for over two hundred years with no difficulties."

"Maybe."

Or maybe not.

I shook hands with Andrew, then he headed toward the podium.

Hmm.

Chapter 10

My finger was beating out a clave rhythm on the Elevator's Up button. The idea was that Otis would find it so irritating he'd pick me up sooner rather than later. So far, the tactic hadn't worked.

I arrived at the Elevator doors of Level Five promptly at eight am. That was early for me, at least early since I'd received salvation. Back when I was a damned Hell's Super and couldn't really sleep anyway, getting up and out the door for work was pretty easy, but these days, well, since I didn't really *have* to get up at a set time, eight was practically the crack of dawn for me. Still, when you've chosen a vocation of easing the suffering of the eternally damned, some sacrifices must be made.

I figured I could afford to wait for Otis at least forty-five minutes. After that, I'd have to hoof it to and then up the Stairway. Five miles in a little over an hour was a brisk pace, but manageable for me. Mostly walking. A little trotting. Whether by stairs or a recalcitrant elevator, though, I could make it to Gates Level by ten and meet my first tour group. Assuming, of course, that anyone showed up at all.

That was by no means certain. Maybe Peter was right. Who in his right mind would choose to leave Heaven and go to Hell?

Of course, Flo and I have done essentially that, but who is to say that we aren't a little cracked? Don't get me wrong. I love Flo – yes, I suppose I've made that pretty obvious by now – but she must have a martyr complex or something. Maybe she's a masochist. (That word again.) Don't know. As for myself, I continue to find new reasons why I chose Hell when I could go to Heaven anytime I wanted. Some of it is my natural contrariness. I've never liked being told what to do and where to go.

Believe me, I've been told to go to Hell frequently, even before I'd died, though I've only been told to go to Heaven a couple of times.

Then there's that relationship thing with Flo. I want to be with her, wherever she is, and since she prefers to stay in the Infernal Realm, that's where I'm going to hang out too. Besides, even if she agreed to accompany me to Paradise, I don't know if they'd let us have intercourse up there, and there's no way I'm going to spend Eternity with Flo in Heaven and not have sex with her. Forget it. Non-starter.

Mostly, though, it's because I have to sacrifice a portion of myself to go to Heaven, the bad portion admittedly, but still part of what makes me me.

I didn't know how the Celestial City's citizens felt about spending all their time there, though. They might be completely content, but I was counting on the innate curiosity of humans, and their tendency to get bored. Also, in the spirit of keeping up with the Jones's, I would think heavenly humans might want to check out Hell and make certain that they were in fact the Jones's. Just to be absolutely sure, you know.

But I really didn't know if anyone would show, so I was anxious to get to GL. (Gates Level. Not Green Lantern. You should know that by now, too.) I wanted to see if a line was forming, or if this whole idea was a great big bust.

And I'd just about run out of time. If Otis didn't show in the next couple of minutes, I'd have to start walking.

DING!

Good. I'd rather cool my heels for an hour Topside than hoof it up five miles of stairs.

Grabbing the handle, I opened the Elevator door and stepped inside.

"Fuck you, Minion!"

"And good morning to you, Otis!" I said gaily, punching the GL button.

"What's with the stupid umbrella?"

"Fashion statement?" Not the real reason, but I didn't see why I should be particularly cooperative with Otis, since he was seldom particularly cooperative with me these days.

That's about all the time we had to chat. We were already at Gates Level.

I craned my head toward the Pearly Gates, looking for possible tourists. None so far, but then I doubted people from Heaven cared to wait in lines. Most everyone, living or dead, saint or sinner, considers that a form of Hell.

Peter was in the thick of it, a large crowd of newly-dead filling the space before his desk. There must have been at least a thousand souls waiting to be processed. Over an hour passed before he came up for air.

When the crowd had finally cleared, and Peter was able to talk, I ambled over to him. "Hey, big guy," I said. "How'd you do at the tournament?"

Peter flashed a big grin, then pulled out of his desk a trophy as big as a guitar amp.

"You won, huh? Well, congratulations!"

"Wait!" he said, opening another drawer and retrieving a powder blue sports coat. "I got this too," he said, slipping it on over his robe, which looked pretty bizarre, but I didn't want to point that out and diminish the afterglow of his triumph.

"Nice jacket! It must have been a major."

He nodded. "It was, it was. That's why getting down there yesterday was so important. I was in the finals against Belphegor."

"Belphegor?" I said in disbelief. "As in Patron Devil of Sloth Belphegor?"

"The very same."

"I've never even seen him leave his bed. Well, okay, once he did, when Satan had him chasing me on Level Six when I'd gone all rogue-demon. But he's the laziest creature in Hell."

Pete shrugged. "He's also the best golfer."

"You're kidding!"

"No. It's all because of a little confusion he had regarding his role when Belphegor first assumed responsibility for Sloth. He thought any leisure activity was fine, just so long as he wasn't at work."

"So for hundreds of years, he was running around Hell yelling, 'Tennis anyone?' Or 'How about a round of golf?' Finally, Satan and Beezy pointed out that by Sloth they meant laziness, indolence. Not leisure activities. Belphegor was a bit disappointed, but being a trooper, he embraced the role. He's a very good devil, you know."

"Well," I opined, "I always liked him. He was generally pleasant to me, but I wrote it off to niceness being less stressful than meanness."

Peter blew through his whiskers, reminding me of Orson, who would do the same thing sometimes. "Not for everyone, but I know what you mean. Before Belphegor became disabused of the notion that leisure activities were, by definition, somewhat active and not in keeping with an indolent lifestyle, he became very good at all sorts of sports. You should see him, for example, in a scrum."

This was all quite a revelation to me. I couldn't picture Belphegor playing rugby, so I thought instead about the giant slug-like devil carrying a set of golf clubs, wearing one of those goofy golf hats. The thought made me shudder. "I wouldn't think the virtuous pagans would want a Jabba the Hutt lookalike oozing all over their golf courses."

"Come on, Steve. You should know better. Belphegor is a major devil, and like all the Princes of Hell, he can assume just about any shape he wants. In fact, he looked quite dapper out on the links yesterday. A bit like Ben Hogan in a cardigan."

"Ah, okay." This was a bit much to process. "So how did he do?"

Peter frowned. "He was the toughest competitor I've had since my Lord stopped playing with me for denying him tee times."

I smacked my forehead. "What? Not that again. I thought it was a joke."

"No. It really happened. It's in the Bible."

I looked at Pete with skepticism. "It said before the cock crows, thou shalt deny me *three* times. Not tee times. Jeez."

"Typo."

"Oh."

Peter shook his head. "Goodness, I just barely managed to beat him. A single stroke in sudden death."

I nodded. "Well, that certainly makes sense, considering the circumstances, the afterlife and all."

The Saint ignored me. "This was a major win for our side, and I have you to thank for it. That and a really super fairway shot on the last hole with my baffing spoon."

"Your *what*?"

"Baffing spoon, baffing spoon. It's a fairway wood."

I pursed my lips. "Baffing spoon. Hadn't heard that one before. Mashie, niblik, even brassie, but not that."

"It one of my best shots. I call it Peter's baffling baffing spoonerism."

"Keen."

Peter harrumphed. "Again, thank you for covering for me."

"You're welcome. It was nice to be able to do a favor for you."

"Any problems?"

"Well," I said slowly. "One. It's that coin of yours."

Peter pulled out his quarter. He held the silver disc between thumb and forefinger, flipping it back and forth as he examined both sides. "What about it? It's served me well for over two centuries."

"What did you do before you got it?"

"Oh, I played Rock, Paper, Scissors with each of the souls in question. But that took too long."

"Maybe you should have stuck with that," I said with a frown. "I think there's something wrong with your coin."

"What do you mean?"

"Well, I think …"

The clarion voice of a trumpet split the air. The Gates of Heaven opened, and over a hundred figures in glowing white robes came through them.

"Uh, oh," I said worriedly.

"What's the problem, Steve? Surely that's your tour group."

"Yeah, but I can only take forty at a time." I hadn't expected so many interested customers.

Peter shrugged. "Well, just schedule the rest for other days."

"Guess I'll have to." I walked to the crowd of saved souls standing before the Gates. "Maay I have your attenshun paleeze!" I shouted. "There is a forty person limit to the tour size, so I'm going to have to break you into groups."

A fair number of grumbles came out of the crowd.

"Look, I'm sorry. I'm sure you're unused to being disappointed these days, but you're not dealing with Heaven now. In all matters concerning Hell, you have to expect a little inconvenience. Sort of like vacationing in Italy, ya know." That comment got me some dirty looks from a couple of guys in the front of the crowd. With a shrug, I separated the flock, so to speak, indicating to the first forty to stand next to the Mouth of Hell. Then I reached in my pocket and pulled out a pile of post-it notes. (Post-its are very handy, like duct tape, and you never know when you'll need some, so I usually carry a stack.) I handed forty yellow stickers to the next group and told them to come back tomorrow. To the remaining, I gave some purple post-its and said to come the day after.

"Again, sorry about this," I said to the individuals receiving the rain checks. "When it's your turn, I promise you a good tour. Today is the maiden voyage anyway, sort of a shakedown period. The next two tours will probably be better," I finished, winking at them. They merely shrugged and headed back through the Gates, which clanged shut ... in a harmonious sort of way.

"You are very fortunate!" I said to the forty waiting for me by the Mouth of Hell. "You are about to be among the very few saved humans ever to witness – though fortunately for you, not to directly experience – the horrors of Hell. This is the maiden voyage of the Circles in Hell tour. I'm sure you won't be disappointed."

"My name is Steve Minion." That were a few chuckles at my expense, but I ignored them. "I will be your guide today. As you know," I said, continuing in my loudest outside voice, "there are in total Nine Circles. There are five ways to enter the Underworld, well, six if you can teleport, but not very many people can do that. I used to be able to, but that's another story."

Drat. I need to watch my tendency to digress. They don't need to know that I was a demon for a while.

I started again. "You can go the original way, which is to plunge into the Mouth of Hell here and then down through the Throat, but I wouldn't advise it."

"Has anyone ever done that, I mean, since the invention of other options?" asked a woman in front. She was beautiful, but I realized everyone in the group looked pretty damn, I mean, darn good. Guess that's one of the perks of being a saved soul.

"Why yes indeed, ma'am."

"Ms.," she corrected me.

"Of course." She probably died after the mid Sixties. "Ms. Though not too many people do it anymore. My former job required it of me, though."

"What was that?" Asked the gentlemen standing next to her.

"Hell's Super."

"No it isn't. Can't be. It wouldn't be Hell if it were super."

"No I mean *I* was Hell's Super, Hell's Superintendent of Plant Maintenance."

"You mean," said a voice from the back, "that you had to fix things that broke in Hell?"

"Yep." The laughter was so loud, I couldn't make myself heard. Finally they calmed down. "Never mind that," I said testily. "Getting back to my point, I've fallen through some or all of the Throat, let's see, three or four times."

"Other ways are by Elevator, the Escalator over there, which is the main approach, so to speak, and then the Stairway, which you can see on the other side of Saint Peter's desk."

They looked over at Pete. He gave them a tentative wave.

"But today we're going first class, via the most evocative, iconic way, that storied passage immortalized by Dante Alighieri in *The Inferno*. We are going to enter Hell by crossing the Styx itself, courtesy of Charon, ferryman of the Underworld."

And then we'll get on the Escalator to go the rest of the way. I didn't tell them that, however.

"And what about seeing the Gates of Hell?" said a clean-shaven man with prominent chin, Roman nose and thick Italian accent.

"Oh, them. Look again at the Escalator." I pointed at the three signs surrounding it. For a wonder, all three were illuminated. "There they are."

"Neon?" sniffed a handsome fellow to my right.

Handsome, attractive, statuesque, stunning, etc. They all looked great, okay? I'll cease with the adjectives now. Or at least the complimentary ones.

"How tacky," said another. "Vegas is more tasteful than this."

I nodded. "The original gates were torn down a century ago, or so I've been told. That happened before my time. These neon signs have been around for decades. You'd best prepare yourselves: Hell is full of horrors, not the least of which is incredibly bad taste. I sometimes wonder which is worse: the fire pits of Hell or the extensive use of chartreuse with white polka dots."

"Heaven help us!" gasped a woman. "Polka dots!"

"Yeah," I said with a nod, "and the Entrance to Hell is just the first in a long list of 'major ugly' you are about to encounter.

107

However, at least there's the famous line from Dante above the Escalator."

"A comma is missing," said the Italian guy.

I frowned. "What are you talking about?"

He pointed at the sign. "No comma. Of course, this is a translation, and an imperfect one at that. The original says, *'Lasciate ogni speranza, voi ch'entrate.'* Your sign..."

"Not my sign."

The man shrugged. "As you wish. But the sign should read 'Abandon all hope COMMA ye who enter here." Or better yet, 'you,' since no one says 'ye' anymore."

Oh a wisenheimer. Thinks he knows everything. "And what makes you an expert? Take a Dante course in college?"

"I know because I wrote it."

"What?" I sputtered. "You're Dante Alighieri?"

"Actually, the name is Durante degli Alighieri. Better you should call me Dante than Dante Alighieri." He looked at me skeptically. "Are you sure you're qualified to be running this tour? Have you even *read* my *Comedia*?"

"Well," I hesitated. I'd read the *Inferno* in school, sort off, though I skimmed the boring parts, and there were a lot of those. By the time I was ready to go onto the next two books, I'd had enough of the *Divine Comedy*. I read the Cliff Notes for *Purgatorio* and *Paradiso*.

Hey! I got a B in that course.

"Ha! I knew it!"

"Listen!" I spluttered. "I read some of it, but, well, I may not have read *all* of your work. Frankly, it was pretty dull."

Dante looked as if I'd slapped him. He started to protest, but there were murmurs of agreement from others in the group.

"See? They agree. Your books are *boring*!! Besides," I continued, pushing my advantage, "you only *wrote* about Hell. I, however, have spent sixty years there, so I think real-life, or rather, real-death experience trumps a made-up poem written over eight hundred years ago. Am I right?" I asked, turning to the rest of the group.

"Bravo!" yelled some Spaniard in the back. He had a long face, and one of those funny pointy mustache and beard combinations made famous by Van Dyke – the painter, not the guy who did that awful cockney accent in 'Mary Poppins.' "I have been listening to this know-it-all for five hundred years, saying my *Don Quixote* does not compare with his *Divina Comedia*."

"Cervantes? You're Cervantes?" I wondered if this was going to turn into the Great Books tour.

"Si, señor. Or more accurately, Miguel de Cervantes Saavedra. We are not supposed to argue in Heaven, so I've just put up with his arrogance for all of these years, yet it's good to have someone put him in his place. And, for the record, I found his *Divina Comedia* boring as well."

"How *dare* you, you cafone! I ..."

"Harrumph!"

I turned to find Saint Peter at my shoulder. "Steve," he said in a quiet voice. "Don't make me regret helping you set this up. Get the group under control, or I'll stop your little enterprise before it begins."

I nodded. He was right. "Sorry. Look," I said, turning back to the crowd, "though I am a saved soul now, for sixty years I was one of the Damned."

The crowd gasped. And stepped back a little.

A really nice suit can only take you so far, you know, and while it was a cool silver-gray, my tourists were all in glowing white.

"My job during those sixty years took me to every level of Hell. All Nine of them." I looked speculatively at Dante. *How did he know there were Nine Circles? Maybe he really had been inspired when he wrote his epic.*

"So the Superintendent of Hell's Plant Maintenance is a damned soul?" Dante frowned at this revelation.

"Yes, but I'm not damned anymore — don't worry about that — and I no longer have the job. My former assistant does it now. But we're getting off track here. My point is that I really *do* know Hell better than most human souls." I glanced at Peter, hoping to get a testimonial or something.

The old saint sighed but nodded.

"See? I promise I'll give you a good tour, but if anyone wants to head back into Heaven and skip this, I'll understand, no hard feelings." I looked at Dante, hoping he'd decide to sit this one out. The Italian poet was still glaring at Cervantes, but he glanced quickly at me and shook his head before turning back to Miguel and giving him some more stink eye.

Wonderful. My first tour, and Dante himself is on it. This will be fun.

I decided to change the subject. "Before we start, I need to discuss with you the price of admission."

Taking their cue from Dante, every one of them immediately gave *me* the stink eye, which they were all really good at, surprising since you'd think dirty looks would be illegal in Heaven. I suppose, though, that they were used to getting everything *gratis*.

I held my hands up. "Don't worry. It's nothing major. In fact, you might like it. I just ask that sometime while you are in Hell

110

you ease the suffering of at least one of the Damned. You can do most anything: a kind word, keep them from getting hit by a pie (I explained), stop a devil or demon from pitchforking someone."

"How will you know we've done it?"

I shrugged. "Mostly, we'll be on the honor system. I figure if you can't trust saved souls, who can you trust? But I'll be watching, and when you ease someone's suffering, you'll get one of these." I took out a gold sticker, shaped like a star, and put it on my lapel.

"Great," grumbled one of my customers. "More tacky stuff."

"Don't worry," I said. "It will probably disintegrate as you re-enter the Gates of Heaven. Things made on this side of the Pearlies can't really make the transition to a higher plane."

"Then how did you get those flyers posted all over Heaven?"

"Saint Peter handled that."

"Oh."

I looked at my watch. This was taking too long. Time to go. "So we don't get lost, I will be carrying this big red umbrella." I opened it. "Can everyone see it? Good, good. Now, try to keep up." With that I headed for the path that lead to Charon's boathouse.

Chapter 11

Firrst stop on the tour was the Well of [Damned] Souls, which is really more like a lake, large pond or city park reservoir than a stone-ringed well with a bucket hanging from a rope over it, like what you might read about in a fairy tale. I find the Well quite an eyeful, but my customers were unimpressed, for they had seen its like in Heaven. Apparently, the Well of Souls, the source of souls for the newly born on Earth, is a popular hangout in Paradise. From someone on the tour, I learned that Heaven's inhabitants sunbathed on a sandy beach that abutted the well; sometimes they went skinny dipping in it.

I find this last factoid a little gross. I've seen BOOH swim in the Well of [Damned] Souls, but those are used, maybe even a little threadbare. Oh, some would contend that characterization isn't fair. Peter says that only unadulterated soul-stuff exists in that damned well, with the bad gunk going down to Hell. He contends that everything in the Well of [Damned] Souls is really as good as new, but I just don't know about that. Sounds like something a used car salesman would tell you during a high-pressure pitch. I mean, come on. Good as new isn't the same thing as new. It just isn't.

Heaven's Well, on the other hand, is full of pristine spirits, that is, souls intended for babies. They really *are* brand new and pure. Knowing that, how could Heaven's Management possibly allow skinny dipping there? I mean, what if one of the swimmers has a bladder condition or something? Seems risky to me.

Okay, I'll get off my soapbox now. I'm just sayin' ...

After seeing the Well of [Damned] Souls, we headed down the path toward the Styx. Soon we were in a cave. The Heavenly host that comprised my tour group was unused to low-light conditions, so even a shadowed cave was pretty cool to them. They also liked the carvings of the Seven Deadly Sins, statues that lined the sides of the cave not far from Charon's boathouse. Personally, I've always found them a bit plebeian, the kind of fare you might see leaning against a pickup on the roadside, next to a painting of Elvis on fabric, but hey, I'm not exactly an art critic.

Michelangelo, who was also on the tour, agreed with me though. Don't know how I managed to get Dante, Cervantes and Michelangelo all in the same group, but I've had so many bizarre things happen to me since dying that I've stopped wondering about them. Anyway, the Renaissance master took one look at the crudely-rendered figures then spat on the ash-covered ground. "Merda!" Upon hearing that, I felt vindicated in my own opinion.

After leaving GL the previous day, I had stopped by to see Charon and give him a heads-up. My old friend was excited about the opportunity to get a few more customers. He was waiting for us beside his boat, which was tied to a post by the shore of the Styx. He didn't say anything, but merely bowed low in welcome. Everyone was appropriately creeped out by his skeletal visage, though they were equally impressed by his good manners.

"Arooo!"

On a hillock to one side, a monstrous creature with three heads overlooked the scene. "Arooo!" it howled a second time.

"Ladies and gentlemen. I give you…" – wait for it – "Cerberus!"

Dramatic pauses always enhance the moment.

They had all been expecting Charon, but I'd kept the Hound of Hell a surprise. Cerberus was doing a wonderful job providing atmosphere, but he just couldn't keep up the pretense. He bounded down to say hello to everyone, his tail wagging furiously, a Frisbee in one of his three mouths.

I rolled my eyes. "Don't worry, folks. He won't bite. Just don't throw his Frisbee for him. A game of fetch with Cerberus gives new meaning to the notion of Eternity."

"I do not understand," said Dante. "Cerberus is supposed to be the guardian of the Third Circle."

"Don't let it trouble you," I said, patting him on the shoulder. "I think you'll find that there's a lot down here that doesn't line up with your book."

Dante looked like a thwarted child, like he'd had his toy blocks taken away or something.

Charon stood silently by through all of this, then he raised a single bony finger and pointed at the gondola. He looked to me more like the Ghost of Christmas Yet to Come than the Ferryman of the Dead, but no matter. It was appropriately creepy and fit the occasion.

The group climbed into the boat. It was a bit of a squash – I wasn't even sure we'd all fit – but Ronnie had assured me that his craft could carry a group of forty, plus one tour guide and a gondolier who was a bit on the thin side. He was right; all of us just managed to fit.

But there was no room for Cerberus, who had been bringing up the rear and, I suppose, planning to join in on the fun. "Sorry, boy. No room at the inn."

Cerberus scanned the boat for an empty spot, but there was none. Disconsolately, he dropped his Frisbee to the ashen beach, and sat down to wait. As Charon, who had assumed his normal position at the boat's stern, pushed away from the shore, the Hound of Hell let out a plaintive, "Arooo!"

Poor fellow. I wished he could come along, but aside from the crowded conditions, Cerberus was a little too friendly. He would have ruined the somber mood Ronnie was trying to evoke.

"Do we need to put coins on our eyes?" said some Brit. "I seem to recall something about coins."

I looked to Charon, who gave a slight shake of his head.

"No," I said, relieved. I had had enough of coins for a while. "No loose change required. Besides, you wouldn't be able to see the view if you did that. Let's go, Ronnie, I mean, Charon."

Silently we glided across the River Styx. Now, when Ronnie and I, usually accompanied by Cerberus, were out on the Styx together, my friend would chatter constantly, his teeth clashing together rapidly like a set of castanets, but when on duty, he maintained a stony silence. It was expected of him. We were leaving the Gates Level and moving across the river into Hell, after all, and you don't expect the Immortal Ferryman to be gabbing like your hair stylist.

"It really is as silent as the grave, isn't it?" said one tourist.

"And the Styx is black, just like everyone says it is," opined another.

"I thought it was called the Acheron."

"You are correct," Dante chimed in. "The Acheron is the first of the three rivers guarding Hell, and since this is the first river we've encountered, it must be the Acheron, q.e.d."

There ensued an argument over this, which I quickly stopped. "In this case, our great poet is not correct."

Dante started to protest, but Cervantes poked him with his elbow, not a difficult thing to do in the crowded conditions of the gondola. "Let the man do his job," Miguel hissed.

"But…"

"Relax, Danny," I said. Dante didn't seem to care for me giving him a new nickname, but he held his tongue. "It's the same river, and both names are used, but we prefer 'Styx' to 'Acheron' because it makes for a better adjective."

"Huh?" said one of the tourists. Judging from his drawl, he hailed from Texas.

"Stygian as opposed to Acheronian."

"Oh. I suppose that makes sense."

From the back of the boat, Charon gave a single nod, and that settled it.

"Sir," I said, addressing the Texan, "you'll probably be interested in this. The reason the Styx is so black is that it's made of petroleum."

The man whistled. "That's a lot of oil, son."

Son. I found that amusing for some reason. "Now, if I may direct your attention to the ceiling."

Everyone looked up to the obsidian surface, far above us. A pale light from Gates Level shone down upon the upper end of the Styx, where a lonely if gigantic pup – still howling occasionally through the gloom – waited for the return of his master. The light was a dull oval, shaped by the tunnel through which we had walked not long before, but the luminescence was enough to make the cavern ceiling twinkle, as if it were covered by thousands of tiny diamonds.

"Ooo!"

"Pretty! I never expected anything pretty down here."

"That's because of the nearby presence of Heaven," I explained. "As we descend into the bowels of Hell, there won't be much that could be called pretty, unless you called it pretty ghastly."

With a soft thump, the boat came to rest on the far shore.

"All ashore that's going ashore!" I yelled.

If Ronnie had eyes to roll, he would have done it. Instead he just stood impassively in the stern of the gondola. A hot wind from Down Below picked up, blowing his charcoal cloak around, giving everyone an especially good look at the skull beneath the hood, and making Charon look eerie beyond eerie. The audience shivered, an involuntary reaction, I knew.

After riding many times with Charon, and seeing this happen every single time we landed on Hell's shore, I asked him once about the Hellish breeze. *Oh, that's in my contract,* he said casually. *I like to leave my customers with an indelible memory, you know?*

Waving goodbye to Charon, I led the group about fifty yards downhill. There we came to a one-way gate, sort of a sluice for souls leaving Charon's area. It was a merge lane for the Escalator. "Hop aboard, everyone." One by one, the tourists did as they were told.

"A moment," said Michelangelo. "Is this the same escalator we saw near Heaven's Gate?"

"Yes," I replied, as the last of the group stepped onto the moving treads. I brought up the rear.

"Let me get this straight," said the Brit. "We walked all this way, took the boat ride, and ended up getting on the same moving stairway we could have boarded back on Gates Level?"

"Uh huh."

"But that's just stupid."

I shrugged. "Maybe so, but if we'd taken the Escalator to begin with, you wouldn't have been able to meet Charon and Cerberus and take the gondola across the Styx."

"Maybe we could have ridden it on the way back."

Still holding my red umbrella aloft, I brought up the rear, stepping onto the Escalator. "Afraid not. The gondola to Hell is only a one-way ride. CAN EVERYONE HEAR ME?" I had to yell, because we were pretty strung out along the Escalator. "WHEN YOU GET TO THE BOTTOM OF THIS STRETCH OF ESCALATOR, STEP OFF THE TREADS. WE'LL REGROUP ON THE NEXT LEVEL."

The Escalator, which moves a mile a minute, had already slipped beneath Limbo. The crowd didn't even seem to notice. The Escalator then turned back on itself and briskly carried us to the surface of the next Circle. "Welcome to the Second Circle of Hell," I said, when we were all at the bottom.

"What happened to the First Circle?" Cervantes asked.

"Limbo," Dante said.

"Dante's correct in this case. Unfortunately, for security reasons, the Escalator doesn't stop at Limbo. In fact, the First Circle is kind of hard to get to, which is why we won't be going there today."

"Oh, come on."

"This is outrageous!"

"Total rip off!"

"Yeah, you promised us a complete tour of Hell!"

After a dozen more similar comments, I raised my hands in surrender. "Okay, okay! We'll go, but we'll have to travel by Hell's Elevator, and it's, well, kind of unreliable."

"Unreliable, how?" asked the Texan.

"Well," I hesitated. "A demon runs it."

"A demon? Cool!"

Everybody now wanted to ride in a demon-possessed Elevator, even knowing that the wait could be long. "Fine. That's what we'll do. Just understand that we may have to wait a while to get picked up."

"No problem."

"I've got all day."

"Dinner isn't until seven anyway, so that should work."

"But!" I said loudly, trying to maintain control over the group. "There is one circle we will not visit, no matter how much you beg and plead."

"What a cheat!"

"Which one is that?" grumbled the Englishman.

"The Ninth Circle," I said softly. "Where Satan resides."

The group got very quiet. "Ah," said the Texan, speaking for all of them, "that's okay. I don't think any of us wants to encounter the Lord of Hell, not if we can help it."

I breathed a sigh of relief. "Okay now, Second Circle." I looked around, getting my bearings. Reno had changed his route again. The Escalator was far away from Lustland, which was a bit of a disappointment for the crowd, though a tour of the capital of lasciviousness would have elicited another comparison with Vegas, so perhaps it was just as well.

Fortunately for me, Reno had dropped us close to some of the more eye-popping scenery on Two. "May I draw your attention to the sky over there."

"What's that? It looks like a giant stalactite."

"That, ladies and gentlemen, is Mount Erebus, a mile vertical drop from its base to its summit, though since the mountain is upside down, base and summit when referring to Erebus is a bit confusing. Erebus provides Hell with its cold."

"Why would Hell need cold?" Cervantes asked.

"For devil minibars, mostly. Also, well, you're from Spain, right?"

"Of course."

"I hear it's warm there. Were you ever cold in your life?"

He frowned. "Yes. I did not much care for it."

"We have our fair share of cold wimps down here, people like you. No offense," I said hurriedly. "I didn't mean you were a wimp, not really. It's just that you are a Mediterranean sort.

Lots of people in Hell are from warm climes. They hate the cold, so you can be sure that Hell will expose them to a good bit of it."

"We use more heat than cold, though," I said, indicating the fire pit nearby. As if on cue, Polyphemus came out with his barbecue grill top and a passel of damned souls. Setting the grill above the pit, he threw the humans onto the hot metal, pulled out his spatula and got to work.

I explained. "Satan really likes colorful characters from defunct religions, especially Greco-Roman. He collects them. That's why we have Charon and Cerberus. That one-eyed monster there is the original Polyphemus, by the way. Come with me, and I'll introduce you to another figure from Greek mythology."

A few hundred yards away was Sisyphus and Bessie, his giant boulder. The ancient king was a friend of mine, and he came down to say hi when he saw me. I introduced him to the group.

"Are we going to get anything to eat on this tour?" asked the Texan. He looked over toward where we'd left Polyphemus. "Anything but barbecue," he said, shuddering.

"Why yes indeed," I said, opening my hidey-hole and pulling out some heavy appetizers, finger sandwiches, chips, fruit and an assortment of soft drinks. "Sisyphus, do you have time to join us?"

"Afraid not, Steve. I've got to get back to work. Nice meeting all of you." With that, he headed back to Bessie and commenced rolling her up his hill.

Dante eyed the repast skeptically. "You don't really expect us to eat food from Hell, do you?"

I stuffed a pig-in-a-blanket into my mouth. "Not to worry."

"You shouldn't talk with your mouth full," said a grandmotherly type who, if her dialect was an indication, hailed from the Great Lakes region.

I rolled my eyes and swallowed. "Since we're saved, my girlfriend ..."

"Your what?" asked the feminist, interrupting.

This sounded like a trick question. "My girlfriend?"

"What is she, twelve?"

"Well, no, of course not. She's, let me see ..." I did some quick math. "She looks about twenty-five, but she died when she was ninety, and that was a hundred and forty-five years ago, so I guess she's two hundred and thirty-five years old."

"Humph! Hardly a girl."

I frowned. "Would you prefer lady friend instead?"

She frowned in turn. "Better, but it's pretty old-fashioned, and besides the obvious class reference, it focuses too much on her gender."

I closed my eyes. *There's a reason for that.* With a sigh, I opened them and mustered a smile. "What would you propose instead?"

She rubbed her chin, thinking up some options. "Partner, mate, friend. Even lady friend if you must, but not girlfriend. That's just demeaning."

"Sorry," I said, holding my hands before me in defense. "I didn't mean to offend anyone." I turned back to the others. "My life, er, after-life partner and I get all of our food from Heaven. Florence Nightingale herself helped me put together this snack for you."

"Oh," Dante said, mollified. "Miss Nightingale ..."

"Ms. Nightingale," said the feminist, correcting him.

"Of course. Ms. Nightingale is well-known to us. If she helped prepare the meal, it should be fine." With that, Dante plopped down in the dirt and popped open a bag of Doritos.

"What should we do with our litter?"

"Just throw it on the ground," I replied. "Hell likes litter." It was interesting how many of the tourists found this liberating.

After our snack, we did a small circumnavigation of the area. As we walked, I pointed out items of interests, like the harpies flying overhead, the ocean in the distance, where, I told them, on a lonely stretch of beach, Prometheus lay shackled. Astride a hilltop a half-mile away was the famous Palace of the Flaccid Phallus, an infernal resort for damned couples, where everyone was guaranteed to have a really lousy time. Farther away still was the jagged skyline of Lustland.

Then it was back on the Escalator.

Chapter 12

Reno hit Level Three on the edge of Ba'al's Outlet Ma'al. There ensued an argument among the tourists as to which devil Ba'al was. After five minutes of hearing absurd theories, including, "Ba'al is the devil associated with either jock itch or foot fungus, I can't quite remember which," I finally put a stop to it.

"No. Mr. Alighieri, sir, would you help me with this?" This was an opportunity to get on his good side, or so I hoped.

Dante had not been paying attention to the argument. He was more interested in the mall's large box stores and the pock-marked sidewalks connecting them, but he looked up when he heard his name. "What is it, Mr. Minion?"

"The Third Circle of Hell: what kind of sinners are punished here?"

"Don't you know?"

"Yes, of course I know. This is an opportunity for audience participation. Please, indulge me."

Got a little stink eye for that, but he responded, "The Third Circle is for the gluttonous."

"That's right. And which devil is most associated with gluttony?"

"Why Beelzebub, of course."

"Thank you." I turned to the others. "Dante is correct. Ba'al is an old Semitic word that means 'lord.' It eventually became used to reference gods, many gods in fact, but particularly Beelzebub. The Circle of Gluttony is overseen by Beelzebub, the great Lord of the Flies himself."

"Ooo," said the Brit. "Will we meet him?"

"Let's hope not," I said. "Beezy, I mean Lord Beelzebub, oversees both this level and the Eighth Circle. He spends most of his time on Eight, though."

"Then why doesn't the sign just say 'Beelzebub's Outlet Mall?'" asked the feminist.

I sighed. "Because Hell's management thinks Ba'al's Ma'al is funnier. See, Hell works this way: first priority is to punish the Damned. Second priority, though, is to amuse the devils who run the place, especially Satan, who has an even more warped sense of humor than I do."

Dante sniffed. "I find that hard to believe."

So much for trying to make nice. I ignored him. "If the Escalator had been on its normal trajectory, we would have landed in Glutton's Gap, where you could witness people being starved, force-fed or made to eat each other."

"Ba'al's Ma'al provides a different type of torment, but as with the establishments in Glutton's Gap, all the stores here emphasize conspicuous consumption." I pointed out the mall's four anchor establishments: Satan's Club, CrassCo, Wailmart and Not-OK-Mart. "Those big stores sell everything cheaply, but you must buy stuff in enormous quantities, like a container-ship's worth of toilet paper or an orchard's worth of prunes."

"Even the boutique stores that connect the anchors specialize in excess. For example, at Starburnt's you can get a mocha the size of a planter for less than the price of a tall. Of course, you have to drink it all before they'll let you leave the shop. Booger King sells a four-pounder, with jumbo jet fries and a five gallon coke, all for ninety nine cents. Men's Bewarehouse stocks suits."

"What does that have to do with excess?"

I shrugged. "All of Men's Bewarehouse customers are fat, but they are required to buy ten suits two sizes too small."

The box stores especially seemed to hold the group's interest, so I took them into the Not-OK-Mart for a brief walkabout. Hundreds of damned humans, all of them on the porky side, wandered the aisles pushing stubborn shopping carts with misaligned wheels. "Now dear," said a demon in a house dress to one of the Damned, a poor guy who was probably in life both a glutton and a henpecked husband. "Here's the grocery list. While I'm getting my hair done, you do the shopping. Get only what's on the list, but get all of it, in the exact quantities indicated."

The "husband" scratched his head. "But, uh, dear, I can never find anything in this store."

The demon snarled at him.

"Yes, sweetums!" he said, sweating. "Whatever you say, dear." And then he moved off, the wheels of his shopping cart wobbling and twitching in a determined effort to keep him from moving in a straight line.

This scene was being played out many times in the store.

"How can I buy only one pack of floss? They don't come in anything less than twenty packs."

"A small jar of capers? They only sell them by the barrel. And are those capers anyway? They look like rat turds."

"Hummus? What the hell is hummus? And where can I find it?"

"Look," I said, pointing to a stand at the end of an aisle near the entrance, where a demon, wearing a chef's hat, apron and wireless microphone, was stirring the contents of twin pots that sat on a two-burner hot plate. "They're offering free samples."

"Samples? What are these samples of which you speak?" Cervantes asked.

"Oh, they could be anything. Let's take a look."

I heard the shuffling of feet. From out of the nearby aisles trudged a dozen damned souls. Behind them was a crew of pitchfork-wielding demons. The souls were being herded, or goaded, into a line before the chef's stand.

"We have two wonderful delicacies for you today," the demon chef said through the PA system. "Now, many gourmands prefer their Brussel sprouts roasted, with a little salt, pepper and olive oil. They like their okra sliced, and either in gumbo or breaded and fried. But the best way to enjoy them both is boiled, preferably for many hours until the vegetables are slimy." The demon chef took tastes from each pot then shook his head. "Not mucousy enough." He sneezed into each hand. "To make these recipes really pop, we will add a secret ingredient. BAM! BAM!" he shouted, as he slung his "special" seasoning from his hands and into the pots.

I swallowed hard. Secret ingredient indeed.

A quick stir, and he tasted again. "Perfect! Would you like a sample, madam?" he said to the first unfortunate in line. The legs of the poor soul tried to scuttle away, but they couldn't, since they were connected to a torso that was attached to two arms, currently in the clutches of two demons. A third held the reluctant glutton's head still, forcing open her protesting jaws. The chef took a ladle and poured a generous serving of Brussel sprouts into the woman's mouth. Soon, the damned soul's cheeks were bulging like a chipmunk's.

"You must swallow now, madam," said the demon, again over the PA system. "We still have the okra for you to sample."

With a herculean effort, the woman did as she was told. Her neck bulged as she swallowed, but slowly her cheeks shrank.

My tour group shuddered and turned away.

"Attention, Not-OK-Mart shoppers," said a voice over the storewide PA system. "For the next fifteen minutes, we have a blue light special on forty gallon drums of cashews. Aisle three million and three. Hurry on over." There was a pause. "This is not a request!"

I recognized that voice and looked toward Customer Service. Yep, there at the counter, microphone in hand, was Laverne, the Devil in a Blue Dress. Normally, she worked at the Luby's in Glutton's Gap, but I guess she was subbing for someone today. Either that or she had gotten a promotion. At that moment, Laverne looked up and spotted me. A wary look came to her hooded eyes.

We had some history together. She lost.

I grinned at her then turned to my tour. "Okay, now is your chance to help some of these poor souls."

"No way," said a young man. "I don't want to get stuck by one of those pitchforks."

"You *can't* be hurt by a devil or demon. It's against the Accords. So use your protected status to break up some of these tormentations."

"Tormentations!" snorted the Brit. "That isn't even a word."

"It is down here. Get cracking!"

To their credit, the tourists accepted this challenge with gusto, spreading out through the store to stop evil and suffering wherever they found it. Cervantes and Michelangelo stood between pitchfork-wielding demons and their prey. The Texan and the feminist knocked over the pots of okra and Brussel sprouts. The young fellow, who claimed to have been an electrician in life, disconnected Laverne's microphone. The Brit popped a single spool of dental floss out of a package and handed it to one of the shoppers, who accepted it gratefully then checked off an item on his list.

The gang even deflected a few pies. I was proud of them.

127

All along, Laverne, who, according to her name tag, was the store manager, looked on helplessly. After fifteen minutes, I stepped up to her. "Hi, Laverne. How's tricks?"

"Minion!" she hissed, of course, then looked around warily. "Is BOOH with you?"

"Nope. If you want to, you can take a shot at me. Your choice. You can slug me, pie me or blast me with Hellfire."

Laverne looked at me with loathing. "You know I can't!"

"Oh, goodness me, that's right! Then get out of the way," I said, approaching her threateningly. Of course, I knew I couldn't hurt her either, but apparently she didn't think of that. A nervous Laverne dropped the microphone and stepped back. "Hook me back up," I said to the kid.

"THIS IS STEVE, YOUR TOUR GUIDE!" My voice boomed through the store. "GREAT JOB, EVERYONE. NOW, IT'S TIME TO GO. MEET UP AT THE ENTRANCE."

I did a quick count inside the automatic doors. A good tour guide knows to count his group regularly. You don't want someone lost, especially if you happen to be touring Hell. Fortunately, everyone was accounted for.

An explosion outside rocked the Not-OK-Mart. "MINION!"

Oh boy. I didn't think he'd come personally.

We stepped through the doors and onto the sidewalk. In the street, in a one hundred foot incarnation, was a very angry Beezy, the remains of a mushroom cloud dissipating above his head. "WHAT THE HELL ARE YOU DOING?"

"Er," I looked quickly back at my entourage. "A guided tour, Lord Beelzebub." I thought it good to show a bit of respect to the number two devil in Hell, especially since he seemed thoroughly pissed off at me at the moment.

"Beelzebub!" said the Texan. "Wow!"

"Where's my camera?"

"Wait until I tell my friends!" said the Brit. "The Lord of the Flies! They won't believe it."

"The flies?" asked the feminist.

"No. My friends."

Beelzebub shrunk down to his normal seven-foot size so he could glare at me more effectively. You'd think that would make him less intimidating, but it didn't. He was buzzing mad. Maybe the noise came from the swarm of flies circling his head, but the anger was all his own.

I stood protectively before my group. "They ... they are from Heaven and may not be harmed."

He scowled at me. "I know that, you twit! But keep them away from my employees, do you hear me?"

"Sure, Beezy, I mean, Lord Beelzebub." Now I felt bad. I had just wanted to do some good. Well, okay, I'd also wanted to antagonize Satan, but I'd not considered that Beezy, as the Patron Devil of Gluttony, might view our actions in the Not-OK-Mart as a personal slight. "Sorry," I said, chastened. "I won't do it again. Promise. I'll confine any more helping of the Damned to Four, where it will be Mammon's problem."

My old boss glowered at me, cracking his knuckles in a most intimidating fashion. I knew he couldn't hurt me, but I was still sweating it. "And you think I'll be okay with that, just because it's on another prince's watch? This is outrageous!" he bellowed. "You haven't heard the last of this." He gave me one final scowl and exploded. I actually felt a little heat from the blast. When the smoke cleared, he was gone.

"Did you see that?" said the Brit.

"Yeah. That's against the Accords. Somebody should report him."

"It's okay," I said slowly, brushing a little bit of ash from my puss. "I'm not hurt. Let's just keep this to ourselves." No way was I going to rat out Beezy.

I escorted the group back to the Escalator. All but Dante had earned a gold star on Three, but I gave him one anyway on the condition that he shut up for the rest of the tour.

Everyone was impressed with the golden facsimile of Rome on the Fourth Circle. I let them make a run on the Pantheon, stopping some of the punishment that was going on there and completely befuddling Mammon, who just sat on his throne and watched in disbelief.

In the Pantheon, Dante earned the star I'd given him earlier. He helped J.P. Morgan off the wall where he'd been hanging like a scarecrow for over a hundred years. I knew some demons would put him back soon enough, but Morgan was grateful for even a brief respite.

The day was nearly spent by the time we made it back to Gates Level. We had taken the Escalator all the way down to Eight, stopping on each Circle to see some of the highlights. The gang, having had a taste of easing the suffering of the Damned, refused to stop helping after we left Four, continuing their good-deed-doing wherever they could, but I prohibited them from taking any action on Eight, reminding them that this was Beelzebub's circle, just as Three was, and that I'd promised we'd leave his employees alone.

Waiting for Otis was a real pain. He kept us cooling our heels for two hours, and I had to keep the crowd entertained with some of my devil impersonations. I wished Orson was with me. He was always better at impressions than I was. Still, I soldiered on.

Finally Otis came. He grumbled the entire time he whisked us up to the First Circle, where, thanks to my Elevator key, we got off. In Limbo, everyone got to meet his or her favorite virtuous pagan. Dante was especially pleased to encounter Virgil and Aeneas. We even spent a little time on the putt-putt course, but when it was time to leave, everyone opted to take the stairs rather than wait for the Elevator again. The door at the top was locked, of course, but my Elevator key fit the keyhole, and we had no problem getting through to Gates Level.

I left them in front of the Pearly Gates, after shaking hands with each one, including Dante, who agreed with the rest, if grudgingly, that it had been a good tour.

My first outing had been a success. Yet, heading down the Escalator for dinner back home with Flo, I felt vaguely dissatisfied.

Chapter 13

"**H**ow can the Saved be so petty?" I asked Flo. It was the morning after my tour. We were in the bedroom getting dressed before she left for the hospital and I headed up to meet my next group.

Flo pointed to the back of her dress. I nodded and zipped it up. "People are people, Steve. Even in Heaven."

"Yeah, but I would have thought that once they had all the bad knocked out of them, they'd at the very least be polite to one another."

She stepped into her work shoes. "Not all the bad. Remember, there can be a good deal of evil in the best person's soul, even a saved one, if it is inextricably alloyed with good."

Flo was ahead of me, dressing-wise, so I hurriedly slipped on my trousers, trying to catch up. It wasn't a contest or anything, though. "That's what you and Peter keep telling me, but I still think the snipes that went back and forth between Dante and Cervantes were uncalled for."

She shrugged. "They are both men of words. I suppose you can't strip away that talent of theirs. You can't just leave them with only the 'good' words, at least I don't think so."

"Maybe you're right. Guess I just expected better."

Flo patted my shoulder. "I understand. Just remember, though: all humans are flawed, even the good ones. Besides, they don't get into Heaven on their own. Grace is the all-important factor."

I nodded. "Right, right. Being as good as you can be, doing good works, faith. Individually, not enough. Together, necessary, but still insufficient. Grace is really the only ticket for admission."

A lot of rules here. It's kind of confusing. But maybe it explains why Mary Theresa didn't win her coin toss. That still didn't feel right, though.

We dressed in silence for a couple of minutes, Flo brushing her hair before putting on her nurse's hat, me slipping the noose of my pre-tied tie over my head. "Honestly. Why do people bother to knot these things every day, when you can just loosen them and slip them on and off like this? Why, it's even better than using a clip-on!" I stared at myself in the mirror, finalizing my look.

"Most ties aren't made with fabric blessed by a saint, dear. Nor does the general male population wear the same tie every day." She gave me a smooch on the cheek. "And clip-ons are just tacky."

"But my question remains: why tie one of these every day? Maybe over time a tie might get wrinkled, but even a non-blessed one could be used over and over before that happened." I warmed to my topic. "You know, have all your ties perfectly knotted and hanging, lined up, in your closet, ready to go? It'd save so much time!"

Florence straightened the knot. "There. You're just saying that because you're no good at tying them. A man who ties his tie each day is telling the world something about himself. Sometimes a man is in a hurry; he has tied his tie with the front too short and has to hide the long, skinny back piece inside his shirt, slipped between two buttons. That means he was tired or late or lazy, because he didn't retie it. Other times, well, the man might have put on a pound or two, so he intentionally ties the front long to cover a little more belly." She poked me playfully in the stomach.

"And what, oh great psychologist of fashion, does mine tell you?"

She kissed me again, this time on the lips. "That you don't know how to tie a tie. Odd, considering you are a self-professed expert in knots."

"A hanged man doesn't tie his own noose," I said with a grin.

Flo slapped me gently on the cheek. "Always want the last word, don't you?"

My grin turned to a grimace. A little embarrassed, I nodded.

She smiled back, fondly. Then her face assumed a serious expression. "But enough of this. Spit spot! You don't want to be late for your tour. As for me, I must fly. See you tonight!" Flo grabbed her purse and headed for the door. I heard it open but not close.

"Steve." Flo's voice held a hint of uncertainty. "There's someone here at the door."

"Who?" I asked, coming up behind her.

Standing in the hallway, right arm raised, fist clenched but caught in mid-air before having had a chance to rap on the door, was a small chap, dressed in what looked like an ice cream truck driver's outfit. Well, maybe it was more like a white uniform. On his head was a close-fitting hat with a small brim. His coat reached just below his waist. It was closed from neck down by gold buttons. On top of the coat, a little above belly-button level, was a white belt with gold buckle. His shoes, and I assumed socks, though I couldn't see those, were white as well. On his coat pocket was an emblem that looked sort of like the Pearly Gates. The same insignia was on his hat.

"Who is it?" Flo gave me a wry smile. "My guess would be an angel."

Oh. I forgot to mention that the ice cream man had a small set of white wings on his back and a golden halo suspended in the air about six inches above his hat. "Good guess," I said.

"Steve Minion?" asked the angel in a squeaky voice.

"That's me," I responded. "What can I do for you?"

The angel lifted his left hand. In it was a white, nine by twelve envelope. "Special delivery."

"Uh, thanks," I said, accepting the envelope. "Would you like to come in?"

He smiled. "Thank you, but no. I need to get back."

I looked to Flo, patting my pockets. "What do you tip an angel?"

She shrugged. "I haven't the foggiest."

"A tip is unnecessary." The angelic delivery boy stared up. "Besides, my ride is here." A bright light shone round about him. When it faded he was gone.

We were not sore afraid, but we were a bit bemused.

"Hmm." The envelope was addressed to me in a fluid hand. The penmanship was even better than Flo's, which I would have sworn was impossible. I turned over the envelope. Stuck to the flap was a lump of red wax; it had been embossed with a design unfamiliar to me, two angel wings separated by a sword.

"Oh," said Flo, who had been looking over my shoulder. "That's Michael's seal."

"The archangel?"

"Uh huh. Must be official business. Go ahead and open it."

I shrugged, slipped my index finger under the flap and broke the seal. Pulling out two sheets of paper, I began to read. My face grew hotter with each word.

"What is it, Steve? What's wrong?" Flo set her purse on a nearby chair.

"Well," I said slowly, "my tour today has been cancelled, for one." I flipped to the next page.

"And?"

I looked up from the pages. "It's a summons."

"What? Why? And why are you clenching and unclenching your fists?"

And in the process crumpling the sides of the paper sheets in my hands. I exhaled heavily. "Because I want to slug someone."

"Who?"

"Satan. He's filed a grievance against me with the Council on Heavenly Accords, whatever the heck that is. Seems he didn't appreciate my activities yesterday. I'm summoned for a hearing on Gates Level."

Florence nodded. "I wondered if this would happen. Shortly after I came to Hell, Satan tried a similar tactic against me, unsuccessfully, I might add. When is the hearing?"

"In about ten minutes."

Florence took my suit coat off its hanger and tossed it to me. "Then you'd better hurry and hope Otis will cooperate for a change."

I glanced out the window. Standing on the corner was a large and furry presence. "Don't think that will be a problem. It looks like transportation has already been arranged for me."

She looked where I was pointing. "BOOH?"

I slipped on the coat then fished my fedora out of the closet. "Yeah. I probably don't merit light beam travel yet, like our angel delivery boy, or like you do. Still, it beats dealing with Otis. Come on. We can walk down together."

Flo grabbed her purse and we left the apartment.

BOOH was slumped against a gas lamppost. It was looking a little bent, reminding me of a similar if electrified streetlight outside my old apartment in the industrial quarter. My batty friend had probably been cooling his jets for a while, but he popped to attention as soon as he saw me.

136

Flo said hi to BOOH, then turned to me, one eyebrow raised. "Good luck," she said. "I'm sure you'll be fine, if my experience is any indication." Then she headed for the hospital.

BOOH had really cleaned himself up. The fur on his forehead had been slicked back, probably with demon spit, which made for a remarkably effective hair gel. He apparently had even taken a bath – most likely in the ocean on Seven – because the scents of offal and sulfur, which normally clung to him like groupies to a rock star, were almost undetectable. Diagonally across his chest was a blood red banner; it made him look like a diplomat. He even sported a leather attaché; it hung from a strap around his neck. That made him look a little like a Saint Bernard, but I didn't say that to him. Heck, he's my friend. I'd never hurt his feelings in a million years. Besides, BOOH had a distinct brand of quiet dignity. He projected "official," in his own vampiric way.

"Looking good, BOOH. I assume you are both my ride and my escort for this morning's festivities."

BOOH almost knocked me to the floor with one of his wings as he swung it crisply to his brow. I think it was intended as a salute.

I smiled. "I don't think I have the status to merit a salute, but I appreciate the gesture. Still, why you? You work for Satan, not Michael."

"Urm, urm, skree." Nose wiggle, left foot raised.

"No, I didn't know Heaven could conscript you on occasion. Interesting. Well, shall we go?"

BOOH nodded, then like a helicopter, he rose straight up, hovering above me, his claws opening to grab me by the shoulders.

I took a step backwards. "No way. I'm not going to be carried to Heaven like a piece of carrion. Besides, we're way past that in our relationship, don't you think?"

BOOH dropped to the ground, looking at me uncertainly. I don't know what his instructions were about my means of transportation, but I didn't care. To be clutched in his claws, for everyone to see, well, it was undignified, like I was already guilty of something. And he might have snagged my coat.

Reaching a decision, BOOH flattened down and let me climb on his back, just like the old days. I took off my hat and clutched it to my chest to keep it from flying off during the journey. My other hand firmly grasped the tuft of hair between BOOH's ears. It was a little slick from all the gel he'd used, but I wrapped a lock a couple of times around my knuckles so I wouldn't lose my grip. In seconds, we were off, jetting upward through the Throat of Hell.

I leaned over one of BOOH's ears. "Do you know anything about this hearing?"

"Skree. Skree, urm, urm. Skree."

"Well, I don't particularly care *what* Satan thinks of my presence down here. And if he's complaining about interference, well, he should talk. I was supposed to do a tour today."

"Urm." Nose wiggle. "Skree. Skree." Shrug. Wing droop.

"No, of course I don't expect you to take sides." I patted his neck, almost losing my balance. I grabbed the neck fur again. "Let's drop it, okay? We can just enjoy the ride. Like old times, eh?"

"Skree!"

"That's the spirit! Now make sure you announce our arrival with one of your famous Bat out of Hell screams, okay?"

"SKREEE!"

"No, not now. When we get there." I looked up and saw that we'd just crested the Mouth of Hell and were coming in for a landing near Saint Peter's desk. "Oh. We *are* there."

BOOH set down precisely, then for effect reared up like a prize stallion. I slid off his back when he did that but, recovering quickly, landed lightly on my feet.

I meant to do that.

BOOH stood at attention while I donned my fedora. "Thank you, BOOH," said the saint, who apparently had been waiting for me. "That will be all. Uh, dismissed."

My batty friend frowned at him. "Skree!"

"Now, BOOH," I said, patting him on the shoulder. "I'm sure Peter meant no offense."

Peter looked from BOOH to me. "What did he say?"

"He said he doesn't take orders from you."

"When he's in my domain, he will," Peter said, shooting daggers from his eyes at Hell's emissary-in-chief.

Not literally, of course. That would be weird, and way too violent for a saint.

But BOOH got the intent. The fur on his back stuck out in all directions, like a cat who was trying to intimidate a dog or something. "Skree, skree. Skree!"

"Calm down, both of you!" I snapped. "I've got enough to deal with without refereeing a fight between two of my friends."

The bat gave Peter the evil eye, which by the way is a patented expression in the Netherworld, though few could do it as well as BOOH. Then he went off to stand by the Gates of Hell.

"Prickly sort, isn't he?" Peter said.

"Really? You're talking about prickly? You practically invented the term."

"How dare you!"

"See? You just made my point. Oh, never mind. But he's right, you know."

"About what?"

"That he doesn't work for you."

Peter glowered.

"BOOH also said something else that I feel compelled to pass on." I paused. Needed to say this delicately. "No offense, Peter, but Gates Level isn't really your domain. It's shared space."

"You got all that out of three skrees?"

"BOOH and I are tight."

"Oh." Peter exhaled heavily. "Maybe he's right. No, he *is* right, darn it, but I have to do everything up here except take care of the entrances to Hell. The floor gets dirty; I have to sweep it. Clouds get in disarray; I have to untangle them."

I shrugged. "Sorry. It's not your domain, but I guess it's still your responsibility. Doesn't seem fair, but on the other hand, I doubt you'd want a bunch of demons up here helping out."

"True dat."

I looked at him with suspicion. "You hang out with rappers much?"

He shrugged.

"You know, Pete, you're really picking up some odd expressions."

He grimaced. "Just trying to keep relevant. I'm dealing with new generations all the time. And speaking of time, it's nearly time for your hearing."

I glanced up at the Pearlies. "What am I in for here?"

"Best you find out at the Council session. I'll be going with you, since I'm a player in this little drama." Peter frowned.

I looked around. "Is Andrew going to sub for you?"

"No," he said, a sour look on his face. "Andrew isn't available. Here comes my replacement now."

A man of medium build descended the steps of the Pearly Gates. He had a closely cropped black beard, a receding hairline that was worse than mine and, most noticeably, a halo. Even though this was my second halo of the morning, the glowing ring surprised me. People didn't normally wear them up here. I think they were out of fashion, or maybe they were worn only for formal occasions. I couldn't tell if the saint, for saint is who he was, wore his as mere affectation or a demonstration of bad fashion sense.

Paul. I'd met him twice before but, other than what I'd read in the Bible, knew very little about him. Except for one thing: Peter didn't like him.

That might not be accurate. Certainly, though, there was an ongoing rivalry between them. Paul was a prolific writer from the days of the Early Church. Heck, he wrote a big chunk of the New Testament. He also traveled all over the Roman Empire evangelizing. Peter, for his part, established the church in Rome and, in effect, created both Roman Catholicism and the Orthodox Church. Both saints played crucial roles in the early years of Christianity.

Yet Paul was not the one who got the most visible gig in the afterlife; Peter did. Not to mention that Peter had known Jesus personally, while Paul had not. These factors had inevitably created friction between them.

"Saul," Pete said without preamble.

"Simon," Paul replied, looking at his rival with distaste.

Without another word, Peter handed Paul the all-important soul-deciding quarter, then turned his back on the man.

Just like Flo said. Even good people are not perfect. I didn't know if that notion made me feel better or worse about humanity.

Pete took me by the shoulder and ushered me toward an embankment of clouds about fifty yards away. "I hate having Paul cover for me," he grumbled. "Hopefully, this won't take too long."

As we closed on the precipitate mass, the clouds parted. They revealed a set of double doors, guarded on both sides by blue-winged Seraphs.

That's as opposed to the squiggly additions to letters on the page, like what you'd get from Times New Roman or Garamond but not Helvetica or Arial. No, we're talking about two members of an angelic order. Wings on a font seraph would have looked stupid. Besides, fonts are terrible guards.

At our approach, the two Seraphim opened the doors.

Chapter 14

We stepped inside an already-crowded room. The décor was all white: white walls, white furniture, white art work in white frames.

"What's that a picture of? A cow eating grass. Where's the grass? The cow ate it all. Where's the cow? Why should he hang around if all the grass has been eaten?"

You know: white art. White stuff.

In the center of the room was a conference table. Around the table sat an array of angels unfamiliar to me. There was one exception: Uriel, the archangel, whom I'd met once on the tarmac of the Gates Level air strip. Of course, Satan and Beelzebub were there. The Prince of Darkness had his arms crossed, and he was frowning. Beezy looked like he'd just eaten an exceptionally sour pickle, and it hadn't agreed with him. My old mentor must still have been mad at me from the previous day, which was unusual. He was not the sort to hold a grudge.

Little Laverne was also in attendance. I figured she was a character witness. Scratch that. Lack-of-character witness. And she had personally seen the antics of me and my tour group at the Not-OK-Mart.

Pete and I seated ourselves in the proffered chairs. "Take off your hat," the saint whispered.

"Why?" I whispered back. "Beezy is wearing his fez, and Satan won't even bother to take off his sunglasses."

"Yes, but they're the bad guys. They're *supposed* to have bad manners."

"Oh, o...kay." I took off my fedora and placed it on the table, but a dirty look from Peter made me put it in my lap.

The room was all but full; only a single empty chair, beside Uriel, was left. There was a commotion outside, and the conference room doors flew open. A light flashed, and I was blinded for a moment. When my eyes adjusted, I beheld a gloriously handsome piece of angel flesh, angel centerfold material, if Heaven had been into that sort of thing, entering the room.

The newcomer's face was so beautiful I felt like weeping at its sheer gorgeousness. Or gorgeousity. Or whatever. He had a magnificent build – barrel chest, powerful yet graceful arms, sculpted hands that Michelangelo himself would have been proud to have carved – and long, blond hair that hung, shimmering, all the way to his shoulders. Maybe even a little below his shoulders. At his hip was a sword that made Excalibur look like a thumb tack.

The newcomer was in a seven-foot high incarnation. For some reason, many angels and devils like that size. Big enough to be impressive yet small enough to interact with humans.

Satan bristled when he saw him. "Uriel!" he snapped. "I thought you were handling the hearing!"

"Michael and I are doing it together, Lucifer," Uriel said mildly. "We're both on the rotation."

The archangel Michael, top dog, I think, in the angelic pantheon, smiled as he went to his seat, a big toothy grin. His teeth were magnificent, like Robert Wagner's after he'd gotten his caps. Michael's pearlies gleamed like miniature spotlights, and I was damn near blinded a second time in under a minute.

Sorry, darn near blinded.

What a magnificent creature, I thought.

Then he opened his mouth. "Uh, hi guys," he said to Satan and Beelzebub, sounding, to my ear at least, like a California surfer dude.

My mind cleared, as reality set in. *Oh, that's right.* I remembered. Michael was beautiful, a real hunk, and a great warrior, perhaps the greatest of all the heavenly host, but he was not the brightest of angels. That was putting it kindly, and he demonstrated his lack of savoir faire almost immediately by tripping over his sword when he tried to sit down. Michael fell forward, landing with both hands on the table. Sitting opposite him, I saw the surface before me hop up a foot.

Uriel smiled indulgently, but I saw the barely suppressed eye roll as he carefully slipped Michael's sword and sheath off his colleague. Uriel patted the other archangel on the back then leaned the sword against the wall. "Thanks, Uri," Michael said and took his seat.

Satan hates oafs, so it's no wonder he dislikes this guy. Well, that and the fact that Michael once beat him to a pulp.

"Go ahead, Michael," Uriel said encouragingly. "It's your turn."

Michael screwed up his face, concentrating hard, but he seemed to come up empty. He leaned over to Uriel. "I'm sorry. I forgot what I'm supposed to say."

His colleague whispered in his ear.

Michael brightened. "Oh, yeah! I remember now. Thanks! Ahem. This hearing is now in session."

Oh brother.

Uriel handed Michael a Manila folder. The blond giant opened it and hunkered over the page. I saw his lips move as he read. "It says here that Lucifer …"

"Satan!" snapped the Earl of Hell. "I'm sure it says Satan!"

Uriel smiled mischievously. "You'll always be Lucifer to us."

Satan's fist slammed on the table top. "That doesn't matter! I filed the complaint as Satan, not Lucifer." Satan reached to his feet and retrieved a leather briefcase, dropping it with an

145

echoing thud on the table top. He popped the latches and pulled out a document. "Why don't you just let me read it?" Michael was staring hard at the page before him, trying to puzzle out the words. Uriel looked at him warily then glanced at Satan and nodded.

"Very well. Ahem. I, Satan, Lord of the Underworld, the Antagonist Supreme, etc. etc., formally lodge a complaint against Steven Minion, formerly one of the Damned, former demon, now," Satan looked at me with distaste, "one of the Saved. In these proceedings, I, Satan, Lord of the Underworld, the Antagonist Supreme, etc. etc."

Sin of Pride.

"...will be referred to as the Party of the First Part. Minion shall be considered the party of the second part, and Beelzebub, Lord of the Flies, insofar as he is a cosignatory of this complaint shall be referred to as the party of the third..."

"Oh, good grief," Peter spoke up. "Can we just part with all these parts and get to the point of the complaint? I've got a desk to run out there, you know."

"I concur," Uriel said. "Lucifer, I mean, Satan, if you would just summarize, that would save us even more time. As it stands," he glanced at Michael, who looked as if his head was ready to explode, "all the legalese in your document could be confusing some in the room."

Satan slammed closed his dossier. "Very well. Here it is then. It's bad enough that you allow Minion to wander around my realm completely unfettered, without me having any say in the matter, but permitting him to give guided tours of Hell is completely unacceptable!"

A chainsaw rumbled to life. It was Beezy clearing his throat. "I have to agree. Hell is our responsibility, given to us by Divine Delegation. The manner of running it is up to us."

Satan shot him a dirty look. "It's up to Me! Me! *I'm* the Antagonist Supreme."

Beezy closed his eyes, sighing. When he opened them again, he stared through half-slitted lids at his boss. "Whatever, Nick. The point is that we have a job to do, and having forty or so of the human Heavenly Host wandering around Hell is very disruptive to operations. It's one thing to have Minion poking around, deflecting pies and sending them back into the faces of the demons who throw them ..."

"Wait! He does that?" Michael broke out laughing. "Ooo, wow! That's pretty funny. Oh, come on Lucifer, lighten up. Imagine a demon getting hit with his own pie. It *is* funny, and you know it."

"Doesn't matter if it's funny or not," Satan responded. "He's getting in the way of the Damned's eternal punishment."

"I hardly think a pie in the face rises to the standard of eternal punishment," Uriel chimed in. "Seems like you're just doing it for kicks. You've always had a twisted sense of humor."

I may not have thought much of Michael, but this Uriel guy I liked. He was one sharp cookie.

"May I finish my sentence?" Beelzebub grumbled. "You know, it's just rude interrupting someone like that. As I was saying, pie deflections are one thing, but when Steve, I mean when Minion, sics an entire tour group on us, with the express purpose of undermining the workings of Hell, well, it's very disruptive."

"An understatement!" Satan said heatedly. "This is terrible for public relations. Hell has an image to maintain, you know, and saved humans wandering through it, as if the excursion was a walk in the park, completely undercuts that image."

"Again, I agree," Beezy rumbled. "And Minion's not just interfering with damnation. He's distracting my employees, like Laverne here."

The devil in a blue dress – she'd put on a nice off-one-shoulder frock for the occasion, rather than wear her work outfit – gave her usual bobblehead nod. She was clearly out of her depth here.

"I won't have it!" Beelzebub slapped his palm against the table. All the arms resting on the surface, mine included, bounced in the air from the force of his blow. We looked like we were doing a wave at a stadium game. Our eyes flew wide, and I wondered who was more intimidating, Satan or Beelzebub.

"*We* won't have it," Satan hissed in a low voice, making everyone shudder.

Okay. It was a tie.

"I want the tours to stop immediately," he continued. "And I want Minion out of Hell for good."

They'd been poking at me long enough. It was my turn. "May I say something?"

Uriel nodded. "It's about time we heard from you anyway."

I stood up and began to walk slowly around the table. It seemed to me that we had a bunch of high-wattage individuals in the room: angels, devils, even a saint. Among such company, I was a pretty humble personage, but I'd always been a good public speaker, and I was better when I moved. Besides, Body Language 101: stand above your audience, and they have to look up at you. Height gives an immediate psychological advantage, and I needed all the advantages I could get.

"I'd like to respond to the second item first and the first item second."

"Huh?" Michael said. "First, second, what are you talking about?

I sighed. "First, about Satan wanting me out of Hell. I claim precedent. Well over a hundred years ago, Heaven permitted Florence Nightingale to descend to Hell in order to provide comfort to the Damned."

"I've *never* agreed with that ruling!" Satan said forcefully, rising from his chair.

"So what? Has Heaven changed its mind?"

The Lord of Hell frowned. "Well, no, but I've appealed."

"Then it seems to me that unless and until the ruling changes, Flo and I and any saved soul who cares to do what we two did can come to Hell."

"He's right, Satan," Peter said. "No one ever expected a saved soul to choose Hell over Heaven, but there's nothing that prohibits it. That's why the Nightingale Ruling went against you, and equally why you haven't any legal basis to deny Steve access to the Underworld. And as long as I'm talking, I might add, since some of you are wondering, that Steve didn't just go off half-cocked with this tour idea. He asked me about it beforehand, and while I had some reservations, I did not object."

"What?" Satan snapped, flames crackling around his fingertips. "*You* gave him permission?"

"No, I didn't, Nick," Pete said calmly. "All I did was distribute some flyers. As I said, Steve asked me, but it really isn't my place to tell him what he can or can't do."

"Except for when you feel like telling him what to do," Beezy said sourly.

I stifled a chuckle. He was right about that. Peter simply smiled.

"And, Lucifer," Uriel chided. "Please remember where you are. Put out that fire."

"What?" Satan looked down at his hands and quickly extinguished the flames. "Sorry, but it just shows you how passionately I feel about all this. Very well, on the point of Minion's presence in Hell, I want to go on record that I object to it ..."

"So noted," Uriel said, writing something on a legal pad.

"But for now, and as long as my Nightingale appeal is in limbo ..."

"It's not in Limbo," Michael corrected "It's up here."

Satan rubbed his eyes. Can't say I blamed him. "Metaphorical limbo, Michael," he said tiredly.

"Oh." Michael leaned over to Uriel and whispered. Uriel whispered back. "That's what it means? I did *not* know that. Thanks!"

Satan and Beezy sighed in unison. Only the sighs, not the pitches, which sounded about three octaves apart. It was an interesting audio effect, though, with Satan as the tweeter and Beezy as the subwoofer.

"For now," Satan continued, "I will grudgingly accept Minion's presence in my realm, but I will not tolerate these tours. They make me, Beelzebub and the staff that helps us run Hell laughingstocks throughout the Cosmos. In fact, I think this whole tour idea is less about easing suffering than it is Minion's mean-spirited attempt to humiliate me and undermine my authority."

"Mr. Minion," Uriel said. "Do you wish to rebut?"

I shrugged. "I acknowledge that maybe, just maybe, there's a bit of truth to what Satan says. Look, I may be a Christian, but I believe in karma. What goes around, comes around. For sixty years, Satan and his staff treated me like hell, unjustly as it turns out. If I want a little payback, can anyone really blame me?"

I guess they could. Looking around the room, I saw that no one was sympathetic, not even Peter, who was frowning at me.

"Besides," I said hurriedly. "I really don't see the harm. Forty saved souls amid thirty billion damned ones. The saved ones couldn't even make a ripple down there."

"Then why do it?" Beezy asked.

Why, indeed. His was the sixty-four dollar question. Now it was my turn to frown. I had no answer to that.

In fact, I still can't convince myself that anything Flo and I do in Hell has any lasting value at all.

Uriel and Michael were huddled together in a private confab. After a minute of back and forth whispering, Michael nodded. He turned to the assembly, frowning at the Earl of Hell. "This is a real bummer, but we gotta go with horn head on this one."

Uriel cringed. "I think what Michael means to say is that, in the matter of the tours, we rule in favor of Satan and Beelzebub."

"What!?" I sputtered. "But I thought you were the good guys?"

"We *are* the good guys, Steve," Uriel said calmly. "But your motives in this are all wrong. You aren't trying to ease suffering here. You're just trying to humiliate Satan."

I opened my mouth, ready to shoot out a hot retort, but Peter chose that moment to put my leg in a viselike grip. "Ouch!" I stared at him in anger, but his severe look took all the fight out of me. Besides ... "You're right," I mumbled.

Uriel nodded. "So the tours are to end. Immediately."

"But, but I've already committed to two more tours. I'd feel like I was going back on my word if I didn't at least do them. Those on my waiting list would be disappointed."

151

"Uri," Michael chimed in. "You know we don't do disappointment in Heaven. They won't know how to handle it."

Uriel stroked his chin. "This is true."

"Oh, good grief," Beelzebub said. "I'll do the two tours, on the condition that no good deeds be done by the tourists while they are in Hell."

I stared in astonishment at my old boss. "You? You'll scare the crap out of them!"

"What? I can be charming when I want." Even Satan looked skeptical at that. "I *can!*" Beezy shrank a foot. A petunia-spotted bow tie appeared around his neck. "See?"

"No offense, Beelzebub," Michael said, "but now you just look like a six foot tall devil, instead of a seven foot tall devil—in a bow tie. And that bow tie somehow makes it worse."

"Crap!" he snapped, transforming into a dead ringer for me. "How's this? I can even do Minion's voice. See?"

Uriel stroked his chin, nodding. "That should be sufficient."

"Could you at least lose the bow tie?" I asked. "I don't do tasteless bow ties."

"No!"

"Okay, okay! Just asking."

Uriel dug his elbow in Michael's side. Taking the cue, the blond archangel dismissed the hearing. "Adjourned. Have a good one, gang. Peace out," he finished with a grin, flashing a Rock On! hand signal.

What a moron.

"What a moron," Satan said, echoing my thought. I hadn't even heard him walk up to me, and sixty years of conditioning kicked in, meaning I nearly leapt out of my skin from fright.

Fear combined with surprise is never good. It's like standing in some peaceful woods then abruptly hearing a rattlesnake doing his maraca impression at your feet.

I took a deep, calming breath and turned to him. "What do *you* want?"

"To gloat mainly," he replied with a sneer. "I stopped your stupid tours. Such hubris from a mere human!"

I pursed my lips. I was feeling better. "You only got half of what you wanted. I'm still living in Hell, and I'll do my level best to be a thorn in your side for the rest of Eternity."

Satan's right hand went back, as if to slap me, but he restrained himself. Instead, he hissed at me.

That hiss, well, it was just one too many in six decades of them, and it pushed me over the edge. Suddenly my anger at the Lord of Hell became a conflagration. I was enraged, enraged for all those decades of torment and humiliation. I wanted to hurt him, to scare him the way he'd always scared me. I almost snarled, but instead lowered my voice nearly to a whisper. "I know what you've done, you know," I said, an unmistakable edge to my tone.

Satan slipped off his sunglasses. His eyes were red today, and they looked puzzled. "What the *hell* are you talking about?"

To be honest, I didn't know what he'd done, not really. There was only this vague suspicion of mine, but I'd always trusted my gut. By now, I was pretty sure the Earl of Hell had managed to rig the system, increasing his harvest of souls at Gates Level, and that the coin was somehow involved. Pretty thin grounds on which to base an accusation, but this was a wonderful opportunity to make him nervous, if such a thing was even possible, and I was going to take it.

In hindsight, what I did next was probably a mistake.

Reaching into my pocket, I pulled out an imaginary coin and pantomimed flipping it in the air, catching it and placing it on the back side of my left wrist. Then I stared at him, eyes narrowed, a look that I hoped appeared threatening.

And Satan blinked.

In sixty years of knowing the Earl of Hell, I'd never seen him blink, but he'd just done it. Because of me. What's more, his reaction gave me confidence that I was on the right track.

The blink was only for an instant, and when Satan opened his eyes, they were no longer red but black, unreadable. His face was impassive.

"Don't count on it, Minion," he said after a moment of silence, donning his sunglasses. "Nightingale I can tolerate in my domain, but you, you have to go. I will figure out a way to get you out of my hair, have no doubt."

"Nick!" Beezy bellowed from the conference room entrance. "You coming?"

"Yes," he said then turned to face me again. "Watch your back, Minion, not that it will do you any good. Bwahahahahahaha!" With that, as I had done to him in his own office, he turned his back on me and headed for the doors.

I hate that stupid laugh.

Chapter 15

"I don't know, Orson. It just didn't feel right."

We were in the trailer. I was perched on the stool, Orson was on the floor, trying to fix a leak in the office sink, and Edison was sitting at the desk, sipping coffee and going through the morning's work orders.

"Why's that?" Orson's voice echoed a little, which wasn't surprising, since it was currently tucked inside the cabinet that housed the drain and water lines. One arm was in the cabinet; the other was flailing uselessly, trying to grab a monkey wrench that was just out of reach. "Say, Steve, could you hand me my wrench?"

"Ah, I don't think I should do that. Beezy is really mad at me right now. He told me to keep away from his employees."

"I'll get it," Edison said, getting up from his chair. "After all, it's my job, not yours."

He handed the wrench to his boss. "Now, Orson, before you fiddle with the trap, let me…"

"Agh!"

"…drain the water out of the sink first." Edison made eye contact with me and shook his head.

Orson's own head popped out of the cabinet, hair and beard soaked. His assistant tossed him a towel. It had a little motor oil on it but was the cleanest thing in the room, other than my suit, of course.

Edison frowned. "I don't understand. Why would you care if Beelzebub is mad at you? I thought that was the whole point."

My hands were clasped in front of me, thumbs twiddling as I thought. "No, the real point was bugging Satan, and," I added hurriedly, still clinging to my feeble excuse for motive, "to ease suffering. But..."

"But what? Here, give me that." Edison took the towel from his boss and dried Orson's hair like a mom might take care of her kid's mop on bath night.

"Well, it's complicated. I don't mind antagonizing almost any devil or demon, and especially Satan, but Beezy, well, he was very kind to me when I was a demon."

"Beezy was kind?" Orson said in astonishment.

There was a warning rumble that we could feel through the linoleum. "When I was a demon!" I shouted, looking wide-eyed at the two of them. "That's a big difference, you know. Devils and demons stick together. And 'kind' is probably not the right word. Let's just say he gave me good advice. Beezy isn't kind to anyone. He's as mean and evil as they come!"

The rumbling at our feet stopped, and I breathed a sigh of relief. *Nice save.* "Let's just say that, because of the years I worked for him, I'd rather not cause Beelzebub any trouble."

After Edison finished his ministrations, Orson continued. "It seems to me that, while an interesting idea, bringing saved souls down to Hell on a guided tour was a bit over the top."

I scowled. "Apparently Heaven agrees with you, or at least they do now, after Satan filed a formal protest with the Powers on High. I've been told to cease and desist."

"Why can't you just do what you were doing before?" asked Edison. "You know, deflecting Hellfire and pies?"

I tried to touch my ears with my shoulders. (That's a shrug. It gets old saying "he shrugged.") "Dunno. That seems kind of pointless. As soon as I walk away, they'll just get clobbered anyway."

"Just a second." Orson's head went back into the cabinet, along with an arm and the wrench. "I need to get this drain flange thingee off."

Edison sighed. "It's not a flange thingee, Orson. It's just a flange."

"Whatever."

"Why don't you put a bucket under the sink?" I suggested. "That's what we used to do."

"Because," Orson said, head and arms emerging from the cabinet again, this time with the flange and an O-ring in hand. "Tom thinks we should fix this right."

Tom inspected the O-ring. "There's nothing wrong with it, so I don't know why tightening didn't work. Let me get some plumber's putty and Teflon tape from the supply cabinet and you can use them when you reinstall it."

Orson looked at me and winked. Meanwhile, Edison walked over to the cabinet, opened it and began pawing through the contents. "Orson, I don't see either putty or the tape I was talking about."

Orson looked at me apologetically. "He's still new at this, you know. Tom, you remember that we're in Hell, right?"

"Of course, and, oh, got it." He slapped his forehead as he processed the staggeringly obvious implications then grabbed a couple of items from the cabinet and closed the door. "So, the closest I could find was some Silly Putty and Scotch tape."

"Give them to me, will you?" Orson asked, hand outstretched.

I nodded. That's what we usually used on plumbing jobs like this, that is, when we were actually expected to fix something, except I always favored duct tape over Scotch tape. Still, I nodded in approval. Edison would get the hang of his new job yet.

As I watched Orson fumble with the putty and Edison clench his fists in frustration for not being allowed to do any of the fixing, a wave of nostalgia passed over me. It was silly, I knew. I loved Flo and spending time with her, and I was very happy not being Hell's Super anymore, but I missed hanging out with the guys. Which was why I was visiting in the first place.

I kept quiet while Orson, with Tom's guidance, reinstalled the flange thingee. Flange. "Go ahead and turn the water on Tom, but first let me...Agh!"

Edison turned red with embarrassment as a soaked Orson emerged a second time from the cabinet. He grabbed the damp towel and dried off again. "Hand me the bucket, Tom." Orson slid it into the cabinet and closed the door. "Told you it wouldn't work."

"Well, it might have, if I'd been allowed to do the repair myself."

"No, it wouldn't," Orson and I said in unison, then grinned at each other.

"This is Hell, remember?" Hell's Super pointed out.

"Okay, fine," Tom groused. "I'll go back to emptying the damn bucket twice a day."

Tom and Orson drank a bunch of coffee. The sink was an important fixture in the office, and a lot of water, as well as coffee dregs, ran through the thing.

Orson took one final swipe at his head with the towel then threw it across the room, where it knocked over a floor lamp, shattering the bulb. Tom gave Orson a dirty look but grabbed the dustpan and broom and went to clean up the glass.

"Now, Steve, what were you saying?"

"That the best I can do is stall the inevitable punishment of a damned soul." I shrugged. "It doesn't seem like much help, Orson."

"It's good enough for Flo. Have you discussed this with her?"

I nodded. "Many times. In her mind, delaying punishment is an important accomplishment, her way of wrestling with the Devil and his minions."

We were interrupted by the sound of tinkling glass as it ricocheted off the insides of file thirteen, aka the waste basket. Edison had finished his cleanup operation. He stowed the broom and dustpan then turned to me. "Steve, I don't really see how you can do any better, short of going to Heaven, I mean. Why is it again that you don't want to do that?"

I shrugged. "Well, there's Flo, for one. She wants to stay here and fight her battles in the Toaster. Where she goes, I go. And besides, well, I'm not sure if I'd even like Heaven. All of my friends are down here, like you guys."

Tom brightened. Over the years, I'd usually referred to him as the Big Prick. This was the first time I'd ever called him a friend, and it was not lost on him.

Orson just smiled. "We would miss you too, Steve, but you'd make new friends. I mean, it's Heaven after all. There must be plenty of nice people there to hang out with."

"Maybe." I frowned, thinking about all the unpleasant individuals who'd been on my tour. "But regardless, I'm not ready to go there. Take it as my ultimate expression of human free will."

Okay, then. I'm here, and I want to help. I don't think I'm quite prepared to expose the coin conspiracy, despite Satan's reaction yesterday, but if not that, then what?

I remembered what Andrew had said to me the day I'd helped out Peter. "Hey guys. Do you think my good deeds need to be confined to damned humans only?"

"Well, I think that's where your greatest opportunities lie," Orson said. He swept his arms out expansively. "Thirty billion and counting, right? But I guess there's no law that says you can only help damned humans. You said you did a favor for Saint Peter just the other day, didn't you?"

"Yes. In fact, I was just thinking about that. It felt pretty good bailing him out, even though he did me a favor in return. Still, it showed that even the big guys could use a little help from their friends once in a while."

Edison frowned. "Other than Saint Peter and the Damned in Hell, who do you have opportunities to do good deeds for? Devils and demons? Hah! Don't make me laugh."

Hmm. "Well I can think of one demon I'd do a favor for. Thanks, Tom. You've just given me an idea." I got up from the stool. "Think I'll go check out my idea with Pete."

"You're spending a lot of time on Gates Level these days," Orson remarked.

"Yeah." I shuffled my feet awkwardly. "I, well, I need people to talk to. During the day, Florence is busy in the hospital, and I can't really spend too much time with you and my other friends down here. You're all way too busy, what with your eternal damnation and all. But Peter is safe. He also gives good advice, sort of a sanity check for me."

"In an insane afterlife," Orson intoned softly. "I completely understand. I'll try not to be jealous."

I grinned at him. "There's only one Orson Welles."

"Too true," he said, with zero false modesty.

"And you'll always be my best friend," I said, grabbing his shoulder.

He smiled. "You too."

One blocked pie later, I was preparing to leave when I had another thought. "Hey, guys. I want to show you something."

I pulled a piece of paper from my pocket and laid it on Orson's desk. This was the sheet that held the impressions I'd made of Peter's quarter. "Have either of you ever seen a coin like this?"

The guys crowded around the paper and examined it. "Not me," Orson said.

Tom picked up the sheet. "I have. In my father's coin collection." He looked at me. "Where'd you get this?"

"Gates Level. These impressions come from the coin Saint Peter used to determine my fate. Yours too, by the way." I told them about looking their names up in the Book of Life.

I stared over Edison's shoulder. "I can see that it was made in 1838, but can you tell me anything else about it?"

"Actually, yes I can," he said. "If memory serves, it's what's called a capped bust quarter. Minted in Philadelphia. They were made in two sizes, large and small. This is the small version, which many people liked, because it fit well in a pocket."

Yes, Peter would appreciate that, as often as he has to reach for the coin.

Edison continued his examination. He frowned. "One thing has always struck me as odd about this series."

"What?"

"Here," he said, handing the paper to me. "Do you see anything missing?"

I examined the paper closely and gasped.

"Yes," Edison said quietly, looking thoughtful.

"What are you guys talking about?" Orson reached for the onion skin.

DING! From the pneumatic tube above his inbox came a whooshing sound, and a work order slapped the top of a growing pile of papers in the tray. Normally, only top priority jobs were accompanied by a DING! so it had to be important. By old habit I reached for the paperwork.

But Orson, forgetting the sheet in my hand, had already grabbed the new work order. "Oh, it's from Beezy. Apparently he finally liked one of my ideas." Orson looked to his assistant. "Tom, go see Dora. According to the order, she's holding some parts we'll need for this job."

"Okay." Tom gave the paper with the impressions one final look, frowning. He started to say something, thought better of it, and headed for the door.

"What's up?" I asked, folding the paper and putting it back in my pocket. Tom's revelation had unnerved me, though it fit the pattern that was taking shape.

"Production values," Orson said, all thoughts of the coin gone from his mind. "Looks like, if you hang with Peter for a while, you may see us up there."

"That would be nice. I guess I'll see you later then."

Orson was staring at the work order in his hand, stroking his goatee in thought. "Later."

And then I was out the door.

Chapter 16

Another hour wait for the Elevator, plenty of time to consider the mystery of the quarter. Yet I resisted. That stupid coin was becoming an obsession, and I needed a break from my own suspicions.

Otis was also driving me crazy. *Man, if I just resided on Two or Three, I'd always take the stairs, but I don't want to walk five miles every time I need to go topside. I'll have to figure something else out.*

But I didn't know what that could be. Without being able to fly or teleport – or ride a light beam, like Flo was allowed on occasion – my options were pretty limited.

Finally Otis picked me up. For a wonder, he transported me to Gates Level without a word. I guess he'd given up on sparring with me, either that or gotten bored. The latter was possible. Demons have short attention spans.

On the other hand, they aren't very bright, so it doesn't take much to amuse them. For instance, take Otis. Please. He's been running the Elevator for at least a hundred and fifty years, without going insane, so he must have gotten a measure of job satisfaction from blasting up and down between Gates Level and Eight and the circles in between.

Not that he had much choice in the matter. This was the job he'd been assigned to, and I supposed Satan had no interest in giving it to another demon. As I pondered Otis's situation, I realized that, on a certain level, it really wasn't all that different from being a damned human in Hell. He was doing the same thing for Eternity, just like everyone else down here.

It's funny that, ever since I'd been saved, I felt more at home on GL than anywhere else, except of course with Flo in the apartment. The cloudy no-man's land fit me in a way. I didn't really belong in either Heaven or Hell, which might have explained why this space in between felt comfortable to me.

Seeing the old Saint at his podium when I arrived on Gates Level, sorting the recently dead into lambs and goats, brought the quarter back to mind, but I again forced it from my consciousness. I wasn't ready to discuss my suspicions with Peter. Instead, I just watched him whittle away at the line before him.

After a few minutes observing, I smiled. He was industrious; he was as honest as a ruler is straight. All those years of acrimony between us no longer mattered. Everything was different. We had become friends. "Hi Peter," I said, when he had finished. "How are things?"

"Steve?" The saint looked surprised to see me. "I didn't expect you today."

"Well, I had another idea and wanted to run it by you."

His expression turned to one of suspicion. "What now? Your last escapade got me in a little trouble, you know."

"Yeah, I *do* know," I said, flushing. "Sorry about that. Still, I don't understand why you got in trouble in the first place for my idea."

"I distributed your flyer, remember?"

I winced. "Oh, yeah."

"This better not be anything like that."

"No, no. It's not nearly so flashy. A simple act of kindness."

"What do you have in mind?"

I told him.

"Well, well," he said stroking his beard. "So I'm not the only person in the universe who thinks that entire situation is unfair. Good to know."

"So you'll do it?"

164

"Yes. Shouldn't be too hard. He's on light duty these days. Doesn't make the trip to Earth as much as he used to. How about tonight?"

"Great! If we could make it early evening, say sixish, that would work well."

"Why so late?"

"She's off work by then. Besides, I'm going to try to make this a twofer."

"How?"

I told him, and he laughed. "Yes, both of them should like that. Hope the logistics work out."

"Me too," I said, turning to leave. "I'm counting on some good luck."

"Well, you're the only damned human to have been reclaimed by Heaven, so I'd say you're just about the luckiest guy I know."

I grinned. "I think so too. Especially with friends like you."

He smiled. "Thank you, Steve."

Next on my itinerary was a conversation with Charon, but before I turned from Peter's desk, I heard a DING! The Elevator had returned to GL. There was a rattling of the ever-recalcitrant Elevator door. Behind it came muffled curses. Then the door flew up, and out stepped Orson and Edison. There were carrying a lot of stuff: their tall ladder, some metal poles and a large box.

I was curious, but with all that gear, I knew they'd be here a while, so I decided to come back and check things out after I'd talked with Ronnie. As Orson and his assistant walked by, carrying their gear, Edison stared at me with a curious intensity.

What put a bug up his butt? Did he have a bad exchange with Dora? That was certainly possible. Or maybe he was still thinking about the quarter.

With a shrug, I headed down to have a conversation with Charon. Ronnie was putting a coat of paint on his boathouse: charcoal gray, his signature color. I told him what I had in mind and asked if he was interested. Beyond being merely interested, he was enthusiastic.

"I'll try to make it happen tonight, Ronnie. If I can't, I'll call you. Otherwise, it's a go, okay?"

Certainly, Steve. I look forward to it.

The whole exchange had taken five minutes. I did a U-turn and went back to see what Beelzebub had assigned to Hell's Super and his assistant.

Orson and Edison were working near the Escalator. The collection of poles, or tubing, that they had brought was now interlocked, forming a sort of frame, perhaps thirty feet wide and twenty high. The large cardboard box they had borne up from Level Five was lying open nearby, its contents, a mass of gray and black fabric, already pulled halfway out of the container. Festoons of the stuff fell on the floor. From opposite sides of the frame, Orson and Tom were slipping the fabric onto the metal. The cloth seemed to be some kind of curtain, and the frame a gigantic curtain rod of sorts.

The work had been going smoothly, suspiciously so, I thought. Back in my day, that frame would have fought me and Orson, and the loop in the fabric through which they were shoving the metal support would have been too small. With a small amount of envy – very small, considering I was spared the work entirely – I realized that Orson and Edison might make for a better maintenance team than Orson and I had in the past.

Or perhaps whatever they're doing is considered important enough that Hell's Management is allowing them to work without the added complications so common in a standard job.

Peter walked over to me, and together we played the part of a crowd watching a construction crew. "Do you have any idea what they're doing?" he asked.

"Nope. They sure are working fast, though, aren't they?"

"Preternaturally fast," he concluded. "This must have the sanction of Those on Low."

"Yeah. I think so too."

In a few more minutes, the two men had the fabric completely unfurled and threaded on the poles. Then they put a set of feet on the bottom poles. That was kind of funny. They were literally feet, made of plastic, but shaped just like human dogs. Dogs: that's a euphemism for feet. I didn't want to use feet too many times in the same paragraph.

Oh, shoot. Did it anyway with my explanation. Sorry.

Edison looked my way and locked eyes with me. I guess he'd been aware of my presence for a while, even though both Peter and I had been pretty quiet as we'd watched them. Tom looked angry about something, though I didn't know what. Perhaps just being Orson's assistant was enough to keep the Wizard of Menlo Park in a perpetual state of mad.

"Hey, Minion! Make yourself useful and help me and Orson put this thing in place."

"Uh, Tom, I don't think that's a good idea," Orson chimed in.

"Nonsense! He is saved and can't be harmed. It will be fine." Edison stared at me impatiently. "Come on and help."

I looked at Peter and shrugged. "On my way."

The whole structure was awkward, and truth be told, they kind of needed my help. We lifted the contrivance and placed it around the Escalator and the three neon signs ("WELCOME TO HELL," "OVER 30 BILLION SERVED" and "ABANDON ALL HOPE etc.") that surrounded it. As a final step, Orson and Edison put

167

together the last three tubes, which together formed a U shape, stuck the loop of the U through a sleeve at the bottom middle of the fabric, then stuck a final foot in the center of the U's middle. They placed the foot about fifteen feet behind the point where the Escalator pierced the cloudy surface of Gates Level. This effectively pulled the fabric back and away from the moving stairs so that people could descend through the hole in the clouds without catching their heads on the fabric. Then we all stood back and examined the finished project.

I whistled. The drapery had been painted with great precision to emulate a massive entryway. From the edges the fabric transitioned from billowy clouds to an ever-graying sky – like staring through thickening smoke – until it flowed into the severe lines of the new Gates of Hell. These were formed by two faux stone pillars that hugged the Escalator signs. Above them was a connecting arch; "attached" to the pillars were beautifully rendered wrought iron gates that looked as if they would slam shut as soon as a damned soul crossed through. Beyond the Gates, the sky graduated from charcoal to pitch. Draped across the top of the arch was what looked like a giant rat, its back armored and barbed, with an occasional tuft of savage rat hair. The rat, a medieval stand-in for Satan or some other devil, clutched a cruel spear.

"Wow!"

"Impressive," Peter said. "Reminds me of the old Entrance to Hell."

Orson nodded. "That was the idea. I always thought the current Entrance looked really cheesy. I had suggested to Beezy that we install an actual stone gate, but that would have put us over budget, so he said no. He thought my alternative was acceptable, though."

"And how!" I said admiringly. "Who did the painting?"

"Albrecht Dürer."

"I thought I recognized his style."

"Yes. He based it upon his own 'Harrowing of Hell.'"

"Your idea too?"

"Yeah. I wish Beezy had let me eighty-six the neon signs entirely, but he refused. This was our compromise."

"Well, it's a darn good one. I ..."

Edison was tugging on my arm. "Minion, uh, Steve. Could I talk to you for a second?"

"Sure. What's up?"

Tom leaned in closely, giving me a whiff of his breath. I almost gagged. He must have been eating garlic or something. "Not here," he whispered. "It's about Orson." Grabbing my arm, Edison pulled me away from the others and toward the Pearly Gates.

We were within ten feet of the steps to the Gates when he stopped.

"All right, Tom," I said. "What about Orson?"

We were interrupted at that point by the ding of the Elevator. Out stepped, of all people, Thomas Edison, looking slightly dazed.

"Goodbye, Minion," said a familiar voice beside me.

Edison Number One had morphed into Satan. With a prodigious shove, the Earl of Hell pushed me gently but inexorably across the cloud floor in the direction of the steps.

There was a mighty roar and then the oncoming of night. I lost all consciousness.

Chapter 17

When I came to, I found myself draped across the steps of the Pearly Gates, surrounded by a nimbus of white light.

A great sense of calm pervaded my soul. I was at peace. Something fundamental had changed.

"You monster!" Peter yelled, though his voice seemed miles away. "You have just broken the Accords!"

"No, I haven't!" Satan snapped back. "There's nothing in the Accords that says I can't touch one of the Saved, only that I cannot do harm. Are you harmed, Minion?"

Slowly, I was coming back to myself. The sense of calm remained, but I was more aware of my surroundings. I stood up, though my legs were wobbly beneath me. My suit, no longer gray, was a gleaming white. I felt … pure … thin … popular. Everything was wonderful!

I looked over at the Earl of Hell. He was an unpleasant sight, and I flinched as I beheld the Evil that seemed to radiate off him.

"I said, are you harmed?"

"No," I replied slowly, looking at Peter, who was rushing to check on me, and Orson and Edison, who stood, troubled but helpless to intervene, behind Satan. I gave them a lopsided grin then made a peace sign. "I'm good. Really good."

"Bwahahahahahaha! See, Peter? Well, this is goodbye, Minion! You and your conspiracy theories will be very happy in Heaven, I'm sure. And you two," Satan said to his maintenance crew, "get back to Five. There's plenty of work waiting for you there." Then he vanished.

"Are you really all right, Steve?" Peter said, grabbing my shoulder.

"Heaven?" I said dazedly. I looked up at the Pearly Gates and felt myself irresistibly drawn to them. I took a step forward, but Peter held me back.

"No. Wait." As if I were one of the walking wounded, he guided me gently back to his desk. I went placidly, though my eyes kept being drawn toward Heaven's Gates and the Rapture that lay beyond them.

He sat me down on his stool. He snapped his fingers before my face. I blinked. He moved a finger back and forth. My eyes tracked it, if a bit lazily.

"Is he okay?" Orson asked.

"I'm good, Orson," I repeated, smiling beatifically. "Oh, hello Mr. Edison. What happened to you?"

"Mr. Edison," Tom said, turning to Orson. "See? That's the kind of respect I deserve."

Orson rolled his eyes. "Never mind, Tom. And answer the question. What *did* happen to you?"

Edison frowned. "I'm not quite sure. I was heading to get those parts from Dora, when a black cloud descended on me. The next thing I knew I couldn't move. And I couldn't see a thing." He shuddered. "I've never experience such darkness."

Orson frowned. "Sounds like Satan's broom closet."

"What?"

"Never mind. Then what happened?"

"The darkness lifted, and I found myself in the Elevator, riding up to Gates Level. I could move again. That was just now." Edison looked to Orson. "So what *did* happen to me?"

"My guess? Satan put you on ice so he could impersonate you." He turned to Peter, who was still hovering over me, testing my reflexes with a tiny silver hammer he'd pulled from a drawer, periodically propping me back up on his stool, as I was showing an alarming tendency to ooze onto the floor.

I was pretty relaxed.

"But what happened to Steve, Saint Peter?" Orson asked. "And why is he so spacey?"

Peter huffed. "He's just disoriented, and it will take him a little while to adjust. Unusually strong reaction, though, especially losing consciousness. It's probably because he was unprepared for it."

"Adjust to what? Unprepared for what?"

The saint indicated the chute next to the walkway leading to the Gates. "Satan shoved him right past the chute, and the unalloyed evil that was in Steve's soul got removed."

"Oh, the chute! I forgot about that."

"We don't allow very much of the bad stuff to enter the Gates, you know," Peter continued, "only that which is inextricably bound up with good and cannot be separated out."

"Yeah, yeah," Orson said impatiently. "I've heard it a million times. So now what?"

"Now Steve is being irresistibly drawn toward the Entrance to Heaven."

A light bulb seemed to go on for Orson. "Getting Steve out of Satan's hair forever."

"Precisely." Peter frowned. "I don't like it. Nobody should enter those Gates until he's ready, and the fact that Satan initiated all this is deeply unsettling. Steve, what did he mean about conspiracy theories?"

I rubbed my forehead, feeling a little woozy. There *was* something, but ... "I'm sorry. I can't remember."

The phone on Peter's desk rang. Still staring at me, the saint grabbed it. "Yes? Uh huh. Uh huh. Really? Will do, Sir."

Peter hung up and looked at my friends. "You two head down to Five like Satan told you. I don't want you to get in trouble."

"But Steve!" Orson protested.

"Don't worry. I'll take care of him. Leave it to me."

"Okay, sir." Orson looked teary-eyed. He gave me a hug; it made me hiccup. "Goodbye, Steve."

Even Edison looked sad. He patted my shoulder.

"Don't say goodbye quite yet, gentlemen," Peter said, still eyeing me closely. "You may see Steve again, sooner than you think."

"Well, that, that would be good," Orson said, sniffling a little. "Au revoir, then."

"Later, Orson," I said, beaming, flashing another peace sign. "Later, Mr. Edison?"

Edison smiled at me gently. "Later, Steve." Then, gathering their tools and cardboard box, they descended through the new Gates of Hell.

I started to ooze off the stool again, but Peter caught me with one hand as he rummaged through a desk drawer with the other. "Here's what I need," he said, extracting a syringe.

"What's that, sir?"

"A little something to clear away the cobwebs," he replied, jabbing it in my arm. "I don't need use it very often, but your extreme reaction to losing all of your major evil tendencies makes it necessary."

The warm, gauzy feeling of well-being that had so quickly overwhelmed me began to recede. My head no longer felt like it had been stuffed with cotton. My suit, which had been glowing like a one gigawatt flood light, dropped into the megawatt range. Soon the light faded entirely. The suit was no longer a pure white, but it hadn't returned to grayness either. It was more of an off-white. "Thanks," I said slowly, sitting up. "That's good stuff."

"Actually, it's bad stuff. Essence of Evil. I have to administer it occasionally to a newly-saved soul who reacts the way you just did. The effect is only temporary, but it should help you handle the adjustment to your newly-purified soul."

"You have an *evil* injection you give good guys?"

"Comes in a cologne, too."

"Keen," I said, rolling my eyes.

"Oh, good," Peter said in a not entirely sincere voice. "Your sarcasm is back, so you must be okay. Now stand up, and let's see how you're doing."

I got off the stool, walked around a little. "I feel fine, though not quite myself."

He nodded. "A little less than yourself, I would imagine. In a way, you're a different person now, without the major evil bits in your soul."

I stroked my chin in thought. "When I was damned, I always felt a bit off, and when I was saved, and had all of my parts back together, so to speak, I finally felt like me again. This is a little like that first feeling, all over again. Rats."

"Sorry about that."

"It's *exactly* why I didn't want to go to Heaven!"

"Well," Peter, said, looking at the phone on his desk, "Heaven agrees with you."

I looked at him, startled. "You mean I'm *still* not good enough for Heaven? After all I've been through, They don't want me?"

"No, no, nothing like that," he said soothingly. "It just isn't your time. I don't know entirely what's going on, but you seem to be needed on this side for something."

174

"Hah! Doubt if I'm good for anything, even with that little bit of Satan Serum you shoved in my veins. Why, I can't even compute a square root in my head!" I frowned. "Of course, I never could do that anyway. That's what calculators are for, but still, damn it! I am not myself!"

"Which is why you need to get your bad stuff back."

"Humph! And how, exactly, am I supposed to do that?"

"By fetching it. Come." Peter gestured for me to follow. He led me toward the Pearly Gates, stopping opposite the chute that had just carted off the evil portions of my soul. "I am about to show you one of the great secrets of the Afterlife. Well," he said, hesitating, "it really isn't much of a secret, except to the human populations of Heaven and Hell. The rest of us just don't talk about it much. We've been asked not to."

"By who?"

"Whom." Peter took a deep breath and blew away the clouds at our feet. This exposed a large iron panel, like a hatchway, hinged on one of the narrow ends, with a big ring on the other narrow side. He grabbed the ring and with one hand lifted the metal hatch.

"Wow! Have you been working out?"

"Saints are strong," he said modestly. "Especially me and a few of the others."

"Like Paul?"

He gave me a dirty look.

I peered down into the darkness, spying in the gloom a long flight of steps. "So where do they lead?"

"To the realm of the dweebils."

"The what?"

"Dweebils."

That was a new one. "And what the heck are they?"

175

The saint pursed his lips. He looked thoughtful. "They are the souls of a race from a far-away star system. Gone now. The star went supernova a millennium ago. Somehow the civilization there evolved without any religious beliefs at all — most unusual — but as a result, when dweebils died, they were more or less stranded. For years uncounted they awoke after death and wandered throughout Chaos, forlorn, homeless, no place to go. Kind of like nerds on a Saturday night." He shrugged. "Top Management here took pity on them and provided an afterlife space. Only one, mind you, since dweebils are morally neutral and don't need to be separated into wheat and chaff, sheep and goats or whatever metaphors you prefer."

"TMI," I said wearily.

"What?"

"Skip it. You were saying?"

He pointed at the stairway. "Down there is a pocket universe, mostly separate from Heaven and Hell, though touching in spots upon both of them. In fact, the dweebils, who were grateful for the kindness the Big Guy showed them, have made themselves very useful. They maintain the infrastructure between the two domains, patching the occasional crack in the Foundation of Paradise or repairing the roof of Hell. Being comfortable, or as comfortable as anyone can be, out in Chaos, they also patrol and as necessary repair the outer perimeters of Heaven and Hell."

"Oh! Kind of like me when I was Hell's Super."

"No, not really. They're actually *good* at what they do."

"Gee, thanks." I sat down on the steps of the Pearly Gates, staring thoughtfully at the stone stairway. This was a new one on me. "Why do the dweebils want their existence kept a secret?"

Peter waved his hands above the opening, sweeping away a handful of clouds that had drifted back over the space. "They are a very shy people. You know, not good at mixers, don't know how to dance, etc. They're great at Trivial Pursuit, superhero backstories and so forth, but if you didn't need those particular bits of arcana, you wouldn't be inclined to invite them to a party. Nor would they want to come. They prefer to keep to themselves."

"So," I said slowly, "we have angels, devils ..."

"And dweebils." He paused, considering. "The good, the bad ... and the awkward."

Jeez. Yet I soldiered on. "And humans, mythical beings, magical creatures."

"Yes. That pretty much accounts for the entire population in the main areas of Heaven and Hell and the rather cramped space in between. But don't forget Doggie Heaven, Bamboo Bliss and the other realms for God's creatures."

"No Doggie Hell?"

He looked at me in disbelief. "Of course not! Everyone knows all dogs go to Heaven."

I groaned.

"Of course," Peter continued, warming to his topic, "that's just our theological neck of the woods. Other religions, other worlds, even other universes have their own Afterlife spaces. Except the planet of the dweebils, of course. That makes them unique."

My head was spinning with the possibilities. "Never mind," I said, willing myself not to think about it. "I get it. So now that I know the secret of the dweebils, what am I supposed to do with it?"

"Just trot down those stairs and ask Doofa to give you your soul stuff back."

"Doofa?"

"The archdweebil who runs the desk down there."

And I'd been feeling so good. I rubbed my eyes with the heels of my hands, trying to massage away the wicked headache that was now pounding deep in my brain pan. "Let me get this straight. This guy's named Doofa?"

"That's right."

"And he's an archdweebil?"

"Correct."

Sigh. "Okay. So Doofa the Archdweebil will give me back my soul stuff, just like that?"

"Ah. You're right of course. Hold on a moment." Peter went back to his desk, scribbled something on a piece of paper and came back to me. "Here," he said, handing me the paper. "Show that to Doofa, and you shouldn't have any problem."

"Uh, thanks." I shoved the note into a trousers pocket as I stared into the dark recesses of the stairwell. "I guess it's down the rabbit hole for me."

"Yes. Don't worry, Steve," he said, patting my shoulder in encouragement. "It will all work out. Say 'hey' to Doofa for me."

I threw my hands up in defeat. "Sure. Whatever. Keep the light on in the kitchen, okay?"

The old saint looked at me, confused. "What? Oh, a euphemism. Yes, certainly. See you soon, I hope."

"Me too." Taking a deep breath, I descended the stairs.

Chapter 18

The stone felt cold against my hand as I plodded down the stairs. I was still a little unsteady on my feet and almost slipped a time or two.

They should install a rail or something else to hold onto. This is dangerous.

I descended about fifty steps before reaching the bottom. Here I found a long hallway. The floor was flagstone; the walls were a rich wood, like mahogany. In the distance was a light, warm and beckoning. I headed for it.

After about a hundred feet, I reached the end of the hallway, entering a well-lit room paneled in the same wood as the passageway. The ceiling was perhaps fifteen feet up. Ladders on wheels leaned against the walls; they could be rolled to easily reach any point on said walls. Three of the four sides of the room were covered with glass-fronted cabinets, filled with all manner of things. I saw a jar with what looked like a dragon fetus in it. There were old knives, powders with labels inscribed in a script I'd never seen. One compartment had an old Nintendo system. I had no idea why all these weird things were together, but my guess was that dweebils were by nature collectors, or packrats.

In one corner of the room was what looked like a pickle barrel. Near the entrance, where I was standing, were two tables covered with open wooden bins. Inside the bins were thousands of comic books. I rifled through a few. Justice League, Spider-Man, Superman, Wolverine. Nothing like Archie, Casper or Scrooge McDuck though. The dweebils seemed to prefer super heroes, which fit with what Peter told me.

In the back of the room was a long, low counter. Behind the counter were rows of shelves, like what you might see in a library, or an auto parts store. In fact, this place reminded me a little of Dora's parts department, or maybe an old apothecary shop.

Between two of the ranges stood a small creature, no more than four feet tall. He had pale blue skin and furry ears shaped like those of a Papillon. The dog, not a French butterfly. The little fellow was putting a large sealed jar on a shelf that was a trifle too high for him, yet rather than grab the nearby footstool, he was managing with a bit of tiptoeing and some shoving at the jar's bottom with his fingers.

"Excuse me," I called.

The dweebil, or what I assumed was a dweebil, started at my voice, and the jar began to topple. With a desperate final push, he shoved it farther onto the shelf. The jar settled down.

Satisfied that the container would not fall, the little guy turned to regard me. His eyes were huge, bulbous things, as big as the lenses on his round, black plastic-framed glasses. He had a long, hooked nose. The dweebil swallowed hard then came up to the counter.

"Hey," he said, holding his hand in a way that looked a bit like the Vulcan greeting on Star Trek. Since he had two extra digits on each hand, though, it was kind of hard to tell if that was his intent.

"Uh, hey. I'm looking for Doofa."

The fellow's ears began to shake. He swallowed hard. "I ... I am Doofa."

Doofa seemed awfully unassuming for an archdweebil. He was dressed in a Green Lantern T-shirt and blue jeans. Doofa was a little on the portly side; looked like he'd had a few too many dweebil din-dins in his time. He held his pants up with suspenders.

"Nice to meet you, Mr. Doofa."

He looked down at the counter, pulling out a handkerchief to wipe some fingerprints off the finely-waxed wooden surface, though I think it was just a ploy to avoid making eye contact with me. "Just Doofa, please."

"Oh, okay."

"What, what can I do you for?" he asked, a nervous quiver in his voice.

"Well, I just inadvertently walked toward the Pearly Gates and lost the bad elements in my soul. I'd like to get them back." This sounded stupid, even to me.

Doofa frowned. The thought of parting with something seemed to trouble him. In that regard, he was definitely like Dora. It also gave him a measure of courage. "Do you have a receipt? No returns without a receipt, you know."

"Well, I have this note from Saint Peter." I fished it out of my pocket and handed it to Doofa.

He read it carefully, mopping his azure brow with his handkerchief. Then he took off his glasses and, holding the paper very close to his nose, read the note again. "This is definitely Peter's signature," he said, a measure of regret in his voice. He donned his glasses. "Very well. Let me check the ledger."

Doofa went to the far right of his counter, where an enormous book sat open. He scanned down the last page. "Name, please."

"Minion. Steve Minion."

"Ah, yes. It just came in. Last one I processed, in fact." He looked up at me. "Sorry. You missed it. All the souls for people whose last names begin with the letter M have just left for long-term storage."

"But I really need it!" I looked at my suit. It had turned white again and glowed a tad. "As soon as possible, please."

"Well," he said, slowly. "This is most irregular. I cannot remember the last time we had to return some bad soul matter."

"But it can be done, right?"

"Yes, yes of course. Dorla!" he cried.

I sighed in relief. The light from my suit faded in a show of moral support.

Another dweebil came from the back of the room, somewhere beyond the storage shelves. This one was a she, though, at least so I thought, since there were some strategically placed bumps beneath her Wonder Woman T-shirt. She also had generous hips, at least for a four footer, on which draped a utility belt of which Batman himself would have been proud. Her outfit was otherwise similar to Doofa's, including the glasses and jeans. Dorla looked quite a bit younger than the archdweebil. Certainly she was cuter, with a button nose instead of the saber schnozz Doofa sported, and thinner; the suspenders she wore were more fashion statement than necessity.

"Hey," she said to me, giving me the hand gesture.

"Hey," I replied. This seemed to be some sort of ritualized greeting among the dweebils. "Oh," I said to Doofa, realizing I'd forgotten. "Saint Peter says 'hey.'"

"Tell him 'hey' for me." Hand gesture again.

"Will do."

The archdweebil turned to his assistant. "Dorla, Mr. Steve Minion here just missed the departure of the M train. He wants his soul matter returned, and I've authorized it. Please take him in the handcart to retrieve it."

Dorla blushed furiously. I guess she was a shy sort, like Doofa. "Yes, Uncle," she said, brushing the locks of her long azure mane to one side.

He nodded then turned to me. "Fear not, Mr. Minion. Dorla is very capable. She will help you find the right stuff."

"You mean the wrong stuff, right? I mean, after all, it's the evil in my soul we're talking about."

"As you wish, sir. Just follow Dorla." With that, Doofa grabbed a jar containing a preserved tongue – from some large and undoubtedly repulsive reptile — and transported the container to the back of the stacks.

On the wall behind the pickle barrel was a door. Dorla opened it and led me through. I ducked to clear the doorframe, since this was a dweebil-sized portal, but I still managed to crack my head against the lintel.

I hope you understand that I'm not talking about a legume here, but the top of a door jamb. That's homonyms for you. They can really confuse things.

We were outside. Sort of. Actually it was more like an enormous cavern; it seemed to go on forever. Bisecting the cavern was a narrow-gauge train track. I could not see its end, no surprise there, since the light wasn't very good. Off the main line was a side track with a handcart. Dorla threw a switch next to the railings and pushed the little cart onto the main track.

Weird thing about the hand cart. Well, not the cart itself. It looked much like the one used in 'Blazing Saddles,' if a might smaller, but sitting on one handrail was a large and rather tubby bird. He looked like a picture of a dodo that I'd once seen in an encyclopedia.

Dorla took off her glasses and placed them in a pocket of her utility belt. Then she opened another pocket and drew out some goggles.

"Prescription?" I asked.

"Yes, of course. Would you like some?" She opened another pocket on her belt and pulled out more goggles. "I have another pair."

"Are they prescription also?"

"Well, yes they are, Mr. Minion."

I smiled. "That's okay. I'll manage without. And call me Steve."

Dorla shrugged and slipped the extra pair back in its compartment. "Okay, Steve."

I walked around the hand cart. "So, how do you want to do this? You want to face forwards or backwards as we pump?"

Dorla blushed furiously.

"That's not what I meant," I said hurriedly, feeling my own face redden. "I mean, do you want me to work the handle on the bird's side so you can work the back handle and see where we're going?"

"N...no. If you want to help, you can help me in the rear. I, uh ..." Dorla's arms had gone rigid at her sides, and she was trembling all over.

I kept quiet. Sometimes it's best to just shut up and let awkward moments attenuate on their own. This strategy worked, and in a minute the young dweebil was able to speak again.

"Dodoo ..." she began.

"What?"

"The bird."

"Oh. Did you say dodo or doodoo?" I wasn't sure I'd heard her right.

"I said Dodoo. That's the bird's name. Ahem." Dorla pulled out a handkerchief not dissimilar to her uncle's and wiped her forehead. "The front is his job."

"I don't understand."

"You will." Dorla gestured for me to climb aboard then followed me. She took hold of the right side of the rear handle, gesturing for me to grab the left. Then she pushed down hard, my hands naturally falling synchronously with hers.

"Bwak!" With a squawk, Dodoo shot into the air, where he flapped his wings furiously. He wasn't much of a flyer, though. With a gasp, he fell back on the handle, shoving it decisively downward. Then Dorla shoved our side down again, once again propelling the benighted bird into the air. "Bwak! Gasp!"

Soon I got the idea; we launched our fine-feathered friend again and again, picking up speed quickly and with relatively little effort. I did feel sorry for the bird, though.

We rattled along for about a mile. At that point, the track split into three, one continuing in the same direction we'd been traveling, another angling upward, and a third turning downward. By the side of the track were three levers. Dorla snagged the last one, which operated a switch, placing us on the downward track. Soon we were blasting down at a ninety degree angle, something impossible on Earth but evidently quite manageable in the land of the dweebils.

"You're in luck," Dorla shouted. "Soul matter is stored all over the Interstices..."

"The what?"

"The Interstices. That's what we call our home. As I was saying, soul matter is stored all over because we use it to patch holes in Heaven, Hell and the barrier separating them from Chaos. Useful stuff. Very tough. Fortunately, the M's are stored above the cavern of the Styx, where we use it on the obsidian dome over the river. We should be there in just a few minutes."

I guessed, based on the increasing amounts of chatter from Dorla, that she was getting used to me.

While riding the rails, we passed cavern after cavern of dweebils going about their days. Each cave was lined with the same richly-hued wood of Doofa's shop. Whenever some dweebils spied me, they shouted out "hey" or sometimes "heeeyy," invariably accompanied with the hand gesture. I "heyed" back as companionably as I could.

"Bwak! Gasp!"

It was kind of hard to talk while propelling Dodoo again and again into the air, but I was curious about the dweebils. "Is Doofa really your uncle?" I couldn't imagine family relations down here. An uncle implied a sister or a brother, which in turn implied a mother or a father for Dorla. That implied sex, and even though Dorla was adorable, I just didn't think she or any other dweebil could manage the act without dying of embarrassment.

"He is the uncle of all dweebils," she said, taking her hand away from the handle and brushing her hair to one side.

"Hmm. Pretty big family your uncle has."

She looked at me with confusion. "Oh. No, not uncle. *Uncle,*" she said. The second time she said it, she made the now-familiar hand gesture. "In our tongue…"

"Which would be?"

"Dweebish," she said.

Sigh. "Of course it is."

"As I was saying, in our tongue 'uncle,'" hair swipe "means 'oh great and powerful archdweebil to whom we gladly swear our fealty.'"

"Uncle means *all* that?"

"Well it does when you accompany it with a hair swipe."

A lightbulb went on. Hand gestures were part of the language. "So 'hey' – Vulcan hand thingie – means..."

"'Leave me the fuck alone' or merely 'go away,' depending on the forcefulness of the gesture. Nice accent, by the way."

"Uh, thanks."

After that exchange, I stopped yelling 'hey' back to the dweebils we encountered. Perhaps these creatures were not as socially awkward as Peter thought. Maybe they were just misunderstood.

In another minute, Dorla signaled for me to quit pumping. We rolled to a stop, a grateful Dodoo gasping for breath as he clutched at his side of the hand pump. Dorla swapped out the goggles for her glasses then hopped off the cart. "We're here." I climbed down after her.

We were outside another cavern that connected to the large one through which the train tracks ran. Above the opening was a sign with a single letter: "M." A warm glow emanated from the cavern, and as we stepped inside, I again saw wooden walls and furniture, though this time the wood had the patina of aged teak.

Apparently, Dweebilville or DweebilWorld or whatever the heck they called it was all enclosed spaces, with lots of wooden compartments, like a curio cabinet stuffed inside a hope chest, or a Chinese puzzle box. Or something. Orson, who suffers from claustrophobia, would have hated it, but I found it cozy. I could see why the dweebils liked it here.

The room was long and narrow, with a high ceiling. It seemed to go on and on. Somewhere inside here was the rest of my soul. Not that that seemed like a very big deal to me at the moment.

Yes, the land of these funny creatures was quaint, but my heart and my mind were turning more and more toward Heaven. If this place was nice, how much more wonderful would Paradise be? I wondered.

Why am I working so hard to get evil back into my soul?

"Mr. Minion..."

I didn't respond.

"Um, Steve?"

"Yes?" I answered lazily, not really paying much attention. My eyes glazed over as I contemplated my ascent into Heaven.

"You're glowing!"

Chapter 19

"Huh?" I looked down at my suit. It was pure white again, and a faint light, which seemed to be slowly increasing in intensity, radiated from the fabric. I felt positively incandescent ... or radioactive.

Peter's Essence of Evil injection was wearing off. I shook my head, trying to clear it. *Why am I here again?* The answer came to me slowly. *To get back the rest of my soul. And why is that important?* This was a harder question, but somehow I knew that getting back my bad was the right thing to do. For one, Peter told me to, which counted for something. It wasn't yet my time to ascend, or so he said. And somehow, by getting my evil returned to me, I would be thwarting Satan.

Well, if I defeat evil by retrieving my own, then so be it. Slowly, I came back to myself. I was clear in my purpose once more, but the glow of my suit was still waxing. I could lose my motivation again very quickly.

"Steve?" Dorla sounded worried.

"I ... I'm okay. But let's hurry and find my stuff, okay?"

"Right." Dorla extracted some clip-on sunglasses from a pouch and attached them to her frames. Then she went to the counter and rang the bell. "Service!" she shouted with authority.

Three dweebils came out from the back. "Hey!" – hand sign – they all shouted.

"None of that, now," Dorla said firmly. "I need to find Mr. Minion's soul stuff ASAP!" After ASAP, she scratched her nose with her left pinkie.

"Psssst," I whispered. "What does ASAP – nose scratch – mean?"

189

"As soon as possible," she whispered back.

"Oh. What was the nose scratch for?"

"My nose itched. Now, would you quit distracting me please? I'm trying to help you."

"Sorry," I said contritely.

"Did you say Minion?" one of the attendants asked, squinting as his eyes tried to adjust to the bright light coming from my suit.

"Yes, Lennerd. It came in on the train a few minutes ago."

"We've already put those souls into storage. Wait a moment, though." Lennerd stepped over to consult his record book. He looked up at Dorla, avoiding eye contact with me and my suit. "I was remembering correctly. We've just had a small breach in the roof of Charon's cavern. Willard left to fix it."

"And …?" Dorla said, foot tapping impatiently.

"And he took Mr. Minion's soul for spackle." He looked at Dorla and shrugged. "It was one less soul to file. Seemed like the easy thing to do."

Dorla's eyes burned with a furious intensity. "Quickly, now! Where? Exactly where did he go?"

"Section C-5."

"Come on, Steve!" Dorla said, grabbing my arm. I think she surprised herself, because she let go as quickly as she grabbed me. Certainly she surprised the other dweebils if their expressions of wide-eyed disbelief were an indication. "We have to stop Willard before he uses your soul. Once it hits the cavern wall, it will be beyond reclamation"

"Wait!" Lennerd said, then went over to a nearby shelf and grabbed a small wooden chest. He handed it to Dorla, who clutched it to her torso. "Give this to Willard to use instead. He still has to patch the hole, you know."

"Right. Let's go, Steve. Hey!" Dorla said to the dweebils behind the counter. She gave them a vigorous Spock Special. Then Dorla and I hot-footed it out the door.

"This way!" she said, turning to the left just a few feet before we reached the tracks.

As we trotted along, a question came to me. "You said 'hey' to them when you left? I thought it was just a form of greeting."

Dorla shrugged, which was pretty good I thought, since she was running at the same time. "Hello. Goodbye. Sort of like 'aloha' ... or 'shalom.'"

"Right."

Dorla led me to a small door off the tunnel. Inside was a spiral staircase. We hurried down it.

Fortunately, section C-5 was not far away. Twenty yards ahead of us, we saw a dweebil, kneeling on the ground, putty knife in hand. Beside him was a box which was the twin to the one Dorla was carrying, though his was open. The blade of his putty knife was already in motion, ready to scoop up the contents of the box.

"No, Willard! No!" Dorla screamed.

I put on a burst of speed and lunged for the box, pushing it out of his hands. "Ow!" I yelled, as the putty knife dug into my arm.

And then I fell down the hole.

"Help!" I yelled, clinging one-handed to the edge of the hole. I looked down. Over three hundred feet below was the River Styx.

"Hang on, Steve!" A silken line fell through the hole. As if by magic, it wrapped itself around my torso. "You can let go now. We have you."

I released my grip on the ledge, and fell about five feet more before the rope pulled taut. There I was, suspended above the Styx, my arms and legs splayed out. Essence of Evil chose that moment to run out completely, and my suit flashed like a small nova. The obsidian walls and ceiling of the cave caught the light of my clothing, and for the first time since Satan last torched the Styx, the cavern was filled with a bright light.

"Arooo!" Below me, Cerberus and Charon were gliding across the surface of the Styx in the gondola. Ronnie threw back his hood and stared at me in wide-eyed amazement, well, wide-eye-socketed amazement anyway.

I heard the sound of a ratchet, and click by click I started to ascend. In a minute, my hands could clutch the edge of the hole. I pulled myself through.

"Ow!" Willard said, shielding his eyes. Even Dorla's sunglasses weren't much good at handling the light of a small star.

It's amazing what a bit of adrenaline will do for a body, even a post-mortem, ectoplasmic one like mine. My little misadventure, dangling by rope above the cavern of the Styx, had scared the bejeesus out of me. I guess my fear of heights, which I thought I'd gotten rid of in recent months, was still with me, a tiger waiting to pounce at the right moment. Good thing, that. A little shot of the old fear juice had cleared my mind momentarily. I knew what I needed to do. "Where's the chest?"

"There!" Dorla pointed at a dark object half a dozen feet away.

I dove for it. The lid had fallen shut in all the confusion, but I popped it open again. Inside was, well, a mass of black, like pulverized coal or heavy soot. It was mine, I knew. I felt a powerful draw, as if it and I were two magnets, pulling toward each other. The motes of black stirred in the chest and began to swirl. Faster and faster they spun, forming a vortex of evil, I suppose. Then they shot into my face. "ACHOO!"

Vertigo overwhelmed me. I dropped the chest and fell to my knees, panting heavily.

"Hey," Willard said. "Nice suit."

I looked down. My custom-tailored Saint Peter special had returned to its original gray.

Dorla removed her sunglasses, folded up her portable crank, rolled up her rope, and slipped all into her utility belt. "Are you okay, Steve?"

I stood, shook my arms, ran in place a little. "So it would seem. Guess I'm back to normal, thanks to you two." I picked up the now-empty chest. "Do you recycle these?"

Dorla grinned, accepting it. "We'll find a use for it."

While we had been engaged in our banter, Willard had grown quiet. He looked at me in a not-particularly friendly manner. Mostly, though, he stared at Dorla, with a moony-eyed expression that was familiar to me. For sixty years I'd often seen it, in my own mirror, when I was shaving or brushing my teeth and pining over Florence.

Oh, ho! I think Dorla has an admirer.

Dorla was now holding two chests, one in each hand. She offered the full one to the other dweebil. "Here, Willard. Use this soul to patch the crack."

For a moment he didn't hear her. He was still too busy staring.

"Willard?" she said more forcefully.

"What? Oh, sorry," he replied, taking the full chest from her. With an effort, Willard forced himself to stop ogling Dorla. He looked down hurriedly and read the label on the lid. "Douglas MacArthur."

"Ooo," I enthused.

"Who's he?" Willard asked.

I shrugged. "Doesn't really matter. He's a good choice, though. Should make for a really tough patch."

Dorla brushed her hands briskly. "Well, our job here is done. Let's go, Steve."

As we wound our way up the spiral staircase, I marveled at the change I'd seen in Dorla since we'd first met. She may have been shy around strangers, but this was one tough dweebil, and once she'd gotten used to me, we had developed an easy camaraderie.

"Dorla, it none of my business, but, I'm curious. Are you and Willard, well, an item?"

We had just reached the handcart, and Dorla was securing the empty chest in the back. "What do you mean?"

I reddened. *Serves me right for being nosy.* "Ah, you know, romantically involved with each other?"

It was Dorla's turn to blush, and she did it nicely; a sapphire circle appeared on each cheek. She pursed her lips, assuming a severe expression. "No." She sighed then added softly, "I wish."

We climbed back aboard the handcart. Dorla lifted Dodoo from his perch and dropped him on the opposite side of the hand pump. Then we took his place and began bwak-gasping our way back to Doofa's office.

The question about Willard had silenced my new friend. Dorla worked the hand pump silently, but she looked troubled.

"You okay?"

Dorla blew an errant lock of hair off her forehead. "Yes," she said at last. "It's just that, well, I've had a thing for Willard for centuries, but he doesn't even know I'm alive. Why are you chuckling?"

"Well, first off, you're not alive. You're dead, just like me. Second, though, I'm sure Willard notices you, because he was staring in admiration at your chest the whole time the three of us were talking."

"The empty one?"

"The other one."

"Douglas MacArthur's?"

"The other one."

"But, what...oh!!" I think her blush entered the ultraviolet end of the spectrum.

Dorla pumped furiously for a moment. It was all I could do to keep up with her. "If that were true, why has he never said anything?"

"Maybe, gasp, because he's shy."

"He's a dweebil. Of course he's shy! We're all shy. Broot!" which I took to be some sort of Dweebish obscenity. "If our sun hadn't gone supernova, we would have died out as a species anyway!"

"Why's that?"

"None of us can get a date."

"Oh." Pump, pump. I looked over at her. "You don't seem so shy to me, Dorla. Here we are talking about a personal matter – sorry about that, by the way, like I said, none of my business. Anyway, we're talking about some pretty deep stuff, but you seem completely comfortable doing it, and ... and could we just slow down a little?"

"What? Oh sorry." We left warp speed and dropped to impulse power. "For some reason, I don't feel shy around you. You're, well, you're easy to talk to."

"Thanks. You too, by the way. Anyway, I'm sure Willard has the hots for you."

"The hots?" She looked at me, puzzled.

"Human expression. It means he is attracted to you."

"Oh. Well. That's great. Good to know." She bit her lip. "Now, if I could just figure out a way to let him know I feel the same way about him."

We had arrived at Dweebil-Central. As one, Dorla and I stopped pumping. With a final bwak and a single gasp, Dodoo fell off his perch, landing with a thud in the wooden bed of the cart. I hopped to the ground.

"Steve?" Dorla was still at her station. She looked almost pleading. "Got any advice? I'd *love* some advice."

I smiled. "Sure. Here it is. You like Willard; he likes you, but he's too shy to say anything. You, on the other hand, seem like a pretty stouthearted dweebil. I'm betting you have the courage to do the unimaginable."

"Which is what?"

"Tell him how you feel."

She stared at me, mouth agape. Then her eyes widened, and she grinned. "Why, I could just tell him! That's … That's brilliant!"

Yeah. Wish I'd thought of it over all those years when I was pining for Flo. It would have saved a whole lot of time.

I helped her get the empty chest out of the handcart, then we went into the office of the archdweebil.

"Sign here, please," Doofa said to me, as I officially took repossession of my evil parts.

I'm talking my soul stuff, here, not those other parts. I usually call those my junk.

"And don't forget to say 'hey' – Spock Sign – to Saint Peter for me," Doofa said. He stuck his hand in my face for emphasis.

I grinned. "Will do, Uncle," I replied, along with a brush to my hair.

He looked at me, surprised. I waved and headed for the stairway.

196

Dorla walked me there. She seemed to have something on her mind, but for a long time she couldn't find her voice. She just kept mumbling "dweeble, dweeble, dweeble" under her breath. I think she was nervous. Finally she spoke. "Thanks for the advice, Steve. It's been really nice meeting you."

"You too," I said with a smile, shaking her hand. She squirmed a little – probably in Dweebish I'd just said something like "you have a piece of spinach in your teeth" – but then she must have figured this was some sort of human custom and gave my hand a firm squeeze. I winced slightly; the girl didn't know her own strength.

"Thanks for all your help," I said, "especially catching me with your rope. That was fast thinking, and even faster action. I would have hated taking a dip in the Styx."

"You're, you're welcome." There was an awkward silence.

She was such a small thing, but she had a big heart. Spunk and brains too. Admiration and, truth be told, a great affection for this odd little person, flowed over me. "How," I began awkwardly, "how does one say 'I have great respect for you,' in your language?"

Another awkward silence, then she spoke again. "Well ... you hug the person."

"Oh? Okay." I bent down and grabbed her in a fierce bear hug, which she returned with equal force.

When I released her, Dorla looked shyly up at me. "We don't really express respect that way. I just like hugs."

I laughed and hugged her again. "Me too." As an added measure, I took the liberty of kissing her cheek. I just hoped by doing so I hadn't said something like "and let me just get rid of that bit of potato salad on your face for you."

Apparently I didn't. I noticed though, when we broke our embrace, that her entire face was quite a nice shade of royal blue. She smiled brightly. "Friends?" she asked, pulling the fur on one of her ears for emphasis.

"Absolutely. Friends." I grabbed my earlobe, like Carol Burnett used to do, hoping I was saying the same thing. "Thanks again, Dorla. Oh, you might want to try one of those hugs on Willard. I think he'd melt in your arms." And then I headed up the stairs.

Peter was pacing near the stairway, but he breathed a sigh of relief when he saw me. "Your suit is back to normal. Are you?"

"Yeah," I said, and helped him close the door. We kicked a few clouds in place, covering the entrance. "Can I borrow your phone?"

"Of course."

Ring. Ring. "Hello, Ronnie. Listen, can we make this for tomorrow? I've gotten sort of side-tracked today."

So I noticed. Cerberus and I saw you hanging from the roof of the cavern. Are you okay?

"I am now. Thanks for asking. Tell you what: let me call you tomorrow, after I've talked with her."

Certainly.

"Okay. Bye for now." Wearily, I nodded to Peter, then took the Escalator home.

Chapter 20

Flo was very interested in my adventures in Dweebildom, but they took a back seat to her outrage over the stunt Satan had pulled. "The arrogance of the man!" she raged as she finished the last sandwich and wrapped it in Saran Wrap. She stuffed it and the rest of the meal in a wicker picnic basket and handed it to me.

I momentarily opened my hidey-hole and placed the basket inside. "Thanks. He's not really a man, you know. Devil, Prince of Lies, Earl of Hell, et cetera. Seems pretty much in character for him."

She looked at me in astonishment. "But aren't you angry?"

"Oh, *yeah*," I said in a quiet voice. "I'm plenty angry. I just haven't figured out how to get back at him yet. For now, I'm just going to go forward with today's good deeds as planned."

"Well." She hesitated, biting her lip. "I'm not sure how I feel about all of this."

I hugged her. "Don't be jealous. You're the only woman in the world for me."

She softened and kissed me. "I know. That's why I wanted to make the lunch."

"You're an angel!"

Flo shook her head. "I'm far from angelic perfection. See?" She showed me the back of her dress. "I still have visible panty line."

I grinned. "That's good, though. You probably wouldn't sleep with me if you were an angel. Now, I've gotta go. Don't hold dinner for me. This is likely to be a long day."

"Mine will be as well." She donned her nurse's cap. "I intend to prevent Uphir from giving Mr. Jagger Botox injections in his lips."

That conjured up an image. "Wouldn't think he'd need them."

"Indeed. He would look like a platypus. Wish me luck!" Then she was out the door.

A few minutes later I made my own departure. Before I headed to Level Two, I swung by the Maintenance trailer to let Orson and Edison know I was okay. They were much relieved.

I'd opted for the Stairway, since Two was only a forty-five minute walk. Heck, I could spend longer than that just waiting for the Elevator.

I emerged next to the Dancing Dildos Lounge. From there it was just a two-block walk to the twenty story corporate headquarters of Lust Unlimited. Through the open doors I stepped, into an atrium surfaced with white marble. In seconds I heard a familiar scuttling. Milhous, carrying his "out of order" sign, raced me to the elevator in the center of the atrium.

"Milhous, relax. It's me."

The old guy skidded to a stop. He gave me a beady-eyed squint, then relaxed. "Oh, Minion." He looked at his sign with regret. "I guess I can't use this against you anymore."

"Nope!" I said breezily. "Saved, you know."

"Yes, I heard." He had a sour look on his face. "And it just seems like the other day you were a demon, making me fall on my ass in this very spot."

I winced. "Sorry about that. Orders, you know. But I'm done with all that tormenting stuff now. It's good deeds only from now on. Here, let me straighten your hat for you." I fixed his bellman's cap so it sat more level on his head, then smoothed out the front of his jacket. "There! Much better."

"Thanks," he said without much conviction. "So, what's it like, being saved?"

I thought for a moment. "Pretty good. Hours are better, that's for sure."

The elevator whisked me up to the CEO's office. As the door opened, I spied a familiar redhead, staring at her computer monitor. But whatever Lilith was doing, she forgot about it when she saw me coming out of the elevator.

"Steve!" she cried, hurrying around her desk and into my arms.

I kissed the darling succubus on the forehead, between her horns. "Hi, sweetie."

Lilith cooed. "Oh, Steve! I'm sooo glad to see you! It's been forever!"

"Lilith, it's only been a few weeks," I said, rolling my eyes.

She shrugged. "Well, it seems like forever. Want to screw?"

Some things never change. Once a succubus, always a succubus.

I smiled and shook my head. "We're not doing that these days. Flo, remember?" It had taken all my powers of persuasion to calm Flo down when I told her my plan. The Mother of Modern Nursing could be jealous, especially of a certain redheaded demon.

"Oh, yeah. I remember now. So, how about a crackhead slammer?" She asked, heading toward the office bar and giving me a full-on view of her killer curves. "I can whip some up in a jiffy for us."

I swallowed hard. Doctor Pepper, peppermint schnapps, cinnamon schnapps. Not my favorite cocktail. "No thanks. We don't have time, that is, if you can get away early today."

"Sure. I have plenty of leave built up."

"How much?" I asked, curious.

She did a little mental math. "About two hundred years, give or take. I'm a bit of a workaholic."

"I'd say."

She looked at me, intrigued. "After work, I was just going to stay home and read, but I'm always up to trying something new. Wait. Is this a seventeen-way?"

"A what?"

"I'm working through the prime numbers. It's a new hobby, which is why I'm only through thirteen sex partners at once."

I blushed. "Well, it's not as exotic as that, but do you remember a certain bony friend of mine?"

"Ronnie! Oh yeah," she said, flushing. "He's really hot!"

Lilith thinks everyone is hot, which is what makes her a good succubus, I suppose. "Well, he's sent me down to ask if you would care to come to his place for an, ahem, intimate meal."

She grinned. She was so adorable when she grinned. "Would I!"

"No, no eye at all, not even a wooden one, just an eye socket."

"Bad joke."

"Sorry. But would you like to go?"

"Sure. When do we leave?"

"As soon as you can get off."

She frowned, looking at her boss's closed door. "I can get off anytime I want to, at will. That's one of the powers of a succubus, you know. However, I can't actually leave work until two. Asmodeus needs me to set up a few appointments."

As if on cue, the door opened, and out stepped the Lord of Lust himself. "Minion!" he hissed.

I believe I've already mentioned that devils are fond of hissing.

202

"In the ectoflesh," I said.

"I heard you'd gotten around Satan's little ploy." He snorted. "Too bad. I'd hoped we'd seen the last of your ugly face."

"Hey!"

"Now boys," Lilith said hurriedly, trying to calm us down. "Play nice."

"Nice? I'm a devil, young lady. I never play nice." I almost laughed. Lilith was thousands of years old, but compared to a devil, she was a mere babe.

Let's make that a major babe.

I put up my hands in mock surrender. "Take the kink out of your shorts, guy. I was just leaving. Think I'll take a walk along Main Street this morning. These days, I have lots of time on my hands, being a saved soul, you know."

Lilith gave me a wink.

"Get out!" Asmodeus snarled.

Remember? Devils do a lot of that too.

I smiled sweetly at Asmodeus. "On my way. TTFN!"

"Fuck off!"

The elevator door opened, and I stepped inside, chuckling.

"Hey, Milhous, can I use your phone?"

The former president came out of his cubbyhole, where he spent most of his time. "I guess." He pointed to the lobby phone near the entrance. First I called Peter to fill him in. Wasn't even sure Hell's switchboard would pass me through, but they did, for a wonder. Then I rung up Ronnie and told him to plan for about five.

I did indeed spend the morning walking Main Street, killing the time until Lilith got off. Not much to see, mostly the same old bordellos, clubs, sex shops and cheesy motels that I'd serviced (as opposed to them servicing me) in my sixty years as

203

Hell's Superintendent of Plant Maintenance. There was, however, a new statue in the city's main square. It depicted the Rape of Proserpina by Pluto. It had been executed by a grand master, Bernini most likely, and it was, ah, a little more graphically violent than was comfortable. That was the point, I suppose.

Shortly after two, Lilith emerged from Corporate. She had taken a moment to slip into a black cocktail dress. "Ready," she said, straightening her hem.

We walked to the Elevator. I figured, with Lilith by my side, Otis wouldn't keep me waiting. He didn't. I slid open the door and we stepped inside.

"Lilith, you gorgeous thing you," he rasped as I pulled down on the door handle.

My friend smiled prettily. "Hello, Otis. How are you?"

I pressed the button for Gates Level, and we were on our way.

"Just fine and ... " DING!

"I've never been up here before," Lilith said, as I worked to open the door of the Elevator. "Are you sure it's okay?"

"Sure. Gasp." I was tugging on the strap used to lift the Elevator door, but the door wouldn't budge. The demon was fighting me. "Otis, what the hell are you doing?"

"I'm not sure I should let you take one of our own to Gates Level," he growled.

"What do you mean?"

"Lilith," he said, grunting. Normally, a human soul would not be able to out-wrestle a demon, but me being saved, well, maybe it gave me a little physical boost. I wasn't sure, but that didn't matter anyway. He wasn't supposed to be resisting me in any fashion, and I told him so. "You know, buckaroo, that I'm saved. You're getting in my way."

"But Lilith!" he protested.

"What about Lilith? Don't you like her?"

"Of course I like Lilith!" he snapped, aggravated. "What's not to like? She's a succubus. But she belongs in Hell."

"Who says? Succubi go to Earth all the time."

"But not by Elevator."

I was getting steamed. "Listen Otis, I don't believe there is any rule that limits where Lilith can or cannot go." I looked over to my friend for confirmation. She just shrugged, which set her spectacular breasts to jiggling. As usual, that distracted me for a sec. When my head cleared, I continued. "And I know for a fact that you can't stop me from going where *I* want to go. So cut it out!"

"Fine!" The door shot up so fast once Otis stopped fighting me that I dangled momentarily from the strap before dropping to the Elevator floor.

Grumble He's just lucky I don't report him. But I've never been a particularly spiteful person, except for when I am, like when I don't care for someone, and ...

Okay. Maybe I *am* a spiteful person. I thought back on the times I'd hassled Edison and Ford, not to mention the little number I'd just played on all devils and demons with my Hell tours. But I'd really been working on that character flaw, and I determined to let Otis's shenanigans slide.

Besides, nobody likes a snitch. *That* is universal.

We stepped out onto Gates Level, and I left the Elevator door open for Otis to close himself. So there.

"Ooo. It's pretty up here!" Lilith walked between two billowing clouds, stroking one gently, and it seemed to me that the cottony wad started purring.

I smiled. *Even clouds like her.* "Lilith, there's someone I want you to meet." I led her over to Saint Peter's podium. He excused himself from the person who was waiting nervously before the Book of Life. "Be right back. What? You're in a hurry? Don't worry, you've got all Eternity. A minute or two won't hurt you."

The guy seemed just keyed up enough that his fate was probably in balance. I thought again about the coin and frowned. Bad enough that someone's salvation hinged upon a random act of chance — as opposed to an un-random one, which actually does exist in places like Vegas and Reno — but it would be far worse if there was something wrong with that quarter.

"Steve," Peter said, digging his elbow into my side. The old guy was smoothing back his white hair, which just showed me that even a saint was not immune to the charms of my favorite succubus. "Aren't you going to introduce us?"

"Of course! That's why we came over. Saint Peter, this is my friend, Lilith."

"Charmed," he said, bending over and kissing her hand.

"Lilith, this is Saint Peter."

My succubus friend flushed prettily. "Mutual, I'm sure."

This exchange puzzled me. Peter was being awfully nice to one of Hell's minions, but then I remembered that, like me, he felt succubi, and perhaps incubi as well, though I don't know the origin story of them, were given a bum rap. After all, succubi may have been the daughters of Adam's first wife and her sisters, but they were also the daughters of an angel, and an important one at that.

"Steve has told me so much about you."

"Oh." Lilith looked down shyly. "I hope some of it was good."

He smiled gently at her. "All of it was, my dear."

"And he," Lilith began, then hesitated. "He's told me a great deal about you, too."

My Sunday, go-to-meeting smile, the one I always used in social situations like this, drooped a little. *Yeah. Like how I used to think he was a supercilious jerk. Or that he was part of the reason I'd been damned for the past sixty years.* I realized that I should have filled her in about my reconciliation with the prickly saint.

But Pete, for all his hyper-inflated ego, being Heaven's Concierge and all, was a pretty sharp cookie. He looked at me knowingly then said, "Well, Steve and I have mended our relationship of late, Lilith. May I call you Lilith?"

He was still holding her hand. I grinned.

"Certainly, my lord."

"Please, it's Peter."

"Or Pete!" I chimed in, earning a dirty look from the guy in the flowing white robe.

Lilith smiled uncertainly. I don't think she'd ever been flirted with by a saint before. "Peter then."

"You know, I'm a good friend of your dad."

She brightened at this. "You are?"

"Yes, in fact, I ..." He looked over at me quickly. "Well, Steve and I have arranged a little surprise for you." With that, Peter put his fingers to his lips and whistled so loudly it scattered a dozen clouds. "Incoming!"

From behind the Pearly Gates a rocket seemed to launch. It hung in the air, far above us, then spun once and descended to a spot ten feet away. The clouds parted deferentially to reveal a celestial being.

The Lord has his way in the whirlwind and the storm, and the clouds are the dust at his feet.

207

Nahum. It's one of the more obscure chapters of the Old Testament. Obscure but with some great imagery. Though, of course, this wasn't the Lord Himself but one of his servants.

"Daddy!" Lilith ran to her father. Samael embraced her with his arms, and his wings engulfed her as if they were two feathery blankets, hiding Lilith momentarily from our view. When he opened them, she stood before us, clad in a simple white robe. Lilith was demure, but beautiful.

Not sexy, though. Hope Ronnie won't be disappointed.

Peter seemed to read my thoughts. "Lilith didn't exactly fit the dress code in that hot number she was wearing. Good thinking on Samael's part to bring something more appropriate for her to wear."

The archangel Samael, bad boy of the good guys, was an imposing figure. Tall, dark and handsome, as the saying goes, with black, curly hair and a full mustache. He looked a bit like Tom Selleck in his Magnum PI days, or would have if he hadn't towered over us by a foot. In Lilith's case, two feet.

She's on the short side. Five foot two, eyes of blue. Horns of pink. Uh, I think.

Samael, noticing the disparity in heights, shrunk down to a less imposing six four. He held his wings at a rakish angle.

Man. Asmodeus has nothing on this guy. No wonder Samael knocked up so many of the ladies. Then I realized I was being disrespectful. I mean, after all, this was an angel. And not just any angel but one of the handful of those that had earned the rank of "Arch," which must have been way higher in status than wall angel or floor angel or any of the other possibilities. The list is endless, no doubt.

"Steve, you darling!" Lilith rushed over and planted a big wet one on me. "You did all this just for me?"

"Hey!" Peter protested. "I helped!"

Lilith grinned and went over to Peter. She stood on her tiptoes and kissed the saint's cheek. He reddened, but her smooch put a big smile on his face.

My hot friend went over to her dad. Apparently, Samael didn't think much of all this kissing. He gave us a warning look and put his arm protectively around Lilith. "This is my daughter, so watch it!"

"Oh, come on," I said, slipping into my reflexive mode of disrespect. "After all, she's a succubus. She gets laid for a living."

The clouds swishing around Samael grew dark, matching the thunderstorm that was growing on his face.

"Show some respect, Minion," Peter whispered. "Like he said, she's his daughter. Besides, you don't really want to antagonize Samael. He has a wicked temper."

"Oh, good to know. Sorry, Sammy."

Pete flinched at the familiarity, as did the archangel, but Lilith quickly intervened. "Daddy, it's okay. Steve is my favorite person in the whole universe." Without taking her eyes off her dad, she gestured for me to come closer, which I did with a little hesitation, like you would if approaching a very large and aggressive dog. She smiled her most ingratiating smile at her father. "Except you of course. I want you two to be friends."

"Well," Samael said slowly. Man. He was just like the stereotypical protective father. "He *did* arrange all this. Very well." Samael extended his hand, which was large and strong. I noticed that he had nice nails.

I shook with him, gasping softly. I felt as if my hand was in a vise; my knuckles were turning white. "Sorry," he said, letting go when he noticed my discomfort. "Don't know my own strength."

"That's okay," I said, rubbing my hand to get the circulation going again.

Lilith was patting her chin with an index finger, frowning slightly. "So, all of that about Charon: that was just an excuse to get me up here?"

"No, not at all. Ronnie is still expecting you, but not for two or three hours, which should give you some time to visit with your dad." I opened my hideyhole and pulled out a basket. "Flo made you two a picnic lunch."

"That was very kind of her," Lilith said, primly, taking the basket. "Thank her for me."

My former paramour had been gracious about me choosing Florence over her, but Lilith's ego was probably a little bruised. Succubi weren't in the habit of losing out to other women.

Still, I should get the two of them together sometime. I think Lilith would like Flo if just given a chance to know her. And vice versa. Not sure how I'd manage it, though. Satan and Asmodeus probably wouldn't want Lilith to do much fraternizing with the enemy. She might get in trouble.

With that thought, I got nervous. I hoped my attempt at doing a good deed or two, with Lilith as the recipient, would not cause her trouble with Hell's bosses.

Samael extracted the picnic basket from Lilith's hands. "Thank Florence for me too, will you, Steve? She's one of my favorite humans."

I guess they'd met in Heaven when Florence had gone there for a conference or something. For years, Flo had visited Heaven periodically. She never told me what it was like up there, though. It was some kind of rule. People who have not experienced Heaven can't be told about it second-hand. I guess it's like a great story that falls flat in the telling. You just have had to be there to appreciate it.

210

Samael kissed Lilith's forehead. "Why don't we have our picnic by the Well of [Damned] Souls? It's a pretty spot. Here, let me give you a lift." The archangel picked up his daughter and flew off. Lilith was in Heaven.

Well, actually, she was in the heavenly DMZ, which is about as close as she'd ever get, I suppose, but you know what I mean.

Chapter 21

"If you don't mind, I'll hang with you a little while then escort Lilith down to the Styx after she's finished her visit with D.O.D."

Peter raised his eyebrows, an impressive feat, since the furry things looked to weigh about three pounds each. "D.O.D?"

"Dear old dad."

"Oh." Peter looked over at his podium. The fellow he'd left waiting was shaking like a leaf. "Well, I'd better get over there and put him out of his misery."

"Yeah. Looks like there's a coin toss in his future."

"No doubt. Excuse me."

As expected, the guy required a consultation with the quarter. Also, as expected, he was consigned to Hell.

Whatever I think about the quarter, that guy was bound for downstairs. He had a really shifty look about him.

"Oh, Steve," Peter called out to me, after he'd dispensed with the man. "A letter came for you."

"A letter?" *Who would be sending me a letter, care of Saint Peter?*

"From Doofa, apparently. At least, this is his stationery." He handed me a pale blue envelope.

With my Swiss Army knife, I slit open the top and pulled out a folded sheet of paper. "Not Doofa," I said, reading. "Dorla."

"Dorla? Who's that?"

"Doofa's assistant."

Dear Steve,

I've asked Lord Doofa to send this note to Saint Peter, since I don't have your address, and I figured he'd be able to get it to you.

It was nice meeting you yesterday. I haven't had much contact with humans, though I have observed them from afar while doing various maintenance projects around the perimeter of Hell. If you are typical of the species, I think I'd like your kind very much. I suspect, though, that you are something special.

Anyway, I just wanted to say 'hey,' so hey. Oh, when we don't accompany that word with a hand gesture, it means pretty much the same thing it does in English.

Your friend,

Dorla

P.S.: I also wanted you to know I took your advice, and ... it worked!

Funny, all those years of wishing that Willard and I could get together. But wishing for it, no matter how hard, never seemed to work. Yet the direct approach did! Willard and I are going to dinner and a movie tonight. We're going to see 'Hot Tub Time Machine.' It's one of my favorites! Thanks again for your help.

I smiled. It was good to know that I was able to help her out. I started humming.

"What's that melody?" Peter asked. "Seems familiar, but I can't place it."

"What? Oh, it's a Beatles tune. 'A Little Help from My Friends.' I've had it on my mind a lot recently. Now, maybe you can help me out. Have you ever heard of a movie called 'Hot Tub Time Machine?'"

Peter rolled his eyes. "Yes, it came out after you died. Three losers go back in time, change their personal histories. They find love, romance and a happy ending. The movie is pretty stupid, but," he chuckled, "kind of funny too."

I smiled again. *Second chances. Love and romance. Go, Dorla, go.*

Lilith and Samael were likely to be gone quite a while. There wasn't much for me to do in the meantime, so I pulled up a cloud and sat down.

Peter was a real pro. When he needed to, he could handle the incoming at remarkable speed, which was good since, based on the mortality rate and the total earthly populations of Christians, Muslims and Jews, I estimated he had to process over eighty thousand souls a day. Did I say remarkable speed? Light speed might have been more accurate. But he did it. Yes, no, maybe so. Out came the coin. A quick flip in the air, and a human's fate was sealed. Check, initial; check, initial; smiley face, initial; frowny face, initial. Over and over again. Soon, he was almost a blur. Maybe he had entered a pocket dimension, where spacetime could be warped, allowing him to move so fast and process all the souls he needed to. Or perhaps it was just an attendant miracle of his sainthood. Funny that I'd never noticed this before, but until now I'd not so closely watched him work.

I thought about my own brief tenure in the role. How I had managed to keep up with the workflow was also a sort of miracle.

Still, in the brief moment of judgment, an eternity had to pass for each soul in question, and so, while Peter may have been fast, I was sure he never short-changed anyone. He was, indeed, the consummate professional.

Yet, I was bothered. First, a depressingly few went to Heaven outright; I estimated one in ten. Eight more went, without question, down the giant Escalator into the waiting arms of Satan.

Not literally. The Earl of Hell is very busy; besides, he couldn't be bothered with such a humdrum activity unless it was for a really important soul, like a former president or a rock star. Besides, Satan is first and foremost a manager and really good at delegation. He lets his staff handle most of the incoming souls.

So nine out of ten had their fates sealed before they hit the desk. That left one out of ten unsettled, and for those times, Pete fished out his coin.

I frowned. It was this last ten percent that continued to trouble me; it just shouldn't have been left to chance. More concerning: after carefully watching Peter work, I was finally and completely convinced that, when the coin flew, more often than not the soul lost the toss. Two times out of three, I estimated, they lost, and that just didn't make sense to me.

I was missing something but couldn't figure out what. I remembered, when subbing for Peter, my practice flips of the coin and the roughly even split between heads and tails. Yet, when it counted, that coin damned far more souls than it saved.

I reached to a pocket and pulled out Dorla's note. There was something in it that she said. Something about Willard. Slipping the sheet from the envelope, I scanned the page.

"But wishing for it, no matter how hard, never seemed to work."

Of course! That's the missing piece of the puzzle!

I jumped off the cloud and hurried toward Peter. My timing was good. There was a lull in the traffic before his desk. My friend seemed bored; he was leaning, slumped against the podium (his desk being a bit of a combination: both desk and lectern), idly flipping his quarter. He was very good at tossing a coin – of course, that would figure, considering all the practice he got – and he could snatch it out of the air without even looking. At my approach, his eyes came into focus, but he continued to flip the quarter. "What?"

"Don't mean to disturb you," – not that it seemed like he was doing anything important – "but when, ah …" – I had to say this as diplomatically as possible – "when was the last time you had your books, I mean your Book, audited?"

Peter's eyes widened. He stopped with the coin flipping, slipping the quarter into his pocket. "Why, the Book of Life has never been audited. It's the Book of Life! Infallible!" He looked at me suspiciously. "Why would I even need to do that?"

I cleared my throat. This was awkward. "Well, to make sure that you yourself haven't inadvertently interjected some mistakes into the Book."

"Harrumph!" Peter shot me a dirty look. "I don't make mistakes. I'm a saint, you know."

"Yes, yes," I said impatiently. "I know all that, and I'm sure you've never made a mistake in your life."

"Actually," Pete said, looking embarrassed, "I did deny my Lord. That was pretty, how do you say it? Oh yes, it was pretty boneheaded of me."

"Oh, sorry. I didn't mean to bring up an embarrassing memory. I was thinking about since your death, since you became a saint. I have every confidence that you've never made a mistake in meting out justice with the Book of Life."

The saint arched one of those massive eyebrows. "Given that fact, I ask again, why would I need to have the Book audited?"

"Well," I said, looking meaningfully at a certain spot on his robe – no, higher than that – "it's that quarter of yours."

Peter pulled the coin back out of his pocket. "You started to say something about it the other day. What about my quarter?"

"There's something wrong with it."

"Ridiculous," Peter said dismissively, blowing a gust of wind through his whiskers strong enough to make the bristles of his mustache stick straight up, like the slats on some Venetian blinds. "Request denied." Peter turned to one side and started shuffling some papers in his in-box, a clear signal that, as far as he was concerned, this conversation was over.

Hmm. I guess I'm going to have to convince him. "Listen, Pete."

"Peter," he grumbled, looking up at me. "Or Saint Peter. Please stop calling me Pete. It's undignified."

"Fine, fine." This was not the time to deal with my friend's ego. "But if I can prove to you that the coin is in some way bogus, will you order the audit?"

"Well, first off, there's no way you can prove it."

"But if I can?"

Peter frowned. "Even if you could, doing an audit would be very difficult. The book has billions upon billions of names in it, you know. And I can't just let someone take it off to a back room. I'm consulting the Book of Life constantly."

"I realize it would be inconvenient. Perhaps there's someone who could audit it at the same time you use it – you know, during slow periods."

He sighed. "I suppose that would be possible. Deucedly awkward, but possible. I can think of one person who could do the job." Pete said this last bit with a grimace then shook his head. "You still have to convince me that it's necessary, though."

"Okay!" I said enthusiastically. "But first, I need something to write on. And with."

Peter pulled out a drawer in his desk, extracting a Big Chief tablet and a crayon. I think it was Cerulean Blue, but I can't be sure. "Will these do?"

"Yeah," I said, grabbing my cloud and pulling it closer to Peter. Then I sat back down.

"So, how do you propose we do this?"

"Flip the quarter, and I'll call it in the air. Oh, this doesn't count, okay?" I said hurriedly. "I mean, I'm still saved, right?"

"Of course. This is a coin toss without consequence."

Whew. "Okay. After each flip, I'll record the result."

"And how long do you propose we do this? I haven't got all day, you know. The Queen Mary (Mother of God) is due in port pretty soon, and then I won't have time for a game of coin toss."

"Well, you're awfully fast with that quarter."

"I've had a lot of practice."

"No doubt about that. I know, to save time, that you usually catch the quarter, but let's let it hit the ground so there are no extra variables in this. Except for the second or two it takes the coin to land, this should go pretty quickly. But not too quickly, okay? I've seen how fast you can work and don't want to miss anything."

Peter exhaled heavily. "Fine, fine."

"Ready?"

Another deep sigh. "I guess."

"Go."

"Call it in the air." And then Peter flipped his quarter.

"Heads," I called, writing this down on a page of the Big Chief.

Peter scooped his coin off the cloud floor. "Nope. Tails."

I put an X next to the word "heads" on my sheet.

Peter flipped the thing again.

"Heads," I said again.

"Yes," he replied picking it up once more. "Wait. Aren't you going to write anything down?"

"I wrote what I called down, but I'll only record a wrong guess." I shrugged. "It's less work."

"For you maybe. I'm the one flipping out and bending over."

"Flipping out," I mumbled. "Funny. Kind of. Go ahead."

Flip.

"Heads."

"No." X mark.

"Heads."

"No." X mark.

"Heads."

"Yes, and are you going to call anything but heads?"

"Huh?" I looked up at the saint. "Oh, no, I'm not," I said, and drew a vertical line down beneath the word heads, signifying that I would keep going with the same call.

"Then this will go a whole lot faster if I just call out my results, don't you think?"

"Uh, yeah. Good idea. Please continue."

"Gee. Thanks."

Flip. Flip. Flip. Flip. Flip. Flip.

"Tails. Tails. Heads. Tails. Heads. Tails."

Peter was very fast with the coin. He was ready to scoop it off the ground as soon as it landed, he never fumbled on the pickup, and he called the previous result as he started a new toss. He did a hundred throws in under four minutes. "Okay," I said. "That should be enough."

"Good. It was getting to my back. So," he said with mild curiosity. "What's the tally, and what's it mean?"

"Give me a sec," I said, poring over my sheet. "I'm still counting. O...okay. Got it."

I looked up at my friend. "First off, a coin toss is pretty binary, right?"

"Yes, just like being damned ... or being pregnant. You either are or you aren't."

"Do you know anything about probability theory?" I asked.

Peter gave me a withering look. "I grew up in the first century, AD. I was a fisherman. What do *you* think?"

"Ah, right. Well, statistically, half the time the coin should come up heads, and the other half it should come up tails."

Heaven's Concierge snorted. "And that's probability? Seems pretty obvious to me."

"Yeah. Some people say the odds are really fifty-one to forty-nine, because there are a variety of factors at play, like which side the coin started on at the beginning of the toss, whether it's caught or let fall to the ground, the fact that the heads side is slightly heavier than the tails side, the wear and tear on the coin you're using, etc., but all of those are in the noise range. An expert coin tosser can influence the outcome of the toss, but ..."

"But I'm a saint and wouldn't do that."

"Right. So fifty-fifty is a close-enough summary of the odds. Now with a small sample, this might not be the case. There could be a statistical blip, but the larger the sample, the closer the results should be to fifty-fifty."

"And where are we? Seems like I flipped a few more tails than heads."

"You got that right." I hopped off my cloud and showed him the results. "Actually, more than a few."

Peter stared at the pages of the Big Chief, and his eyes widened. "Seventy-three tails out of one hundred tosses?"

"Yes, that seems pretty high to me too. Of course, like I said earlier, that could be a result of the small sample size. You can refine the results by continuing to flip the coin, assuming I keep choosing heads, but I'd like to try something else … if you have the time, that is."

Peter stared into the distance. "I see the Queen Mary coming now, but we can probably do about a hundred more tosses."

"Okay," I said, sitting back on my cloud. "Toss it."

Up went the coin.

"Tails."

"No. Heads."

"Tails."

"Tails."

"Tails."

"Tails."

Etcetera. Peter got the idea and kept flipping. Once again, we did a hundred of them. By the last flip, he was holding his two thousand year old aching back. "Well?" he groaned.

"Seventy were heads this time."

"Well, that means we are at about fifty-fifty between the two sets of tosses, right?"

"No," I said slowly, sure that I was right. "I don't think that's what this demonstrates."

"Then what?" Peter asked. A large crowd of incoming had just stepped off the boat and was heading our way.

I nodded, remembering Dorla's words. "I think what this shows is that the coin toss is biased against the wishes of the person making the call."

"Meaning? Oh! Damnation!"

"Right."

Peter was shaking. "I'll, I'll order the audit."

Chapter 22

As the crowd from the ship approached, Peter put his coin in his pocket, handling the undecided souls with a simple question ("I'm thinking of either a zero or a one. Which is it?") He had thought to use the old tried and true rock-paper-scissors method, but I pointed out to him that he would be better at that game, having played it about a bazillion times more than any of the incoming.

Pete's question to each of the Undecided wasn't particularly creative, but zero and one is, in fact, just as binary as damnation, and I'd defy anyone to try to monkey around with a saint's brain. For now, he had a good workaround.

Soon he finished processing the crowd. "Peter, when did you get your coin anyway?"

The saint frowned, trying to remember. "Let's see. Oh, yes. It was in 1840. A fellow came up here who was on the brink. I started to sort him with rock-paper-scissors. By the way, I always chose my option in sequence, rock one time, paper the next, scissors, then repeat, so I think it was pretty fair. Anyway, he suggested a coin toss instead, even offering me a coin from his pocket."

"Wait a minute. He had a coin on him?"

"Oh, don't be so surprised. People come up here with all sorts of things: chewing gum, tic tacs, a used Kleenex, lipstick, a condom, and yes, the occasional coin."

"Did he win or lose the toss?"

"Lost, if memory serves." Which of course it always did. Saint, you know. "Told me to keep the change."

I took a look at the coin carefully, just to make certain I hadn't missed it when I'd made my impression, but I hadn't. I thought about things for a sec then nodded, confident in the conclusions I had drawn. It was time to tell Peter what I believe happened. "Sounds like you got played."

"What do you mean?"

"I think the coin got planted on that fellow by Satan or one of his underlings."

"Is this the conspiracy theory Satan was talking about yesterday, after he pushed you up against the Gates of Heaven?"

In the wake of all the confusion the previous day, I'd forgotten about that. "Yeah. Satan knows, or suspects, that I've figured this out."

"Why would he know?"

"Ah," I said, running my index finger along the inside of my shirt collar. It suddenly seemed tight around my neck. "I may have given him a clue on that score when I talked with him after the hearing."

"Well, *that* was stupid."

I shrugged. "I was mad at him, but I can't argue with you. It was dumb, and I almost paid for it with eternal salvation."

Peter gave me a wry look.

"Skip it. Anyway, you've been determining people's fates with a rigged quarter for over two hundred years." I remembered the detail Edison had brought to my attention. "Take a look at both sides of the coin."

He shrugged but did as I asked. "Looks like a quarter to me."

"To me too," I agreed, "except it lacks a certain phrase I'm used to seeing on U.S. coins."

"Which is?"

"In God We Trust."

"Oh no!" Peter put his head in his hands. "How many people have gone to Hell because of that quarter?"

I patted my friend on the shoulder. "Sorry. It's not your fault. And perhaps things are not too bad. Let's get the audit done and find out."

For once, Saint Peter was speechless. But he nodded.

A wind picked up, and Samael came flying back from the Well of [Damned] Souls, Lilith in his arms.

"How was your picnic?" I asked.

"Wonderful!" Samael replied. "It was nice of Flo to remember that I like peanut butter and jelly sandwiches."

"What did you have, Lilith?" Peter asked. He was trying to be a good host, but there was the tiniest hint of despair in his voice. Samael doubtless heard it, judging from the questioning look he gave me, but his daughter, who did not really know the saint, missed it.

"The deviled ham."

I stroked my chin. "That would figure."

"But only a little. I didn't want to spoil my appetite before dinner."

Samael looked at his wristwatch, which was a nice Rolex job. I bet it kept perfect time, much better than my Casio. "Oh! Look how late it is! Pumpkin," he said giving her a kiss on the forehead, "this has been wonderful, but I have to get back to work."

Lilith wiped a tear from her eye. She really did love her father. "That's okay, Daddy. It's been great seeing you. I've missed you *so* much."

"You too," he said with a smile. "Give my love to the family."

"I will."

"And, ah, don't tell the others, but you've always been my favorite."

"Hah!" Lilith yelled triumphantly, pumping her fist. "I knew it!"

"Maybe we can make this happen again sometime soon?" Samael looked at me hopefully.

I smiled. "I'll do my best." *For Lilith.*

"Thank you son. And now, I really must fly." The archangel shot to the sky and streaked back behind Heaven's Gate. Lilith waved her goodbyes.

"Are you ready for your date with Charon?" I asked

The succubus took off her white robe and handed it to Peter. Have to say that, while she looked like an angel, well, one with horns, in the smock, I liked her better all decked out in a black cocktail dress.

She turned, saw my appreciative glance and grinned. "I used to be Snow White, but I drifted."

I chuckled. "Good one. Stealing from Mae West now?"

"Where do you think *she* got it?"

"Ah. Well, let's go. Oh, Peter, I'll swing back by after I drop off Lilith."

The old saint was staring thoughtfully at his quarter. He nodded.

Lilith had never walked the path to Charon's boathouse before. Just like most of the tourists from Heaven, she was impressed with the statues of the Seven Deadly Sins. I just shook my head.

"Thank you again for arranging things with my dad," she said, giving my arm a squeeze and submerging it in the valley between her breasts.

"Uh," I said, trying not to have my reflexive reaction to this way-too-sexy female, "you're welcome. What are friends for?"

She smiled archly. "We're a little more than friends, you know."

I nodded, a soft sigh popping from my lips. "Yes. We'll always be more than friends, given our history together. But we are certainly friends too, right?"

Cupping my head in her hands, she kissed my cheek tenderly. "Always."

We reached the banks of the Styx. Ronnie's gondola was tied up along the shore; a gentle radiance flowed from the windows of the boathouse.

I opened the door and gasped. The boathouse was set up with a wooden floor that covered the Stygian waters beneath. Atop the planks were thick rugs, actually more like shag carpeting, though it wasn't nailed down. In the corner of the room, a fire burned gently. Lava lamps had been set in sconces upon the wall. I thought it an odd design choice, but at least the light they emitted was muted, green but soothing. Pretty romantic, I reflected.

A large, well-used couch was set before the fire. I wondered how Charon had been able to put that much wear on a piece of furniture. After all, he spent almost every second on the river, except when he was throwing Cerberus his Frisbee.

That's when I noticed there was no bed in the boathouse. *Oh.*

Speaking of Cerberus, I wondered where he was. Usually, by now, I'd be on the floor, my hair full of dog drool.

"Arooo!" came a mournful cry from the doghouse. Ronnie had probably tied up his pet to keep him out of the way.

Charon was leaning over the dining table he'd set up in the room's center, lighting some candles. Gone was his normal charcoal cloak. He was sporting a gray smoking jacket, David Niven style, and an ascot. I rolled my eyes.

No pants though. Just a whole lot of femur going on.

Lilith. Steve. He added my name as an afterthought. Can't say I blamed him. *So good to see you, though Steve, I didn't make enough for three, I'm afraid.*

"Not staying," I said with a smile. I didn't want to horn in on his action. "I just escorted her here, since she's never been before. Oh, Lilith, when you're ready to go home, I'm sure Ronnie will give you one of his epic gondola rides across the Styx. Then you can take the Escalator down to Two. Okay?"

"That's fine," Lilith said with a smile. "Big girl here. Used to taking care of myself. Ronnie, you have a lovely place."

Why thank you my dear, he said, leaning over and kissing her extended hand. *I hope you're hungry. I thought we'd start with oysters and a bottle of Veuve Cliquot.*

"What's the main course?" She asked. "It smells fantastic."

Bull nuts.

"What?" I said in shock.

"Ooo," Lilith enthused. "They're one of my favorites."

Time for a hasty departure. "You two have fun," I said, though a small part of me hoped not too much fun.

It was silly. I loved Flo. I didn't want anything but a platonic relationship with Lilith, but I'd always have a soft spot for her. And feel a little jealously, I supposed. Still, if I were to have her seeing anyone, I couldn't think of a better person than Ronnie.

I hoped they hit it off. They had the makings for a nice couple.

"Oh, Ronnie," I said as an afterthought. "Remember back when the ancient Greeks put coins on the eyes of the dead, like what that Brit was talking about on my tour the other day?"

Yes, of course. That was my payment for ferrying them across the Styx.

"Got any of them left?"

Coins, eyes or dead bodies?

"Coins."

Why certainly. Excuse me for a moment, my dear, he said, leaving Lilith at the table and walking over to an ancient footlocker that was sitting in the corner of the room. It reminded me of a pirate's chest. Charon popped a couple of latches and opened it. The thing was full of coins.

"Wow! Pretty keen treasure trove you have there."

Well, they gathered for a long time. Would you like to have a souvenir? He buried his phalanxes deep into the hoard, pulling out a coin at random. *How about this one?* He deftly flipped it in the air, and I caught it.

I held a silver coin in my hand. It was a little cruder in construction than its descendants but still pretty nice. I noticed that it hadn't tarnished, an effect no doubt of being here in the afterlife rather than, oh, I don't know, buried with a bunch of Greek urn shards at some archeological dig in Ephesus or sitting on an ocean bottom in the hold of a storm-savaged trireme. On one side was the head of a bearded man that looked like it was being gobbled up by another head, that of a lion. "Hercules, right?"

Actually, Herakles. That's a Greek drachma.

I flipped it over. On the other side was a bearded dude sitting on a throne, staff in hand. *Zeus,* Ronnie offered, trying to be helpful.

"Thought it might be," I said, examining it more closely. "What's it worth?"

Well, by the time the Greeks abandoned the drachma, when they adopted the Euro, you couldn't even buy a gumball out of a machine with one. You'd need about twenty for that. Back when this coin was minted, though, a drachma represented a day's pay for a skilled laborer.

"Interesting. What year was it made do you think?"

About three hundred BC, during the reign of King Phillip III of Macedonia. Fun fact: he was the older half-brother of Alexander the Great.

I flipped the thing, snatched it out of the air and placed it on the back of my left hand. I shrugged. It felt like a regular old coin to me. "Is there anything wrong with it?"

What do you mean?

"I don't really know." I frowned, then quickly told him the story of Peter's coin. I kept my voice down so Lilith, who was waiting patiently for our conversation to end, couldn't hear me. Ronnie was immune from Satan's mental eavesdropping, but Lilith wasn't. Better to be safe than sorry. Fortunately, she had gotten interested in one of the lava lamp sconces and was paying no attention to us.

Let me have the coin. Charon looked carefully at the drachma then bit it. *No, there's nothing wrong. It's a good coin. I'd stake my life on it,* he finished, handing it back to me.

"Bold words, coming from a skeleton," I opined. "Still, I trust your judgment more than just about anyone."

I appreciate that. Besides, it was made hundreds of years before Satan hired me, while I was still working for Hades, and the Greek god of the Underworld didn't like cheats and charlatans. The coin's good.

"Okay. Thanks." I put the drachma in my right trousers pocket. "I'll let you get back to Lilith now. Bye, sweetie!" I waved at my succubus friend, who looked up from her examination of the sconce. She blew me a kiss from across the room. Charon led her back to the table.

Bull nuts are quite the delicacy, Ronnie explained to Lilith as he popped the champagne and pored her a glass. *They are considered by many to have aphrodisiac qual...*

I stepped out of the boathouse, closing the door behind me.

Chapter 23

As I hurried up the path back toward Gates Level, I worried about Peter. He'd taken the revelation about the coin pretty hard.

The saint wasn't at his desk when I reached the Realm of Clouds. His little "on break" sign was hanging from the nail hammered into the front of his desk for that purpose. A few souls awaiting judgment were milling around, at loose ends, and more than a little nervous.

Pete didn't take many breaks, especially if people were waiting on him, but I found him not far away, sitting on the steps leading to the Pearly Gates, arms propped on his knees, chin propped up with his hands. His brow was a knot of worry.

I stayed a few paces away from the steps, since I didn't want the Heavenly Chute opening and sucking all the bad out of me again. "Peter," I said softly.

"Huh?" he said, looking up. "What? Oh, Steve. That's right. You said you be back." Then he sighed deeply and continued staring into space.

"Are you okay?"

"No," he intoned softly. He pulled the quarter out of his pocket. "Not at all. How many people have I wrongly condemned to damnation with this execrable coin?"

"We don't know what the damage is yet. Besides, it wasn't your fault. Oh, you have some customers waiting," I said, gesturing at his desk.

"Oh." Peter hopped off the steps and went to deal with them. It was an unusual batch. None of them required a coin toss. "Thank goodness. I'm going to have to find something better than, 'I'm thinking of a number between zero and one.'

231

But I can't go back to using this thing," he said, looking in disgust at his quarter.

"How about this?" I asked, pulling out the coin Ronnie had given me and handing it to Peter.

"A drachma? Heavens, I haven't seen one of these in two millennia. Well, not one that had any value. The Twentieth Century drachma was a bit of a joke."

"So Charon told me. That's where I got the coin, by the way, and Ronnie swears it's legit."

Peter was holding the drachma in his right hand and the quarter in his left. "If Charon says it's okay, that's good enough for me." Without looking, Peter tossed the bad penny, or rather, bad quarter. It made a perfect arc in the air, falling dead-center into the Mouth of Hell.

"Good riddance to bad rubbish," Peter mumbled. Then he flipped the drachma a few times in the air. "Has a nice feel." He pocketed the coin.

"Well, at least going forward you won't have to worry about a fixed coin. Though, just to be extra safe, have some of your numismatist friends in Heaven check it out for you."

"I will, but I'm sure Charon's judgment is dead on, as usual."

I glanced at the Book of Life and frowned. "What about the past two hundred years, though?"

"Indeed," Peter agreed, exhaling heavily. "We'll start the audit right away. In fact, here comes the auditor now."

The Gates of Heaven opened, and out stepped an old man. He was shirtless, with a slight pot belly, and a red cloak wrapped like a towel around his waist, as if he'd just stepped out of the shower. He wore a hat — it looked a little like a gaucho's or something José Greco would wear when he did the flamingo, ah flamenco. Well, not exactly. The brim was too big — more platter size than dinner plate size — and it was red, not black, with scarlet cords that ran from each side of the brim, tied together almost at waist level. I suppose if a strong gust of wind hit him, that hat might have flown off but been caught by his neck, so that was sort of like a gaucho, or at least his American analog, the cowboy.

In one hand was a book – I had a feeling this fellow never went anywhere without a book – and in the other was a leather valise.

"Hello, Junior," Peter said.

The man snorted. "Junior, junior, why are you always calling me that? I've been around for seventeen hundred years, you know."

"Which means you're still junior to me."

"Har, har. How droll," the stranger said, as he put down his valise.

Peter tried to suppress a smile. "Steve, meet Eusebius Sophronius Hieronymus, known in most quarters as Saint Jerome."

"A pleasure," I said as we shook hands.

Patron saint of librarians, translators and other bookish sorts, Jerome had a beard that was even more spectacular than Peter's. Not better. Crazier. It was iron grey and stuck out in all directions. He looked like someone had glued a frightened cat to his chin.

"I don't know how this is going to work," Peter muttered. "I'm consulting the book constantly."

"Don't worry, Peter," Jerome said, opening his valise and putting his book inside. I noticed idly that it was an Agatha Christie mystery, not what I'd expect a saint to be reading, but whatever. Then he began digging through his case, looking for something. "I'll slip in and check a few pages during the downtimes, doing my best to stay out of your way."

"It will be hard for you to get anything done that way."

"No problem. I work fast. And I'm a speed reader, you know. From what date should I begin my examination?"

Peter thought for a second. "All Hallow's Eve, 1840."

"Halloween? How appropriate." Jerome still rummaged around in his bag, finally pulling out a pair of readers, a pile of legal pads, some pencils, a couple of black garters and a green visor. He slipped the garters over his arms, a pointless activity in my view, since he wasn't wearing a shirt with sleeves to keep out of his way. He took off his hat and hung it off the side of Pete's desk.

Jerome was as bald as an ostrich egg. The visor he donned in place of the red hat looked funny on his hairless pate. The light from Heaven's Gate shone through the plastic, creating a green crescent moon on his brow.

Jerome put on his readers then reached toward the Book, which Peter was clinging to a bit possessively. "May I? I can't do this without looking at the pages, you know."

"What? Oh, sorry." Peter had wrapped his arms around the Book of Life, almost in a sort of embrace, but with an effort of will he placed the book on the desk and stepped away. "Go ahead. I expect a number of incoming souls soon, so see what you can get done before they get here."

Jerome smiled indulgently, then opened the book to the first page and began his examination. The pages flew beneath his left hand, while his right made notes on one of his legal pads. In seconds, every page on the pad was full. He grabbed another and started filling it too.

Boy. He really *could* work fast.

"I'm going to need more legal pads, I think," he mumbled.

Peter frowned. That didn't sound good.

There was a rumble in the distance, and a train appeared out of a tunnel in the clouds. Pete frowned a second time. "I'll get some from the supply cabinet in a minute, after I deal with the Orient Express."

The Orient Express – not the original, but its celestial counterpart – transported Christians from Armenia, the Philippines, India, in short from any Asian country with a substantial Christian population. (Isolated Christians in other Asian countries had to take cabs. Some of them took Über or Lift, where those services were available.)

Jerome stepped to one side while Peter took over the book. For a while he was in the thick of it, but as we've already established, he could work fast also, and in no time he dispatched at least three hundred souls. I was pleased to see that the Drachma was working well for him.

Then Jerome stepped back up to the plate, and Peter went to get him some more legal pads.

And so it went, back and forth between the two saints, for several hours. There wasn't much I could do. I made trips to the supply closet periodically to replenish Jerome's supply of legal pads, occasionally grabbing a box of pencils. Funny that I'd never noticed the cabinet before, but it had been artfully disguised by some excellent renditions of clouds that had been painted, so Peter told me, by J.M.W. Turner.

The rest of the time, I sat on a real cloud and watched. Jerome was plowing through the book at an astonishing rate. Tens of billions of lives were represented in its pages, but soon he was nearly halfway through. I really wanted to learn what he would find, so I determined to wait until he was done and at least hear his initial assessment.

After a few hours, Jerome closed the book on the Book.

"Well?" Peter asked.

"Well?" I echoed.

"Gentlemen, please," Jerome said, doing a quick total of the page he was working on. "Let me collate my results." He went over to what had become a mountain of legal pads and started totaling up each one. As he worked, he frowned in concentration, but he was very quick. Seems he was as good at math as words. And his clerical accuracy skills appeared to be astonishing, which would make sense, since he was the patron saint of librarians. I bet he was a good typist too.

After another twenty minutes, he wedged the last legal pad between an arm and his torso. He took off his readers and pinched the bridge of his nose. He probably was going to have a wicked headache from all that figuring.

"Hmm," he said at last. "It could be worse, I suppose."

"WELL?" Peter and I both shouted.

"Okay, okay! Keep your shirts on."

"Why? You haven't?" I quipped.

"Very funny, young man. It just so happens I have a skin condition. But never mind."

"First off, let's put this in context. Over a hundred billion humans have ever lived, most of them in the past couple of hundred years."

I stroked my chin in thought. "I've not paid much attention to the history of human population growth, though I've glanced at charts on the topic. From what little I've seen, the rise is so rapid, it looks almost exponential."

"Looks like it, I agree, but it isn't. Nor is it geometric. Humans and societies are a little too complicated and irrational to pigeonhole so neatly. The increase has been impressive though. In 1840, the world's population was about a billion, and here, in 2055, it's about ten billion."

"Of course," chimed in Peter, "only a portion of them are Christians, Jews or Muslims, or should be, if they had stayed true to their faiths."

Jerome nodded. "A little over half. Another factor to consider is the infant mortality rate: it's about four point two percent." He frowned. "They go to Limbo, so I suppose I'll have to figure out how to factor that in."

Peter's chin dropped to his chest. "This math is way beyond me."

Jerome glanced around, as if looking for a solution, then smiled. He patted Peter's shoulder companionably. "Not to worry. This becomes much easier if we start with that." Jerome pointed at one of the signs around Hell's Escalator. "Of the thirty billion who have been consigned to Hell, about one and a quarter billion – four point two percent – are infants, and they go to Limbo. So we're dealing with not quite twenty-nine billion, most of which have been damned since the coin, well, came into play. Let's work with twenty-five billion."

"Why?" I asked.

"Makes the math easier."

"Oh." Seemed a little heartless, considering what was at stake, but Jerome was right. Right now, we weren't looking for a precise count. We were just trying to understand the scope of the problem.

Peter stroked his beard. "His number is high, anyway. After all, not all of that twenty five billion went to Hell after 1840."

"That's true."

Our auditor continued thinking aloud. "From my analysis, eight point seven out of every ten people have been damned since then. Eight of them outright and the point seven sent there by a coin toss."

"I guess I never noticed," Peter said with a frown. "I mean, of course I know more people go to Hell than Heaven, but I'd never done the math. Guess I was too busy processing souls to count them."

"Probably," agreed Jerome. "Hard to count when you're in the thick of things. Can't see the forest for the trees, as they say. Now, of the twenty-five billion, the fates of about one ninth, or two and three quarter billion people, were consigned to Hell because of the coin toss."

"Gaah!" gaahed Saint Peter. "That's more than I ever imagined."

"Well, wait a bit, wait. Peter, you said seventy percent or so lost the coin toss, which squares nicely with my point seven number, please note. Now, according to Steve, it should be more like fifty percent, so twenty percent went there who shouldn't have. Let me do some figuring." Jerome leaned over his pad with his pencil and ran some numbers, the tip of his tongue held tightly between his teeth in concentration. Finally he looked up, a big smile on his face. "Good news! I SWAG it this way. At the very most, only about eight hundred million went to Hell who shouldn't have."

"And how in the name of all that's holy is that good news?" Peter yelled.

Jerome shrugged. "Well, when you consider the total number of people who have gone to Hell, it's practically a rounding error."

Peter lunged at Jerome, and I had to step between them to keep a little saint-on-saint violence from erupting. "A rounding error? Are you out of your mind? A single soul damned to Hell that shouldn't have been would have been too many. Eight hundred million is an atrocity!"

Peter sagged against his desk, held his head in his hands. "And even worse. We don't know which of the three billion..."

"Two point seven five," Jerome said helpfully.

I sighed. "We don't know which of them got a bad call." I looked at Peter, who just stared at me mournfully.

Finally my friend began to do what he always did when he was truly worried; he began to pace. "What can we do? What can we do?"

"Relax, Peter," Jerome said. "I don't think you'll lose your job or anything like that."

"Do you think I *care* about that? All that's important are those unjustly damned souls. What can we do about it? What can *I* do?" He looked toward Heaven. "I need to talk to my boss." He grabbed his phone and made a call. "Thanks, Andrew," he said and hung up.

Jerome stuffed his gear back in his bag then put his red hat back on his head. "My job here is done. Nice meeting you, Steve."

"You too, Jer, er, Jerome."

I really need to stop doing that.

Jerome patted Peter on the back again. "It will work out somehow, you'll see."

Peter looked up distractedly and nodded, though he looked as if he'd just been kicked. Then with a wave, Saint Jerome left us.

In a few minutes, Andrew showed up to take his brother's place. Then my old friend – well, new friend but still an old dude – took a deep breath, straightened his spine, and headed firmly up the steps toward the Pearly Gates.

Andrew shook his head. "Goodness. I haven't seen him so upset since THEN."

"When?"

"THEN."

"Ah." Peter's role leading up to the Crucifixion, no doubt. "Can I check a couple of things in the Book?"

"Help yourself."

I looked up two names. As I suspected, there had originally been a question mark next to each.

"Andrew, what do you think Heaven will do about this situation?"

He shook his head. "I honestly don't know."

"Well, I can't really imagine the Big Guy not knowing about this. Omniscient, right?"

He smiled, looking a lot more optimistic than his brother had. "Yes indeed. There's always something inscrutable going on with the Divine Plan, but things inevitably work out."

"I suppose so, but meanwhile, can I ask your opinion about something?"

"You mean 'may I,' of course."

"Geez! I get this from Orson all the time, but since he was like that in life, I expect it from him. But I also get corrected by Satan and Peter. So tell me, are all you eschatological big shots grammar Nazis?"

"Pretty much. Your question?"

"I have an idea. Something that may help in a small way." I explained myself.

Saint Andrew stroked his beard. "Interesting, interesting."

"Do you think Peter would mind?"

Andrew shook his head. "No. I'm sure he'd appreciate any help he could get."

"Okay. Thanks!" With a nod to Andrew, I headed toward the Escalator.

I think I've finally found my calling.

Chapter 24

"Oh, Steve. How horrible!"

Flo and I were talking while having a late evening of cocktails in our living room. After what Peter, Jerome and I had figured out topside, a stiff belt was required.

Seems like there were only two places in the universe where I could have a private conversation: Gates Level and our Fortress of Solitude, which is to say, the living room of our apartment. It would have been nice, at least occasionally, to take a walk and talk about things, maybe chat while jogging (ugh, maybe not), go get coffee, but with a devil or demon on every street corner, private tête-à-têtes in public were pretty much impossible. I didn't realize how big a deal this was going to be. When I was damned, privacy didn't really matter. Satan could monitor my thoughts whenever he wanted to, though back then, I didn't really have many thoughts worth keeping private. Not so now, and while he could no longer read my mind, he could read the minds of the Damned who I talked to in Hell.

Like he did no doubt with Edison when we were discussing Peter's quarter.

I slammed back half my martini. I'd need a refill soon. Fortunately, anticipating this, I'd made a pitcher.

"You said it. Can you imagine? There may be nearly a billion people in Hell who don't deserve to be here."

Flo ran her finger around the edge of her martini glass. She was deep in thought. "What will the Powers do, I wonder?"

"Don't know. Poor Pete is taking it pretty hard."

"Peter," she said absently. Flo knew my penchant for shortening people's names. She also knew that Pete didn't like it when I did it to him. Come to think of it, few people liked it, unless it happened to them when they were kids, like when their names were shortened from Richard to Rick or Rich or Dick (the last one a little unfortunate, I always thought) or William to Bill or Will or Billy or Willy (again this last one unfortunate).

I don't know why I do that. I just do.

"Saint Peter has been the steward of the Book of Life for two millennia. He would of course be devastated by something like this. Anyone would." She looked at me. "Surely the Almighty knew about the coin."

I nodded. "That's what Andrew thinks too. An all-seeing, all-knowing God is unlikely to be blindsided by such a shoddy scheme."

Flo arched an eyebrow. "Say that three times fast."

"Such a shoddy scheme, such a shoddy scheme, such a shoddy scheme. Oh," I said, grimacing. "Sorry. Sometimes I take the whole alliteration thing a little too far. But anyway, He had to have known about it."

"Yes," Flo agreed. "But why did He allow it to happen?"

"Andrew believes it's all part of the Divine Plan."

"And what do you think?"

"I think I need another drink." I grabbed the pitcher and refilled my glass then freshened Flo's martini. I could feel the effect of the gin, one of the nicer if unexpected benefits of being a saved soul. I would have thought that nobody drinks in Heaven, but Flo assures me that they do. It seems saved souls enjoy a slight buzz as much as the next fellow. They just don't get drunk. No hangovers either.

After topping off our glasses, I glanced at Florence. She was giving me the hairy eyeball, buttressing it with a frown. "What?" I asked.

"Could you answer my question? What do you think about this being part of the Divine Plan?"

"That's two questions," I responded idly, making Flo's frown deepen. "Sorry, sorry. It probably is part of the Plan, and things will most likely all work out in the end, but meanwhile, I intend to try to help things along in my own, small way."

The frown disappeared, and she smiled at me. "That's my boy. What do you have in mind?"

"Well!" I said with enthusiasm. "You know how I've been searching for something meaningful to do in Hell?"

"You mean beyond easing suffering?"

"Yes. I'm glad to give someone a break ..."

"Respite."

"Yes, respite. Better word. I'm glad to give someone a brief respite from eternal damnation, but as I've said before, it's just a stalling tactic. Eternity is Eternity, and everyone down here is going to get it in the end." Not to mention the face, the midsection, the genitals, etc. No point pointing that out to Flo, however. She and her Victorian sensibilities would just get offended.

"Not to mention the face, the midsection, the genitals, etc."

My head popped up like a prairie dog poking out of his hole. Flo grinned at me. "I spend a lot of time with you these days. Honestly, I believe I'm beginning to follow how you think."

I grinned back. "You have no idea, Miss Mindreader."

She sobered. "You know that I too get frustrated at times by the minimal impact of my ministrations in the hospital. So, out with it man! What do you intend to do, as you put it, 'to help things along?'"

I leaned towards her, almost spilling my martini on the carpet. Even though we were in our own private oasis in Hell, and I was pretty confident no one was listening in, the last thing I wanted was some devil or demon hearing what I had to say next. Heck, if I could have dropped a Cone of Silence on the room, I would have, but of course that only worked for Maxwell Smart.

Come to think of it, it didn't work all that well for him either.

"Do you remember how you helped me get my do-over?"

"Of course! And in the process you became the first person in history to have been damned and then saved."

"Well, I intend to do the same thing for others. Give them a chance to get a fresh coin toss."

Flo frowned. "With that execrable coin?"

"No, no. Pete…"

"Peter."

"Right. Peter ditched that thing as soon as he found out it was rigged. I got a drachma from Charon, who swears it's on the up and up. Both Peter and I believe him, so ties are now being determined by a neutral coin pressed three hundred years before Christianity began."

"Granted that you have an impartial coin, and no doubt a willing saint in Peter, who would give anyone who might have been improperly consigned to Hell a second coin toss, but …" Florence frowned. "I see two problems with your plan. First, how do you know who should be given this second chance?"

"That's easy. We just look in the Book of Life. I already did that and have a handful of potential clients."

"Oh? Who?"

"Tell you in a sec. What's the second problem, or rather, challenge?"

"What's the difference?"

I chuckled. "Oh, just a little management mumbo-jumbo. You're not supposed to discourage employees who offer up good ideas, so Management 101 says to call all problems challenges instead."

"Seems like a juvenile thing to do."

"I agree. You'd be amazed though by how many motivational speakers make money off the idea. Management consultants too."

"Never mind," Flo said, sipping on her drink. "The second problem, or challenge if you prefer, is, to put it in the vernacular, 'how in all Hell are you going to get your client up to Gates Level without being stopped by Satan and his minions?' No offense, Mr. Minion."

"None taken." I pursed my lips. "That second challenge is a bit harder than the first."

"Well," she said, standing up, "it will be easier with me helping you."

"You want to help?"

Flo started pacing. Her face was flushed, but she looked very excited by the prospect. "Certainly! I cannot think of a better use of my time."

"So, it's partners then?"

"My love," she said, coming over and hugging me, "we've already established that. Partners. For Eternity."

"You know, I really like the sound of that." I hugged her back.

We talked late into the night, while preparing an evening snack, during the meal, as we washed dishes afterward. Getting someone out of Hell would be a formidable task. While Flo and I could pretty much go anywhere we pleased between Heaven, Hell and the Pearly Gates, most of the Underworld's denizens were limited in where they could travel. Generally, the Damned weren't really supposed to leave the Circles to which they had been consigned.

Oh, if their damnation required it, they had some limited mobility. For example, Orson and Edison, while stationed on Level Five, had to travel routinely between the Pearly Gates all the way to the bottommost circles of the Underworld. The work orders for Hell's two Mr. Fixits could require changing a lightbulb on GL, unclogging a toilet on Three, fixing an old Atari system owned by some nerdy devil on Five, even unsticking a drawer on Bruce's desk down on Nine.

Or, another example: those whose Deadly Sin was Greed. All of them, no matter which circle they inhabited, had to travel to the Fourth periodically to pay their respects to Mammon, Patron Devil of Avarice. Paying respects in this case also included paying him with the currency dearest to the hearts of the greedy. For Dora, my avaricious former coworker who ran the Parts Department, that currency was cigarettes, like Lucky Strikes and Camels. For others, it might be Starbucks Frappucinos or painted military figurines or whatever. "Render unto Caesar that which is Caesar's." In this case, Mammon was Caesar.

But if Dora had tried to go to any Circle other than Five or Four, she would have been stopped either by a devil or demon or an entire squadron of both. This is Hell, after all. Unsurprisingly, the Damned are kept on a pretty short leash.

Shit, I mean, shoot, it had even been a little tricky for me to get Lilith up to the Gates, and she wasn't even human.

Not that there's anything wrong with that.

And that brought us to the other main challenge. Besides the watchfulness of Hell's horde of devils and demons, there were only a few ways to get to Heaven. If you had the chops, like Satan or Beezy or one of a handful of Hell's Elite, you could teleport there. Once upon a time, I was capable of doing that, but that was back in my demon days, and when I lost my horns and tail, I lost that power as well.

BOOH could fly me and a damned soul to Saint Peter's desk in a jiffy. Unfortunately, at least publicly, I was *persona non grata* to my batty friend. Besides, I'd never want to get him in trouble with Satan.

The Escalator was no help; it only went down. I still thought it possible to run up the thing – I did that in shopping malls when I was a kid – but going up the down moving staircase for thirty feet was a might different from doing it for a mile or five. Just the prospect of it was pretty tiring.

Charon would probably be willing to break precedent and row me from the Hell side to the Heaven side, but you couldn't even *get* to the Hell side of Level 0.5 without Charon rowing you there in the first place, so that would be stupid and pointless.

You could jump down through the Throat of Hell, but not up, not unless you had something like a rocket-powered pogo stick.

That left the Elevator or the Stairs. But the Elevator was not really a possibility. Otis would never transport one of the Damned without Satan's permission. Even I could see that my protected status as a saved soul would not extend to a damned human who happen to be sharing the lift's car with me.

Shit. That left the stairs.

Flo concurred. "The Stairway to Paradise is the only option. I don't mind walking up five miles, though perhaps I'll trade out my work shoes for some cross trainers, but I think we will have problems getting one of the Damned to Saint Peter without being detected."

I frowned. We were back in the living room, sipping on some espresso. "Perhaps if we sneak up the stairs when no one is looking. After all, we're invisible to Satan."

"Yes, but whatever soul we decide to Save is not."

I scowled. "You're right. Satan will be able to read that person's mind. Humph."

We sat quietly for a moment, frowning. Not that we were mad at each other, but this was a poser. Finally, Flo said softly, "The trick, I think, is to keep our client unaware of what we are doing. Then Satan won't be able to read the person's mind and figure what we are about."

"And how do you propose we do that?"

"I'm not entirely sure. Certainly we would need to confuse them. Maybe ear plugs and a blindfold?"

That sounded lame to me, but ... "Well, that helps me decide who should be our first escapee on Flo and Steve's Underground Railway."

"Who?"

I pursed my lips. "So far, I've checked five names that I wondered about in the Book of Life. As I suspected, all of them were victims of that infernal coin."

"Who were they?"

"Orson, Edison, that nun I told you about meeting the other day. And just this evening, I checked on Louis Braille and Nicky Tesla."

"You're thinking of starting with Louis, aren't you?"

"Yeah, since he won't be able to see what we're doing to him. We'll still need earplugs, though."

"On further reflection, I think we'll need more than that," she said.

"Like what?"

"I think we'll need to kidnap him."

"Why, Miss Nightingale, I am shocked, shocked! How can you even suggest something of the sort?"

"Yes, well, my love," she said, taking another sip of espresso, "I fear that my association with you has had a less than salutary effect. Besides, I see no other way to effect Monsieur Braille's departure from the Nether Realm."

"Uh, why do you say that?"

"Because, as you said, we have to ensure that Satan cannot learn from Louis that he is being sprung from this joint."

"You really have gotten into Thirties gangster movies, haven't you?"

"Oh, *yes!*" she said with enthusiasm. "Cagney, Bogie, George Raft, Edward G. They are all such larger-than-life figures. Their movies are just thrilling! But, to continue, Louis is used to going through Hell blind. And he's a cabbie, so his other senses are likely even more honed than they were in life."

"Sort of like Daredevil."

"Who?"

"Comic books, dear. Another aspect of popular culture that you missed out on, having been born too early, you know." Though, I reflected, she really didn't seem the comic book type. "But you don't think earplugs will be sufficient?"

She shook her head. "If we have him walk up five miles of stairs with us, he will figure out what is going on, and in the process, so will Satan."

"Shit, you're right."

"Lang..."

"Shoot, you're right," I amended. Covering his ears alone wouldn't do much to hide our activities, not if we marched him five miles up the Stairway. There was only one stairwell like it in all of Hell. Louis would figure things out quickly, and Satan or Beezy or a thousand demons would be on our heels in no time at all. "What's more, if Satan, through Louis, is aware it's us, he will put out an APB."

"Yes, so we will have to keep Louis confused about what's happening to him."

I sat for a moment thinking about it then brightened. "I think I know how to kidnap him, but ..."

"But what?"

"But I don't know how we're going to get him up five flights of stairs. I mean, we can't exactly carry him."

"Maybe we can," Flo said. "We just need something from the hospital." Quickly she explained what she had in mind.

"Do those things even work? I just assumed they were for torturing the Damned in the Toaster."

"Honestly, Steve, I've never understood why you liken the place of my employ to a toaster."

"Old habit. Sorry."

"I've never had a problem with them. Let me obtain one tomorrow. We can pick it up from the loading dock when the time comes. So, that's the transport. What about the caper?"

Caper. Jeez. She really needs to spend less time with the Blu-ray player.

I explained my idea for kidnapping Louis. We then spent the rest of the evening planning things out.

"We'll have to do this after work, Steve. If I change my patterns, Uphir at the very least will get suspicious."

"Okay. Do you think we could try this tomorrow?"

"I don't see why not. He who hesitates is lost."

"No, we'd still be saved, but I understand you. So tomorrow it will be." I stood up and stretched. It had been a long day. "Let's go to bed."

Flo was lost in thought. She looked up at me distractedly. "I'm really not sleepy yet."

"Who said anything about sleep?"

She blushed. It was charming that after all this time she was still a little modest. "Oh. That's different."

She took my hand and led me into the bedroom.

Chapter 25

Flo was out early the next morning. I think she wanted to take care of her extra errand before the work day began.

I had my own challenge. How could we dependably find Louis as he drove the streets of the Fifth Level? As a cab driver, he could be dispatched anywhere. Hell was like that. Sort of unpredictable.

Then I remembered: Louis was predictable in one regard. He was a bit anal about the condition of his cab, understandable, since he could get into a bucket of trouble back at Dispatch if he returned with a damaged vehicle. Several times a day, Louis would park across the street from the abandoned steel mill and check over his car by feel alone. I'm not sure what he would have done if he'd found anything seriously amiss – it's not like he had access to a body shop or anything like that – and I'm not sure why his boss, a gruff demon also named Louis – or an American variant thereof: Louie – would even have cared. Hell's fleet of taxis, piloted by an all-blind corps of cabbies, was pretty beat up. Most of the cars were ancient, like those driven by Cubans after the U.S. trade embargo was imposed in the mid-Twentieth Century, except unlike the lovingly tended Chevy's on the streets of Havana, in Hell you tended to have Yugos and Gremlins, as well as Fiats that wouldn't start in hot weather, which we have a lot of down here. All were painted yellow, a sickly yellow, like that of an invalid suffering from jaundice. This last detail was wasted on the cab drivers, but the passengers certainly noticed.

The interiors of Hell's cabs were nothing to write home about either. The upholstery was ripped and stained and pockmarked by cigarette burns too numerous to be accidental.

The carpet on the floorboards smelled as if a demon had upchucked on it.

Probably not, though. Demon barf is caustic. It would have eaten through the carpet and, likely, the metal underbody of the car. No, the smell of bile was probably from the poor riders who didn't have nerves strong enough to handle flying blind along the streets of Hell.

So there wasn't much Louis could do to keep his car in shape. He *did* carry around a little whisk broom – and a mop for use when warranted – and he kept his cab cleaner than most. If there was some bird poop on the fender, he'd wipe that off with his sleeve. Little stuff, but it had probably kept him off the other Louie's shit list a time or two.

Just to confirm that Louis's habits had not changed, I hiked over to the steel factory. As I recalled, my friend usually showed about mid-morning. I was not disappointed. I waited less than an hour before he drove up.

Last time I'd seen Louis, he'd been driving an AMC Pacer. Today he was in a 1957 Ford Edsel. He must have won cabbie of the month or something to get such a nice car. The Edsel was good news. The plan would work better.

Louis put on the emergency brake then got out of the car and started feeling it up. Well, that's what it looked like to me, anyway.

As he stepped around the car, I noticed that the trunk was unlatched. Louis noticed it too; he cursed then opened the lid, digging around in there until he grunted then pulled out a small, multi-colored snake. It probably wasn't a real snake, though it certainly looked like one from a distance. He attached the snake, which was likely a bungee cord, though you can never tell down here, to a loop that had been welded to the top of the trunk, then reached under the bumper with the other end and

253

attached it to something down there, probably one of the metal rings that car manufacturers are so fond of putting under cars, for reasons I've never understood. The bungee cord held the trunk closed.

I nodded. The trunk probably had a broken latch or at least an inconsistently working one. This must have been a chronic problem with this particular cab, judging from the aftermarket loop on the lip of the trunk and what was apparently a large collection of bungee cords in the boot itself. More evidence of Hell's unpredictability. Some things could be broken all the time, but more frustrating was for something to be broken sometimes and working others. Yet this was a hallmark of Satan's realm.

Satisfied that the trunk was secure and that everything else was okay, Louis opened the driver's door to get inside. At that point, the emergency brake disengaged on its own and the car started rolling. Louis had to run along the street for half a block before he could jump in, but he appeared to be an old hand at this particular maneuver, probably due to lots and lots of practice. Once he caught up with the vehicle, he deftly swung himself into the driver's seat then slammed the door, put the Edsel in gear, gunned the engine and took off.

I was pacing the living room floor when Flo came home. "Did you get it?" I asked.

"Yes," she said, slipping off her pumps. "It's waiting for us at the loading dock. Do we need anything else?"

"I don't know. I guess not. But, I feel like something's missing." I patted my pockets then brightened. "I know!"

I went to the living room closet and rummaged through the contents of the top shelf. Flo had a small collection of tools up there: screwdrivers, a hammer, some pliers, even some WD-40. And one other item. "Aha! I thought I saw some in here."

I pulled out a roll of duct tape. Not the Hellish version, of course. I'd had to give that up when I'd stopped handling Hell's maintenance. What I had in my hand was good, old-fashioned Earth-style duct tape, maybe not as indestructible as the Infernal version, but still useful. I slipped my hand through the roll and slid it up my upper left arm until it stayed in place, like a dull gray bangle.

"What's that for?" Flo asked.

I shrugged. "Dunno. I'm just used to having it when I'm working. Feel kind of naked without it in situations like this. Besides, duct tape is the most useful substance in the Cosmos. It could come in handy. Are you ready?"

"Half a second. I just want to change my clothes and put on some sensible shoes."

"Okay."

It took a little longer than half a second, and I had restarted my pacing by the time the bedroom door opened.

"Wow!"

"Do you like?" Flo asked.

She was dressed in a white, tight-fitting body suit and white sneakers. She looked like a superhero in a spandex outfit. There wasn't even a visible panty line, taking her a step closer to angelhood, I suppose, though the absence of one was also a hallmark of female superhero suits. "Wait a minute. Are you wearing a bra?"

She blushed. "Well, no. I tried it, but I could see the bra strap, and it undercut the look I was going for."

"Which is what, other than 'sex goddess dressed in tight, white body suit,' of course?"

She shot me a dirty look. "Didn't you ever see 'To Catch a Thief?'"

"Well sure!"

255

Flo spun around on her Reebok's. "I thought if we were going to skulk around, I'd dress like Cary Grant."

"Er, he was all in black."

She shrugged. "White is really more my color, you know. Do I look all right?"

"Yes. Wonderful. Luscious in fact." I gave her a hug.

Not exactly inconspicuous, though. Not with a body like that. Still, it made little difference how she dressed. Flo was noticed wherever she went.

Flo pulled her hair back into a ponytail, tying it off with a rubber band, then put on a white beret. "Ready?" she asked.

"Ready. Oh, grab one of the steak knives, would you?"

"Why?"

"All I have is my little Swiss Army knife. We might want something more substantial."

We were waiting for Louis when he pulled up to the curb for his second inspection of the day. Luck was with us. There wasn't a soul in sight. That didn't mean there weren't some demons hiding behind a corner – they always looked for opportunities to cause some grief – but we were counting on our luck to hold.

Before Louis got out of the car, Flo, at my direction, used her steak knife to saw through the bungee cord.

The trunk flew open just as Louis opened his driver's door. He heard the noise of the flapping lid immediately. "Merde! Stupide automobile!"

As quietly as we could, Flo and I stepped a few feet back from the car. I held a forefinger to my lips. She nodded.

Louis was puzzled to find the bungee so cleanly cut through, but he probably wrote it off to some demon playing a prank. He started to fish in the trunk again, searching for another cord.

The trunk was very large. After all, this was a Fifties vintage American automobile. They were fucking huge. Sorry. I mean very big. (Sometimes I really miss swearing.) Anyway, you couldn't even put one of these monster cars in a garage without four feet of vehicle sticking out onto the driveway.

Louis was on his tiptoes, trying to reach the back recesses of the trunk. That's when Flo and I slipped up behind him and flipped our friend inside. We slammed the lid closed. It didn't latch of course, and Louis, cursing loudly, tried to push it open. Flo hopped on the back of the car, holding the lid down with her weight.

In triumph, I whipped my duct tape from my arm. "Aha! Told you!"

"Shh!" Flo whispered. "Hurry up, but don't let him hear your voice. He mustn't know who's doing this."

I nodded then, while Flo foiled Louis's increasingly frantic efforts to push open the lid, secured the thing with half a dozen straps of duct tape. Florence hopped off the trunk. "Did I get any dirt on my outfit?"

I didn't see any, but this seemed like a good opportunity to pat her divine ass, so I gave it a good dusting. Then I looked at her and gestured with my head toward the car. "Let's beat it, doll face," I said in my best Bogie voice. Florence gave me the a-okay signal then got in on the passenger side.

I hadn't driven in over sixty years, but it's not really a thing you forget how to do. The Edsel's PeRNooDLe (Park, Reverse, Neutral, Drive, Low) was a little weird. It was set into a disc in the center of the steering wheel. Worked okay though.

Biggest problem we had was dealing with the streets. Traffic was just terrible, even worse than driving in Manhattan on a Wednesday. I was lucky to average ten miles an hour. Every delay, every red light, one-way street, traffic snarl, jaywalker — of which there were many — increased my anxiety, and by the time we got to the hospital, my nerves were shot.

I pulled up to the loading dock. None of the demons who regularly hung out there smoking were around. We had counted on that; this was the time of day when all the demons in the hospital gathered in the Waiting Room to hear Uphir blather on about the next day's work schedule.

Leaving the car idling, I followed Flo to a closet at the back of the loading dock. She opened the door and revealed our other set of wheels: a hospital gurney. There was also a small white paper bag sitting atop it.

"What's that?"

"Gauze," she said. "I forgot the surgical tape though."

"No problem," I said, patting my roll of duct tape, which I had transferred from my arm to my belt.

"Oh! That's going to sting."

"No doubt."

We rolled the gurney to the edge of the dock and then — bumpity bump bump — down the short flight of stairs to the level of the asphalt.

"Do you think it will fit in the back seat?" Flo asked, worrying.

I bit my lip. "Hope so. It has to, unless we want to tape it to the top of the trunk with duct tape."

Louis's pounding grew louder. I don't think he heard us. He was just pounding on general principle, the principle being a strong desire to get out of a car trunk.

Other than dealing with the awkwardness of the gurney, getting it in the back seat was easy. Shoot. The Edsel was as big as a Winnebago. An exaggeration I suppose, but the Ford seemed that way to me.

Getting out of the loading area and back onto the Road to Hell was difficult; a demon bus driver had abandoned his vehicle. It lay stretched across the loading dock exit like a dead thing, and I had to drive up on the curb to get around it.

After that was more congested traffic. Seems like we took forever to make it to the Stairway. Things got worse when people started trying to hail us; I'd forgotten to turn off the "AVAILABLE" light on top of the cab. This wasn't a big deal – available cabs ignored fares all the time down here – but we didn't need any more attention than necessary. Flo put her beret on a wheel of the gurney that was shoved up against the rear passenger window, then I flipped off the "AVAILABLE" sign. Our fare looked decidedly inhuman, but at least it wore a stylish hat.

After thirty minutes of me fighting traffic and cursing, and an equal amount of time for Flo to chide me over my swearing, we finally reached the Stairway. My partner in crime retrieved her hat, and together we wrestled the gurney from the back seat.

"Okay," I panted when we were done removing the beast from the car and raising it to about the level of the trunk. "This next part will be a little tricky."

"You mean the part where we attempt to get an enraged Frenchman out of the trunk and onto the gurney?"

"Yeah. That part." I pulled out three long strips of duct tape, sticking one end of each strip to the underside of the gurney. "I'm counting on the fact that Louis will assume we're just a couple of demons getting our jollies."

"Oh, dear," Flo dithered. "I hate doing this to him, though I suppose we have no choice. How shall we proceed?"

"I'm hoping Louis will do most of the work for us. Oh, if we have to talk, can you whisper in a low register?"

"Like this?"

"Lower."

"Liikke thisss?"

"Good. You sound like Batman."

"Who?"

"Never mind. Point is, Louis shouldn't recognize your voice if you talk like that. I'll do the same, though we should keep our talking to a minimum. Okay. Ready?"

She sighed. "I suppose."

Louis was making so much racket now with his poundings that I was afraid he'd attract attention. Quickly, I peeled the duct tape on the car's bumper away from the metal. Our captive used that moment to shove with all his strength. The lid popped open and Louis, like a child's jack-in-the-box, came flying out.

He landed right on top of the gurney. With lightning speed, I flipped a strap of duct tape over his body then pulled the gurney away from the car. Flo slipped in the space I'd created and secured the strap across Louis's belly, catching his arms in the strap at about elbow level, and fastening the tape to her side of the gurney. I flipped over the other two straps to her, and she did the same with them, effectively pinning our friend to the bed of the mobile bed.

"Incroyable! I have been tortured by many demons during the time of my damnation, but you sickos are the worst!" He spat.

Got me right in the face too.

Flo sighed and went back to the driver's side of the cab. She returned with her bag of gauze.

"Have your fun, you wretches, but you shall not break me! I will rail against your perfidy for … mmph!" Flo stuffed a big wad of gauze in his mouth.

Sorry, Louis. It's for your own good. Ours too, I think.

I taped the gauze to his face so he couldn't spit it out. Flo tore off two smaller pieces of gauze and stuffed them in his ears. These I secured with more duct tape, of course, wrapping it around his head like a bandage. Things were going to really sting when we pulled all that off, especially where the tape was stuck to his hair. Oh well, couldn't be helped.

Louis was fairly well immobilized, except for his arms from the elbows to his hands. He was flailing like a T-Rex trying to grab a triceratops, in other words, pretty ineffectually. I taped his wrists to the gurney. My friend's feet also had a little mobility; they were looking for something to kick, so I strapped them down too. When he could move nothing more than his eyelids, he sagged in defeat.

Our friend lay helplessly on the stainless steel gurney. He reminded me of the salmon Flo had prepared for dinner last week. She had served it on a silver platter, not unlike the stainless steel of the gurney. Poor Louis.

"Are you ready?" I whispered in my best Batman voice.

She nodded.

I opened the door to the Stairwell and propped it open with a rock. Then we rolled our friend onto the landing.

We looked up. The stairs went up and up and up, flight after flight, for what appeared to be eternity. With a sigh, I kicked the rock out of the way. The door slammed shut behind us.

Chapter 26

"Oh, man, this is murder!" I gasped.

We were on a break.

"Yes," Florence whispered, panting slightly. Flo almost never got winded, but this was certainly doing the trick. Her cheeks were red against her otherwise milky complexion; a faint sheen of sweat made her face glisten. "But we are making good progress."

True enough. We'd traveled all the way to the Second Circle of Hell and were currently taking a break on the stair landing at that level. The gurney was making what seemed an impossible task merely a very difficult one. The gurney was intended to climb stairs through an ingenious design based upon a set of three wheels placed equidistant from each other. In their collective center was an axle around which the three could pivot. Each of the four corners of the gurney was supported this way. The first wheel in a set would roll until hitting a step, which, combined with the forward momentum, would turn the axle connecting all three. This would place another wheel on top of the next step. Of course, this was going on at all four corners of the gurney — the whole activity would have been pretty pointless otherwise. Roll, hit a step, pivot, climb the step, roll, hit the next step, pivot, and so forth. Worked pretty well, at least for us, though I'd never seen it do anything but frustrate the human hospital workers who had tried to use one. Those poor schmucks would just push against a gurney that refused to move, or get clothing caught in the wheels, fingers pinched from trying to extricate said clothing, feet crushed from the wheels suddenly spinning out of control, ribs broken when the entire gurney would slam against the pour soul pushing it.

I was in the back, doing most of the pushing, but Flo had the job of guiding us up the stairs, which couldn't have been much fun. This was kind of like what people used to say about Ginger Rogers: "She does everything Fred does, but in heels going backwards." That must have been killer on the back, but Florence, good sport that she was, did not complain.

Over halfway to Gates Level, and it had only taken us about an hour. That seemed kind of miraculous to me, but weights and distances and inclines, even when a gurney and an immobilized Frenchman were involved, we're not the insurmountable obstacles to me and Flo that they would have been to any of the Damned. As saved souls, we were on the buoyant side, and this was serving us well. Still, the effort was a bit of a slog, even for us, and we had to break occasionally.

"All of this exercise is making me a bit peckish," Flo commented.

"Me too. Wish we'd made sandwiches."

"Ah, yes, a lovely picnic on the Stairway to Paradise. Very romantic, Ste...ahem." Even though we'd been talking in our raspy low whispers, we were being careful not to use each other's names, just in case Louis, who had exceptionally keen hearing, caught a name through the gauze, and put two and two together. That would add up to disaster for all of us.

Flo stood up first, brushing off her own fanny, much to my disappointment. "Shall we? Wait. What is that noise?"

I got to my feet. A rumbling rose up the staircase from a source far below. The sound grew and clarified, resolving into a rapid "thud thud thud" that crescendoed with each "thud."

"Shit!" I cursed. Flo, for a change, did not chastise me for my language. "Flo, we have to get off the Stairs ASAP!"

"But what is it?"

263

"Demons," I said through gritted teeth. I pushed open the doorway leading to Level Two, and we pulled the gurney through. The door had just slammed shut when the thudding reached a fortissimo, like a percussionist doing some really loud pounding on a timpani. Occasionally the drumroll was accompanied by a grunt or a hoot or a yip.

Flo looked at me, bemused. (Flo was almost never puzzled, but she could on occasion be bemused. I think it had something to do with her Victorian upbringing.) "What in the world?"

"Beast Barracks. The cadets sometimes train on the Stairway, racing from the Eighth Circle all the way to the top and then back down. It's good exercise." Again I remembered, with fondness, my own time in demon boot camp. I had blasted up and down the Stairs on more than one occasion, though only as far as Limbo, since at that time, the risers were still missing between the First Circle and Gates Level.

"Well, what are we going to do? And where exactly are we?"

"Don't worry. The cadets will reach the top of the Stairs in short order and then start back down. All we have to do is stay out of sight for five minutes or so." I looked around. Unlike the Escalator and the Elevator, the Stairway almost never moved, but apparently it had done exactly that overnight. The Dancing Dildo was nowhere in sight, and it took me a moment to get my bearings. "This is the warehouse district for Lustland."

"Why would Lustland have warehouses? I thought all of those were on Five."

"Most of them are, but you can find storage facilities on nearly every circle. Each cardinal sin requires its own unique supplies, and it's more efficient to store them close to where they're going to be used. Here, let me show you."

264

This particular facility was like a self-storage franchise back on Earth. I walked over to one of the garage-type doors fronting one of the units, pulling it open. Inside was a sea of condoms, at least three feet deep, covering the entire floor of the unit. "Team Asmodeus likes to keep its supplies, uh, handy." I grabbed one of the flat, square packages, tore it open and pulled out a latex condom, unlubricated of course. I blew it up to about salami size. "See?"

Flo was not amused. "So are you going to twist it into a horsey now?"

"Ah, well," I said, embarrassed. "I don't know how to do that."

"Why is it pink?"

"Beats me. Probably to emasculate the wearer."

I heard a sound. Hurriedly, Flo and I shoved Louis and his gurney into the heart of the sea of rubbers. Then I grabbed the handle on the door and pulled it closed. A few condoms had fallen off the pile, but Flo grabbed most of them and flung them into the shadows.

Three demons in guard uniforms turned a corner and came into view. As one, they whipped out their pitchforks and yelled, "Freeze!"

Flo looked at me wide eyed. I just shrugged and hoped for the best.

All three demons sported goatees and slicked-back hair in pathetic attempts to look like Asmodeus. Regrettably, these three didn't have as good bone structure as the Lord of Lust. Nor the bodies. One demon was a tall scarecrow of a fellow. Another couldn't have been more than five feet high. The last, who acted like the boss of the crew, was an unusual sight in Hell: a chubby demon.

"Hey!" he said, lowering his pitchfork. His subordinates followed suit. "What's a succubus doing out in the streets?"

"Yeah," said the scarecrow. "You're made more for indoor work, if you know what I mean." He winked at his colleagues.

It was all I could do not to laugh. Logical mistake, though. Succubi were, after all, just about the only attractive females in Hell.

Florence was blushing furiously, but she had the presence of mind to go with the situation. "Not that it's any of your business, but I'm giving this gentleman a quickie."

Grinning sheepishly, I gave the three a wave.

"And who are you?" said the demon chief. "You look familiar."

I tried not to gulp. My face was pretty well known among the demon crowd, since I'd been one of their own not that long ago. And since they put out that APB on me, after I'd gone rogue, my face was probably familiar to all of them.

The chief stared at me and frowned. I looked down at the ground, spotted a condom and slammed my foot on it.

That startled the three guards. "What are you doing?"

"Killing a roach." On cue, a hundred roaches, disturbed by my foot stomp, scurried out of a nearby dumpster.

Fortunately for me, demons have short attention spans. They also, as I've told you before, aren't usually very bright. My "roach" interchange distracted them.

"What...what was I saying?" the chief asked his friends.

"Sorry, boss. Don't remember," said the scarecrow.

"Me neither," added the shrimp.

"Well, doll," the chief said to Flo. "I'll let you get back to work."

Flo put on her haughtiest expression. "Thank you."

"You know," said the scarecrow. "You're not as nice as most of the succubi I've met."

I sniggered.

"Ah, well." Flo was uncharacteristically flustered. "It's a quickie, right? The clock's running, and Lord Asmodeus will have me in chains if I don't get this done soon."

The shrimp looked puzzled. "I thought you liked chains."

"Do me. Do me," I chimed in, looking as lustful as I could, in hopes that I could bolster Flo's story.

"Sorry," said the chief. "Don't want anyone to get in trouble with Lord Asmodeus, Miss, uh..."

Flo gritted her teeth. "Lilith," she grumbled.

He turned to me. "What's so funny, you?"

"Nothing. Sorry."

"Well, as you were. Come on boys." With that, they left.

As soon as they were out of earshot, Flo turned to me. "Steve! How could you?"

"How could I what?"

"How could you think that was funny?"

"Because it was." My chuckle became a full-throated laugh. Lucky for me, though, before Florence got thoroughly miffed (another Victorian attitude – I might get pissed off, but Flo would get miffed), a sound like thunder came from the Staircase, then quickly faded. "Coast's clear. Come on. Let's get Louis and scram."

"Humph!"

"Now, darling. Be a good sport."

In a trice, we had Louis out of the lake of condoms. Then we headed back to the Stairway and continued our ascent.

The next fifteen minutes passed without incident as, stair by stair, we trundled upwards toward the Pearly Gates. Pushing the gurney seemed harder to me now, as if we were struggling

267

against some invisible will. I hoped not, for in that event, the will in question could only have been Satan's. In a cosmic wrestling match with the Earl of Hell, a human soul, even a saved one, seemed unlikely to prevail.

Fortunately, though, it was all in my head. I was just getting tired of, and a little bored with, pushing the damn gurney up about forty thousand steps. Flo, who always displayed more patience than I, seemed to be having no additional difficultly.

We were about thirty steps shy of Limbo Landing when I again felt a vibration in the Stairway.

"Shit!" Flo hissed, then she stared at me wide-eyed.

I almost lost my grip on the gurney. Flo never swore. "Language!"

"But they're coming again!"

She was right. The vibration turned into a rumble then grew into a roar.

"Hurry!" I gasped. "We have to get off the Stairs! Now!"

Flo nodded, joining me at the bottom end of the gurney. We pushed with all our strength, propelling the contraption rapidly, if wildly, since no one was topside to steer, up the Stairway. We slammed the gurney against the door leading to Level One. On most floors, that would have depressed the pressure bar, opening the door, but I forgot. This one was routinely locked to keep out any of the great unwashed. You needed a key to get in here.

My Elevator key didn't fit this particular lock. I patted my pockets, but of course, now that I was no longer Hell's Super, I had nothing else to unlock it with. I looked helplessly at Flo.

But she was already in motion. Reaching to her hair, she pulled out a hairpin then began working on the lock. To my amazement, she had it picked in three seconds, then held open the door for me. I shoved the gurney through, and Flo slammed the door shut, just before the Beast Barracks Special arrived at Platform One.

"Where did you learn to do that?" I said in amazement.

"The hospital. I've had to get pretty good at picking locks to get at medical supplies I need. Now where are we?" she asked.

Chapter 27

We were standing beside an oval of brilliant green zoysia. Near the center of the oval was a hole with a pole sticking out of it. On the pole was a triangular red flag. In the distance we spied a large, single story building, the walls of which were formed by twelve foot square panes of plate glass. "Looks like the eighteenth green of the Clubhouse Course."

We heard a whizzing, and a little white ball appeared overhead. It reached the end of a graceful arc and dropped onto the grass, not three feet from the cup. In rapid succession, three more balls followed it, all landing close to the first one, in a tight grouping that would have made Jack Nicklaus proud. "We need to get out of here before we're spotted!"

"But where? The nearest trees are that way," she said, pointing in the direction from which the balls had come.

Two golf carts, driving in tandem along the cart path, crested a hill. They were heading straight toward us.

The golfers were just pulling up to the green. In the passenger seat of the first cart was a one-year old. With difficulty he climbed out onto the grass. He must have been one of the unbaptized babies who had taken up the game of golf after Limbo had been converted to a gated golf community. Usually, the babies would traverse the courses in diminutive golf carts built more to an infant's scale, but since he was filling out a foursome, I guess he decided to ride with one of the big guys.

I didn't know him, but the other three were familiar to me. *Great.*

Flo grabbed my arm. "Let's just stand in front of the gurney. Maybe they won't ask any questions."

"Not likely," I said, sighing.

"Why not?"

I pointed at the bald, bearded fellow in white tunic and azure cloak who had been driving the infant. "That's Socrates."

Flo hung her head. "We're doomed."

Steve? Socrates called out in ancient Greek – translated here for your convenience – as he got out of the cart and walked toward us. *Steve Minion? Is that you?*

Please note that he said my name in Greek, with a pretty thick accent. That was a stroke of luck. If Louis had understood Socrates, my immobilized friend might have figured out what was going on, spelling disaster for our enterprise.

Giving the philosopher a slightly curdled smile, I held out my hand. *Good to see you,* I answered in his own language. This was not true, of course. Well, the speaking in Greek part was, but being happy to see the old Greek? No way. Oh, Socrates was okay, but his particular approach to philosophy involved a lot of ques …

Who is that with you? he asked, as the other three golfers joined him. *And what are you standing in front of? And why are you whispering?* He tried to look around Flo. She shoved her hip to one side in an attempt to block his view. Her strategy wasn't particularly effective, but it made her look sexy as hell. Perhaps that would distract Socrates, but then I remembered that he had had an unpleasant marriage, back in his youth, when he was still a sculptor in ancient Greece. His wife, Xanthippe, was famous for being a bit of a shrew.

He said one time, "By all means, marry. If you get a good wife, you'll become happy. If you get a bad one, you'll become a philosopher." I guess we know how that turned out for him.

That's probably why Socrates started spending so much time with young men. All of which is to say that a fetching damsel in white, formfitting clothes might not be much of a distraction to him.

In any event, politeness required an introduction and an explanation. *Ah, I'm whispering because I have a bit of laryngitis. Need to use my quiet voice for a while. My companion is Florence Nightingale, founder of modern nursing.* I didn't see any benefit to lying about it, and Flo's name in a thick Greek accent sounded just as confused as my own, so no clue for Louis there either. I pointedly ignored Socrates's third question. Well, actually it was his second question, but I suppose that's just splitting hairs.

A tall, dark man in ancient battle armor pushed Socrates out of the way.

Oh good. We might have a chance after all.

The previous paragraph represents a thought I had at that particular moment, not a bit of dialog. This can get confusing, I know, with me using italics for my own thoughts as well as the translated words of the ancients. Hope you can keep up.

Hello, Steve!

Hey, Al.

Won't you introduce me to your charming friend also?

Of course. Flo: This is Alexander the Great.

Florence in her life had received an excellent education, being the child of well-to-do parents. Her Greek was a little rusty though; she looked like she was catching maybe one word out of three. To compensate, she smiled fetchingly and reached out her hand to shake.

Alexander kissed it instead. *I have not seen such beauty in many years.*

Unlike the rest of Hell, Limbo actually has its share of attractive women, in the form of virtuous pagans, but I would stack Flo up against any of them. Actually, Flo handled her own stacking, and her white skulking outfit showed off said stacking to wondrous effect.

"What did he say?" Flo whispered to me.

"Essentially that he thinks you're really hot."

Flo smile was a little strained as, with difficulty, she extracted her hand from Alexander's grasp.

These other gentlemen are Socrates, as I told you a moment ago, and Tacitus, the famous Roman historian.

Tacitus, who hung out with Greeks a fair bit, had no problem following the conversation. He was, after all, a well-educated man. *Hi,* he said in Greek, instead of Latin, no doubt to show off his language skills.

He was also famously tight-lipped; it's no surprise that his name and the word "taciturn" share the same root. We were not likely to hear another peep from him. Unlike the Greeks (well, one Athenian and one Macedonian), who tended to favor traditional garb, Tacitus was dressed in an IZOD polo, khaki slacks and modern golf shoes. I always thought he had great hair, which he sometimes wore long, though at present it was cut short. It decorated his skull with little brunette ringlets. Sometimes Tacitus would sport a beard, but today he was clean-shaven.

I looked to the baby, but he was ignoring the conversation, having gone to the back of his golf cart. He was focused on pulling a putter out of his bag. *I'm sorry,* I said to the pagans, *but I don't know his name.*

Oh, that's Roger, said Alexander. *He's not much for chit-chat.*

Roger gave us a wave then crawled toward the green.

No, Socrates agreed. *Great golfer though. Now Steve, what is that contraption behind you?*

Oh, nothing, nothing, I said, as Flo and I closed ranks, trying to obscure their view.

How can you say that? he persisted. *And is that a person strapped to it?*

By Jove! Tacitus exclaimed, this time in Latin, in an uncharacteristic bit of loquaciousness.

You're right, Socrates. Who is he, Steve? Al asked.

Uh oh.

Yes, did he come with you? Where is he from?

Well, it can't be heaven, and he's no pagan, for sure. He must be from Hell.

Shit. Outed. "Quick, Flo!" I hissed. "Distract them! Do something sexy!"

She gave me an irritated look. "How about something dramatic instead?" Flo put her hand to her forehead and pretended to faint.

Miss Nightingale! Socrates cried in dismay.

Stand back! Al said, muscling to the side Socrates and Tacitus, who had both knelt next to the sumptuous and prone figure of my girlfriend ... partner. *She needs mouth-to-mouth resuscitation. Perhaps a vigorous chest massage too.*

I heard a little choke come from Flo – thorax is both the Greek and Latin word for chest, so she had no problem translating that – but trooper that she was, she stayed down.

There were only seconds to act. I had to do something with Louis, had to hide him, now, while everyone's back was turned. Problem was: there *was* no place to hide.

And then I had a flash of inspiration.

Alexander was just beginning to lock lips with Flo when I stopped him. *I think she'll be okay,* I said, tapping her foot with my own. "You can wake up now, Flo," I said in English.

We all helped her to her feet. "Tell them I'm fine," she said impatiently. "Especially Alexander. I don't need him pawing me anymore."

She's fine.

Alexander looked greatly disappointed.

Socrates looked around. *What happened to the damned huma ...?*

In the sky above us, a small sun appeared. Right on cue.

Ah. The Lightbearer.

Lucifer himself!

Satan, in his Lucifer persona, complete with twenty-foot white wings, landed gracefully on the ground before us. For PR reasons, he almost always appeared before the pagans in Lucifer form.

Satan is the most consummately evil creature I've ever encountered in my long existence. But he wasn't to these guys. To the virtuous pagans, he was just their landlord, and it looked like they were glad to see him.

Lucifer had a fake smile plastered across his face as he greeted each of the three pagans in turn, but his eyes shot lightning at me. No doubt reluctantly, he chatted with the guys for a few minutes, then he said, *Please don't let me interrupt your golf game. Besides, I need a word with Mr. Minion and Miss Nightingale.*

Okay, said Alexander. He reached in his pocket and pulled out a business card, which he handed to Flo with a wink. *Call me.* With effort, Flo managed to give him a smile.

Bye! The three shouted, then, grabbing putters from their bags, went to join Roger on the green.

"Minion! Nightingale!" Satan hissed, when we were alone. He looked in all directions. "Where is the damned human?"

Flo looked around too. "Good question," she said, eyeing me in surprise.

"And *who* is the damned human?" Lucifer asked, a puzzled look on his face. "No, don't tell me. Let me think." The fallen angel stared downward, Hell-ways, as if he were doing a rapid count of all the billions of the Damned. I didn't think even he was capable of that, but he was smart enough to start with my friends, I was sure, and it wouldn't take him long to...

"Braille. Yes. Where is Louis Braille?" He frowned at me. "What have you done with him? I can't even read his mind!"

I shrugged. "Don't know what you're talking about."

"You do too!" he retorted. "Minion! Your arrogance knows no bounds! How dare you abscond with one of my own?"

"One of your own?" Flo snapped. "How do we know that's even so?"

"He lost the coin toss!" Lucifer snapped back.

"That may very well have been rigged," she replied.

Satan grew very still. He looked closely at Flo, then at me, and frowned. At last he spoke. "I'm sure I have no idea what you're talking about."

"Then I'll spell it out for you," I said. "No more pantomimes. No more guesses. You're busted Satan. I know all about that loaded coin you had someone slip Peter back in 1840. I know what it does. I know how it works."

Satan looked like a fish who had just been caught and was now flopping around on the shore, meaning his mouth opened and closed spastically. He quivered a little too. "That's ... that's ridiculous!"

I gave him a withering look. "Nice try, but Peter, Jerome and I figured out that as many as eight hundred million of the

Damned don't belong down here. I'm willing to bet money that Louis is one of them."

"You have no proof!" he spluttered.

Flo looked triumphant. "We have statistics!"

Lucifer snorted. "Statistics? Give me a break. You can make statistics show anything!"

"Sir," she said formally. "I happen to know a bit about mathematics, probability and statistics included, as does Steve. In this case, the numbers don't lie. Peter has shown the evidence to the Powers on High, they have been convinced, and you have been exposed!"

The three pagans and Roger had just climbed back into their golf carts. They gave us a wave then drove off to the Nineteenth Hole.

Once they disappeared over the last hillock before the clubhouse, Lucifer transformed into a giant cobra, his snake of choice, because of the cool neck cowls and the association with scary parts in scores of movies. He towered over us, hissing.

"That may have worked back when I was damned, Nick," I said calmly. "But you know you can't hurt me. Besides, if you're so sure we have Louis, where is he?"

The snake transformed into the man in black. He pointed a long claw at me, stamped a cloven hoof on the turf, so hard, in fact, that the grounds crew would need about a wheelbarrow full of soil to fill the hole. "Damn you, Minion!"

"Sorry," I said, with a fake yawn. "Been there. Done that. Think I'll just stay saved."

"And safe from you!" Flo retorted.

"Look, Red." I'd never called him that to his face. He frowned at me. I guess he didn't like it much. "If you can find Louis Braille, you're welcome to him. Meanwhile, Flo, let's take the Stairs up to Gates Level, okay?"

"Ah, all right," she said, looking around a final time. She caught my eye. Her lips were pursed, an unspoken question on them, but I just smiled.

"You will not leave!" Satan said in his most authoritarian voice. "Not until you have returned that which is mine!"

I chuckled. "You hang onto that thought, Nicky, my boy. You know you can't stop us. Come on Flo, let's go talk to Peter. Maybe he knows what punishment Management has devised for Satan's two centuries of malfeasance."

"I believe it's more like two hundred and fifteen years." Flo was always one to be precise.

"Indeed," I said with a smile, looking at the Earl of Hell. His mouth was open again, as if to say something, but he snapped it shut, scowling at us.

Well what do you know? For once I've left him speechless. Not an easy thing to do.

With that, we stepped to the Stairwell door, opened it and slipped inside. Before the door slammed behind us, I looked back. A very puzzled Satan was talking to himself, trying to figure out how two humans had just managed to best him.

Chapter 28

"**B**ut where's Louis?"

We were climbing the last mile of stairs between Limbo and Gates Level. I put my finger to my lips. I had no idea if Satan had figured out a way to spy on us this last mile. I wouldn't put it past him, so it was best to keep her in the dark for a while longer.

"Trust me."

"But..."

"Please."

She looked thoughtful but nodded.

Without the encumbrance of the gurney, we made fast work of the Stairway. We were at the door leading to Gates Level pretty quickly, but it was locked. This lock I knew about, so I pulled out my dual-purpose Elevator/Stairway door key. That's when I noticed that the lock was new. I looked at Florence questioningly. With a shrug, Flo pulled out her trusty hairpin and started to work.

"Uh, I'm having a bit more trouble with this one than I did with the door to Limbo."

I looked closely at the lock. The model was unfamiliar, nothing that I had ever seen in the Parts department from my time as Hell's Super. "I have a feeling Satan just had Beezy put an especially secure lock on this door."

"That he did," said a rumble behind me.

We turned and were facing the Lord of the Flies himself.

Beezy was leaning against the wall of the stairwell, ten steps down, using a claw to scrape some wax out of an ear. "You know," he said calmly, "Nick is really pissed off at you right now."

"So what else is new?"

He snorted. "Too true. Ever since you gave up being a demon, reclaiming your immortal soul, you've been on his shit list."

"Like I give a crap."

"Steve!"

"Sorry, Flo. Like I give a darn," I amended, though darn just didn't seem to have the same panache as crap, especially since I was talking to a prince of Hell. I just hoped Beezy didn't think I was henpecked or something.

"He's also really puzzled by what you've done with Braille. I was too, for a minute at least, but I think I've figured it out." The Lord of the Flies held up his right forefinger and wiggled it at me, grinning evilly. Or maybe that was just his version of a mischievous look. It was kind of hard to tell with Beelzebub.

I gulped. "You're, you're not going to tell him, are you?"

Beelzebub frowned. "Depends. Why are you messing around with another human's damnation?"

Flo shouldered me to the side. "Because for two hundred years …"

"Two hundred and fifteen," I corrected. She shot me a dirty look. "Hey, you started it!"

Flo nodded, accepting the justice of that. I'd just interrupted her moment of righteous indignation, though, and she'd lost her rhythm. I nodded at her, encouraging her to continue.

She began again. "For two hundred and fifteen years, Saint Peter has been using a rigged coin to decide borderline cases, a coin that a lieutenant of Satan tricked Peter into accepting."

"What?" Seldom had I seen Beelzebub caught by surprise.

"You mean he never told you?" I asked.

"No." My old boss frowned.

"You didn't even read it in his mind?"

"What? No. Of course not. We can only read each other's minds if we are allowed to by the other party. It's part of the rules of etiquette that Hell's Elite follows."

"And you expect me to believe that even Satan follows these rules? Really, now. Forgive me for being skeptical, but we *are* talking about the Prince of Lies."

"Ever hear the expression, 'honor among thieves?'"

"Oh." He had me there. "Then he's not reading your mind right now?"

"No. Oh, he's trying. He always makes the attempt, the big snoop. You're right that Satan is the only one of the princes who tries to cheat, but I'm not letting him."

I sighed in relief. "Well, in brief, back around 1840, he got a guy to offer a rigged quarter to Peter for use as a way to settle borderline cases. Before that, Pete used rock-paper-scissors."

Beezy nodded thoughtfully. "I remember Petey used to play that game a lot. Satan must have talked a human into doing that, someone who probably didn't have much confidence in making it through the Gates of Heaven."

"He didn't. He's in Hell somewhere. Maybe Satan promised to make it easy on him. Anyway, I don't much care. He was just a stooge. However it went down, the coin toss has been unfair for a long time."

"May I finish please?" Flo said, losing her patience. "Millions of souls have been unjustly damned because of Satan's perfidious act."

"And why are you surprised?" Beelzebub countered. "Perfidy is his middle name. Or one of his middle names, anyway. He's got so many I've lost track."

"But this is unjust!" she finished.

The old devil used a claw to poke through his forked beard, scratching his chin in thought. Then he frowned. "You know, you're right."

Florence gave him a look of disdain. "But you, sir, being a devil, will just allow this injustice to stand, will you not?"

I looked closely at my former boss. Knowing Beezy the way I did, I wasn't so sure. At last, he sighed. "No. It ain't cricket."

"Indeed it is not!"

He looked closely at the two of us. "I can't really stop you from going to Gates Level anyway, though," he added, pointing toward the lock, "I can make things difficult for you. Tell you what. I'll stay neutral. I won't open the door, but if you can get through it without my help, I won't stop you."

"As if you could," Flo sniffed.

"Please, Flo," I said gently. "Beezy has treated us fairly. No point insulting him."

He smiled wryly. "You still have to get through the door, though."

"Oh, *that!*" I said with a smile, then I turned around and rapped loudly on the metal surface. "Knock, knock!"

"Who's there?" said a voice from the other side.

"Steve."

"Steve who?"

"Steve Minion, that's who."

"Ah," said Peter, opening the door. "That Steve. Hello, Flo. Hi, Beezy."

Beelzebub broke out laughing, black tears flowing from his eyes. "The direct approach! I didn't think of that."

"Peter's been expecting us," I said by way of explanation.

The three of us followed the saint to his desk. "I thought Andrew said you'd be bringing up a damned soul for a do-over."

"I did."

"So, where is he?"

"Right here." I concentrated and opened my pocket universe. It took a bit of effort to open it big enough, but I managed, a second time in under an hour, which I thought was pretty good since I was new at the maneuver, then pulled out the gurney. Louis, who had long since resigned himself to this bizarre form of torment, lay docile on its surface. The gurney's surface, not the surface of torment. Well, maybe that too.

I reached inside my hidey-hole again and pulled out my foam rubber "We're number one" finger, the one Beezy had bought for me at Fenway Park, back when I was a demon, and put it on. Then I wiggled it at my old boss.

In a repeat of his gesture on the stairway, Beelzebub wiggled his right forefinger at me. "Clever, Steve."

"Thanks. Flo, do you still have that steak knife with you?"

"Of course."

"Well, cut our friend loose. I suggest you cut him free from the gurney first, and then we can work on his head. Less screaming that way."

She nodded, cutting off the straps of tape holding him to the gurney's surface. We didn't have to take off the tape covering his mouth and ears, though. He ripped them off himself.

"Ow! Merde! That hurts!"

I looked to Peter, hoping he wouldn't take offense at Louis's outburst. The Saint, seeing my glance, just shrugged.

"You okay, Louis?" I asked gently.

"Steve? Is that you?"

"Yeah. Sorry about kidnapping you."

"You did this?" he sputtered.

"Me and Florence."

"Hello, Monsieur Braille. Forgive us, but it was necessary."

"Where am I?"

"You are once again before my desk, Saint Peter's desk," said Heaven's Concierge. "And Beelzebub, I would appreciate it if you'd stop leaning against that cloud. I just had it cleaned."

Beezy shrugged and stepped away from the precipitation.

"The Lord of the Flies is here too? But why?"

Quickly I explained the situation with the coin, what we intended to do, and why kidnapping him had been necessary.

"And now, Monsieur Braille," Saint Peter concluded, "I'm going to give you another chance at salvation. But we must be quick about it. I don't have all day."

"Peter," I corrected, "you have Eternity."

"Well of course I have Eternity, but I also have a jet full of souls arriving in a few minutes, so let's get to it, shall we?" He pulled out his coin.

"Ooo, a drachma!" Beezy said with interest. "Cool coin. I haven't seen one in a long time. What did you do with the rigged quarter?"

Peter frowned at Beelzebub. "I tossed it into the Mouth of Hell. Monsieur Braille, I'm going to flip my coin now. When I say 'go,' call it."

"Oui, Saint Peter. Merci."

"Pas de quois." He flipped the coin. "Go."

"Tails!"

"And ... wait for it ... You are in luck sir. It's tails!"

"Oh, Louis," Flo said, embracing him. "You're saved!"

"I ... I am?" he intoned softly. "Just like that?"

The old Saint beamed. "Just like that. And, anticipating a good outcome, I have arranged a special someone to guide you to the Gates of Heaven."

Coming down the steps was a lean, clean-shaven man. His eyes were milky white, though his feet took him unerringly to our side.

"This is John Milton."

We all shook hands, even Beelzebub, though Milton flinched when he smelled the sulfur beneath Beezy's claws. "Big fan of yours," the devil rumbled.

"Uh, thank you, sir."

"As am I," Louis said. "And, you sir, will lead me to the Gates of Paradise?"

Milton smiled. Louis couldn't see it, but that's what he did. "Yes, of course."

Louis stretched out his hands toward me and Florence. We each took one. "Steve, Miss Nightingale: thank you for everything you've done for me."

All of a sudden, I choked up. Louis was a close friend of mine. I'd always felt he was too good for Hell, but now that he was going to Heaven, I didn't know how often I'd get to see him. "I, I'll miss you, Louis."

Louis embraced me. "Mon ami, you are the best friend anyone could ever have. We will find times to visit. After all, are you not a saved soul yourself?"

I wiped a tear from my eye. "That I am. You're right. See you soon, okay?"

"Au revoir, Steve, Florence. Give my regards to our friends."

"Ready, Monsieur Braille?" Milton asked.

"Oui. Yes."

Hand in hand, Louis and Milton headed for Heaven's Gate.

"The blind leading the blind," Beezy said. "Nice touch, Petey."

"Will Louis have his sight restored when he gets to Heaven?" Flo asked. "For that matter, why is Mr. Milton still blind?"

Peter shrugged. "You don't need eyes to behold the Wonder of Wonders. Most blind people opt to stay that way when they go to Heaven. To them, blindness is normal. Same thing with deaf people." Heaven's Concierge looked at the Lord of the Flies. "You seem remarkably calm, considering the fact that you've just lost a soul from your inventory."

It was Beezy's turn to shrug. "It's just a job, you know. I don't take this stuff personally. Besides, while Nick might be willing to cheat to win, I'm not." Beezy dug one more time into his right ear, finally getting to the gob of wax he'd been fishing for. It came out with a slurp. He started to drop it to the ground.

"Don't even think of it," Peter said sternly.

Beezy shrugged then put the offending wad, which was about the size of a grapefruit, by the way, in his pocket. "Also, last time I checked, we were winning this contest by almost nine to one."

"It's not a contest," Peter snorted.

"Try telling that to Nick. Later." There was a small explosion. When the smoke dissipated, Beelzebub was gone.

Peter waved his hands in the air, trying to dispel the intense fumes of burning sulfur. "I hate it when he does that."

Chapter 29

The 7:15 flight of souls from ORD had just landed, and a long stream of the newly-dead, each looking a bit disoriented, was heading toward Saint Peter's desk. "You two stay close for a minute. I have to attend to these new arrivals, but then I'd like to talk."

"Uh, okay." I wondered if our little stunt had somehow gotten us in trouble.

While Pete sorted out the souls, Flo occupied herself by rearranging some of the clouds in the area, asking me on occasion to help with the bigger ones. "Try it over there, darling. No. That doesn't look as good as I thought it would. Be a love and move it over there."

If these were couches, it would have bothered me, but they were as light as clouds. Okay. They were clouds.

After helping with the big stuff, I was cut loose. I spent most of the time before Pete was ready to talk pacing nervously behind his desk. I doubt my nerves were helping the new arrivals. Peter looked at me and shook his head. I went back to helping Flo.

Soon he was ready to talk. "As you know, I had a meeting with Top Management about the situation with the borderline cases."

"And?" I looked at Flo. She seemed as worried as I was. Not that I was really nervous about what we'd done. Mostly, I was afraid Peter might lose his job. Admittedly eight hundred million possibly mis-assigned souls was a pretty big deal, but it wasn't really his fault. I should know. I'd been on the receiving end of Satan's deceptions on multiple occasions. You had to give the Devil his due. He was a master of trickery.

He smiled ruefully. "I needn't have worried. Divine Plan, you know. Apparently, Management has always known about the coin."

"And they let this continue, all these years?" Flo said, aghast.

Peter nodded. "Turns out there's an important piece of the Plan about which I was completely oblivious."

"Really? I would have thought this was all worked out a long time ago."

"It was, Steve, but some of the Plan is on a need-to-know basis. In any event, here's the skinny."

"The skinny? Where'd you learn that word?"

"Crossword puzzles."

"Oh."

"Management is all about second chances, and thirds and fourths for that matter, so they decided to give people an opportunity to redeem themselves, even after death."

"But I thought anything we did in the afterlife was of no consequence," Flo said.

"Generally that's true, Florence, but in the case of those individuals who were on the edge and sent to Hell, The Powers have made an exception." Peter took a feather duster from his drawer, went over to the cloud Beezy had leaned against and commenced dusting. "Of course, they couldn't improve themselves in Heaven – at the time of their sorting, they couldn't pay the entry fee to get in – so they had to go to Hell to work on their self-improvement. Satan's coin sending a few extra to Hell was all part of the Plan."

"A few? Eight hundred million seems more than a few."

"Yes, but don't you see? The standard for Heaven is really quite high, so Management sent these extras to Hell to give them time to earn a place in Heaven."

There was a "pop," and a white three-ring binder materialized in mid-air. Peter deftly caught it. "Oh, good. I've been expecting this."

"What is it?"

He showed me the cover, on which was printed *Book of Life Addendum: Newly Saved Souls.* He handed it to me. "These are all of the individuals in Hell who are now worthy of Paradise." My friend pointed to the Book of Life, which was lying open on his desktop. "The Book itself will auto-update. I suspect it's already fixed Braille's entry. He's probably not listed in this binder at all."

With Flo looking over my shoulder, I started examining the book. "Actually, he is," I said looking up. "So am I." I showed the listing to Peter. At the top of the first page was Steve Minion with a checkmark next to my name. Louis was right beneath me, also with a checkmark.

"The list isn't in alphabetical order," Flo said.

"Of course not," said the saint. "It's in redemption order. Steve was first, for obvious reasons. I think Monsieur Braille was next as a favor to you."

I scratched my head. "Why is it obvious that I would be first?"

"Don't you see, Steve?" Flo said. "You were the first damned soul to be reclaimed. That's correct, isn't it, Peter?"

"Yes, Florence, though there's more to it than that. I'll explain in a minute," he said, reacting to our quizzical expressions. "And only the two names have checks next to them because they are the only two brought up from Hell so far."

I looked at him skeptically. "There can't be more than a few thousand names here."

"That's right. That's all at this point who have earned the right to come into Heaven. However, the list will automatically grow as more people prove themselves worthy."

I shrugged and offered the binder back to him. He held up his hands as if to push it away. "No, Steve. Keep it. That's your copy."

"I don't understand," I murmured, taking the book back. I scanned some of the entries and saw, with relief, that Sister Mary Theresa was on the second page.

I showed Peter and Flo the listing. "That's nice for your new friend," he said, "but she'll have to wait her turn. You'll have to bring everyone up in redemption order."

"Then," I said slowly, "it's okay for me to smuggle souls out of Hell for a do-over?"

"Oh, we won't need to do coin tosses like what I did for you and Monsieur Braille. Now we know exactly whom you should bring up and in what order. They are already saved. They just don't know it yet."

"I'm still not quite getting it," I said, eyebrows raised.

"Oh, come on," Peter said, with some of his old impatience showing through. "This is your new job. Stop being intentionally thick."

"Hey!"

"Now, Steve," Flo said, soothingly. "This is a great honor. Apparently, you have just been given a unique role."

Peter nodded. "You see, Steve, you too have been part of all of this, your time in Hell, your salvation. You were the first to have his Eternal Judgment reversed, and it had always been the Plan – once you obtained salvation – for you to serve Heaven as Emissary Plenipotentiary to Hell."

"Emissary Plenipotentiary? Me?" It sounded awfully high-fallutin', even though I didn't quite know what it meant. Well, I knew what an emissary was, but that second word, heck, I'd never been able to keep its meaning in my head. It sounded like something you'd run across at the United Nations, or a word the Wizard of Oz might have thrown out while dispensing goodies from that bag of his. I'd have to look it up later. "Well, uh, that's cool, I guess."

"Cool?" Peter said. "That's all you can say?"

Flo nudged me in the ribs. "Thank the nice saint and the Powers that Be for this incredible honor." She whispered in my ear. "Steve, being Emissary Plenipotentiary means you are Heaven's official representative in Hell, with full powers to conduct business on behalf of the Powers."

"Oh, that's what it means? Wow!"

Peter rolled his eyes. "You *sure* you're smarter having both the bad and good elements of your soul?"

I ignored the question. "Does this also mean Satan won't give me any more guff?"

"That I can't promise," the Saint said. "He is the Antagonist Supreme, after all, so giving people guff is what he does for a living, but he can't stop you from doing your job."

"Like bringing up all these saved souls!" I thumped the binder in triumph.

"Yes."

"Keen!"

"I suggest," Peter said mildly, "that you work on your diplomatic vocabulary. 'Guff' and 'keen' are not typically used by ambassadors, at least not in their official capacity."

There was another popping sound. A silver ring had materialized. Without taking his eyes off me, Peter snagged it.

"What's that?"

"Your badge of office," he said smiling. He held up the ring, which was about the size of a dinner plate.

"A halo?"

"Yes."

My hands came up, as if to ward off a blow. "Like I said, I'm no angel."

Peter shrugged. "I'm not either, but I have a halo. It's right here, in my desk somewhere." He rummaged around and pulled it out. He shined it on his robe then put it on. Well, actually, he set it about six inches above his head, where it floated in place, glowing impressively. "Halos have been out of fashion for a while, but we're all starting to wear them again."

Reluctantly, I took the ring from him. It was silver, not gold like Pete's. "I'm, I'm not sure I'll be comfortable wearing this in Hell."

"You don't have to wear it at all. It is merely a talisman, or as I said earlier, a badge of office. However, I recommend you wear it whenever you are bringing up a soul, or a group of souls, which you can do as well, provided you can gather them all in one spot. The halo will make you even more untouchable than you are now. I doubt that Otis himself will give you any, ah, guff."

"Satan's going to hate this."

Peter grinned. "I know. His little scheme with the rigged coin backfired. Why, in his way, he has given souls time and space to improve, to be worthy of Heaven."

"Doubt he'll see it that way."

"Probably not. He's being given the Word now."

From the Mouth of Hell a great howl erupted.

"Apparently as we speak," Flo said clinically. "He doesn't seem to be taking the news very well."

"You think?" I said with a wink.

"Well, you two should head on home." Peter gave Flo a hug. "Florence, it's been wonderful seeing you. Take care. Steve, I won't say goodbye to you. We will be spending a good amount of time together from now on. For me, though, it's back to work." Peter picked up his letter opener and started to whittle away at a pile of correspondence in his in-box.

"I'm *so* proud of you, darling!" Florence enthused as we descended on the Escalator. "Heaven's official Emissary to Hell."

I looked at the binder and halo in my right hand. Never in my wildest dreams had I thought something like this would happen.

"Go ahead," she urged. "Put it on."

"What?" I said, coming out of my reverie. "I don't know. It's kind of embarrassing."

"Please? For me?"

I sighed and put the halo above my head. I had a little trouble getting it balanced right. When I finally hit the sweet spot, though, it settled and began to glow, coloring my vision, so that everything, even Florence, took on a silvery hue.

"Oh, Steve. That is *so* sexy!"

"Sexy? A halo?"

"Oh, yes," she said huskily.

"Well, I don't know about that. I think I like my fedora better."

We argued about it all the way home.

89307150R00161

Made in the USA
Columbia, SC
12 February 2018